*To Milica*

GW01190738

The Kennedy Boys

# Seducing Kaden

The Sixth Novel

*Happy Reading* :-)

## SIOBHAN DAVIS

www.siobhandavis.com

*Siobhan Davis*

Printed by Createspace, an Amazon.com Company
Paperback edition © May 2018

ISBN-13: 978-1987790900
ISBN-10: 1987790901

Editor: Kelly Hartigan (XterraWeb) editing.xterraweb.com
Cover design by Robin Harper https://wickedbydesigncovers.wixsite.com
Cover photo by Sara Eirew Photographer
Formatting by The Deliberate Page www.deliberatepage.com

# Note from the Author

While you don't need to read the previous books in this series to enjoy *Seducing Kaden*, it is advisable. For those who are up to date with the series, *Seducing Kaden* starts off in the same timeframe as *Saving Brad*, with the exception of those chapters that reference the past.

Happy reading and enjoy!

# *Prologue*

## Past – Freshman Year of College

### *Kaden*

I join the line in the coffee place, stifling a groan as I count the numerous heads in front of me.

Note to self: Get here earlier in future.

But even the lengthy line can't dampen my mood. I'm *finally* starting college, *finally* free of the stifling atmosphere in the house. Ever since Mom and James broke the news to me on my eighteenth birthday, I've been drowning, suffocating, and I desperately need to start a new chapter in my life. Harvard has always been Mom's dream for us—she attended, along with her father and his father before and so on—and God help any of my brothers if they don't want to follow tradition, but I've never minded.

Not until they dropped the bomb, and now I'm so freaking angry at my mother that all thoughts of joining her in the family business have flown out the window.

But I'm not sorry I'm here. This is the fresh start I so badly need.

The line moves, and I take a few steps forward, still mulling it all over in my head. I can't believe Mom's lied to me my entire life. And now she expects me to do the same to Keven. I was *this* close to telling him last week before I left Wellesley to settle into my dorm. I think I would have too, only all that shit went down with Cheryl and he's devastated. I won't deliver another gut punch, so I'm keeping my parents' secret.

1

For now.

A guy brushes past me, in a huge hurry, holding a paper cup in each hand.

"Aaggh!" A woman cries out behind me, and I spin around, watching the guy scowling at her in annoyance before he pushes through the door out onto the sidewalk. A cup is on the ground, hot liquid seeping all over the floor. "Oh no!" The woman has her head bent, her long dark hair shielding her face, as she frantically plucks at her jacket and blouse, both covered with coffee stains.

I run to the front of the counter, swiping a few paper towels and return to her side. "Here." I hold them out to her. "These might help."

She lifts her head, and I stop breathing. Warm, brown eyes the color of rich whiskey meet mine. Framed by thick, long lashes, her eyes are the kind that suck you in and leave you spellbound. As I stare at her, definitely for longer than is socially acceptable, I see the moment a fresh layer of panic sets in, and I desperately want to remove it. "Are you hurt?" I ask, concerned the coffee may have scalded her skin, but she shakes her head. She barely reaches my chest, but as I quickly scan her body, there's no doubting she's all woman. She may be a tiny little thing, but she has curves in all the right places.

"My jacket absorbed most of it." Her voice is unintentionally sultry and every bit as hypnotic as her face. With her voluptuous mouth, golden skin, and sexy body, she reminds me of a younger Sophia Vergara. Only sexier.

Way sexier.

She sighs. "But it's ruined, along with my blouse. I look a hot mess." She drags slender fingers through her thick hair, sighing again.

"Can I do anything else to help?"

"I think I'm beyond help at this point." Her lower lips wobbles and her smile is shaky. She looks down again, and her chest visibly heaves as a shuddering breath escapes her tempting lips. "Hell. Could this day be off to a worse start," she murmurs, looking crestfallen. She starts dabbing at her clothing, scrubbing at the stains, but she's right—they *are* ruined.

"That guy is a jerk. The least he could've done is offer to pay for dry cleaning."

"I agree." She continues trying to blot the excess liquid from her blouse. "But that wouldn't help my current predicament."

She looks on the verge of tears, and I want to eradicate that strained expression from her face—I've always been a sucker for a damsel in distress. "I'll hold your place in line if you want to go to the restroom and wash out the stains."

She nods. "That's a great suggestion and thank you." She starts rummaging in her bag. "In case you make it to the front before I return, I'll have a latte." She thrusts a five-dollar bill in my hand. "And a pack of valium too," she jokingly adds.

"I'll see what I can do," I say, curling the bill back in her fist. "And I don't need that. It's on me."

She looks flustered. "I can't ask you to do that."

"You didn't ask." I grin. "I'm offering, and you'll offend my masculine pride if you turn me down."

She laughs, a light, tinkling sound that reverberates through my bones. "Okay, if you insist. I don't want to be held responsible for any damage to your male pride." She sends me a shy smile before she backs away, clutching her bag to her chest. Nudging her way through the crowd, she makes a beeline for the bathroom.

My eyes are stuck to her retreating form like glue. She wears that fitted gray skirt suit like it was spray-painted on her gorgeous body. Lust stirs deep inside me, and I can't remember the last time I had such a visceral response to a girl. Although it's clear she's all woman and most definitely a few years older than me. Judging by the way she's dressed, I'm guessing she works on campus. She's way out of my league, but that doesn't stop my hormones from going crazy. If anything, that only elevates my interest in her. My brother Kalvin recently lost his virginity to an older woman, and he said it was hot. Now, I'm imagining all kinds of scenarios and getting worked up.

The line moves forward, and time seems to slow to a crawl. I almost give myself whiplash alternating my gaze between the line and the restroom. When I reach the counter, I place both our orders and then move to the back of the room with our takeout to wait for her.

She appears a couple of minutes later, scanning the line anxiously for me, and, damn, if that doesn't please me no end. When she spots me, a relieved smile spreads across her lush mouth, and I have to coax my dick to stay down. Her jacket is slung over her arm as she advances toward me in a hip-clinging skirt and almost transparent white blouse. White lace peeks through the flimsy material, and the sight of her ample tits barely contained by her bra does nothing to dampen my ardor. My dick surges to life, and I'm praying she doesn't notice the monster bulge in my jeans.

"Thank you so much," she says in a breathy voice as I hand her a cup.

"Did the stains come out?" As much as I want to look, I daren't risk it, because I'm already painfully hard.

She gestures at her chest, seemingly unaware of how transparent her blouse is. "It's not as noticeable on my blouse, but my jacket is ruined. At least it's warm, and I can forego it." Her laugh is nervous, and as she looks down at her feet, I realize she understands the situation perfectly—she's just trying to make the best of it.

"My Jeep isn't far from here. I don't mind driving you home if you want to change?" I offer. Who cares about being late for my very first class?

Tipping her chin up, she smiles at me from under thick, sultry lashes, and I fall into a daze. I've never believed in the whole "love at first sight" bullshit, but I think I'm about to eat my words. She is the most beautiful, most captivating creature I've ever laid eyes on, and I'd burn the world down to keep that gorgeous smile on her face.

"You're so sweet, but unfortunately there isn't time." The smile drops off her face, replaced with her earlier panic. "It's my first day here, and I can't be late. I'll just have to make do." She rolls her eyes, exhaling noisily. "Way to make a first impression."

"You'll do great." I rush to reassure her, even though it's an empty platitude because what the hell do I know? Every guy in the place is going to be sniffing around her all day.

"I guess we'll see." She attempts to put a brave face on, but I can tell it's for show.

"At least let me walk you." *Please let me walk you. I'm not ready to let you go yet.*

"No, it's fine, honestly. Thank you for all your help ..." She arches one elegant brow.

I hold out my hand. "I'm Kaden." I deliberately omit my surname, because I've seen the effect it has on people. Especially women.

4

She places her tiny hand in mine, and the instant her soft skin touches my flesh an electrical charge whips through my body like lightning. Her eyes pop wide and she jumps a little, so I'm guessing I'm not the only one feeling the spark of attraction between us. Two rosy spots bud on her cheeks, and I'm a goner. I want this woman under me, over me, and in every way I can have her. My boner strains against my jeans, and if she looks down, there's no way she'll miss it.

"I'm Evelina, but my friends call me Eva."

"A beautiful name for a beautiful woman," I say, taking her hand and lifting it to my lips. I kiss the tips of her fingers, wishing it was her mouth. She visibly shivers, and my answering grin is automatic. "I'd love to take you out some time." My eyes drill into hers, so I notice the instant they turn anguished. My brow furrows in confusion, and I don't understand what I said to upset her.

She slants a sympathetic look my way, sliding her hand from mine. Switching her coffee cup from one hand to the other, she waves her left hand at me. "I'm married." She smiles, but it doesn't quite reach her eyes.

My brows climb to my hairline in surprise. I know she's a bit older than me, but not that much older. Disappointment slaps me in the face. "I'm sorry. I didn't realize, or I wouldn't have said anything."

"It's okay." She clutches her bag tightly. "It happens a lot."

I'll bet.

Eva is a stunner and I'm sure she turns heads wherever she goes. I hold the door open for her. "After you."

"Thank you, Kaden."

We step outside, bathed in glorious sunshine, and she turns to me, the sun highlighting her exquisite form like a halo. "It was so nice to meet you, but I really have to run." She wiggles her fingers at me. "Have a good day." She offers me one last smile before turning around. "Oh," she calls out over her shoulder, looking back and gently shaking her cup, "and thanks for the latte."

"My pleasure," I holler, watching her pick up her pace, heading in the same direction I'm going.

I walk behind a group of students, keeping a reasonable distance between us in case she notices me and thinks I'm stalking her or something.

Mom would blow a gasket if I did anything to damage her precious reputation. The Kennedy Apparel brand is her whole world, and, sometimes, I think she loves that business more than she loves me and my brothers.

When Eva turns into the same red-bricked building I'm heading for, my interest further piques. Well, shit. She works in the Arts and Sciences faculty? Guess I'm going to be seeing a lot more of the lovely Eva.

What a pity I can only look.

A thought occurs to me suddenly, and I stop at the bottom of the steps, quickly glancing at my watch. I'm early for my first lecture so I have enough time. Calling Courtney, my mom's assistant, I quickly tell her what I want. From the initial pregnant pause, I can tell she's dying to pry, but she knows better. She confirms she'll get onto it immediately, and I hang up, hoping I'm right and that there's only one Evelina working here.

My morning classes go quickly, and I connect with a couple of guys who seem solid. After lunch, I join my new buddy Duke in a row at the back of the auditorium as we wait for Professor Garcia to show up.

Duke emits a low whistle, sitting up straighter in his seat. "This class just got a whole lot more interesting." He bumps my shoulder, and I silence my cell, slipping it in the pocket of my jeans. Looking up, I blink repeatedly, straining forward in my seat, struggling to accept what my eyes are seeing.

Well, hot damn.

The professor clears her throat, addressing the dumbstruck crowd. "Good afternoon, class. I'm Evelina Garcia and I'll be instructing you on the principles of economics for this semester." She projects a course outline, proceeding to discuss each item she plans to cover, but her words filter in one ear and out the other. I'm still stuck on the fact the woman I've been lusting after all morning is my professor.

Duke chuckles under his breath. "Dude, I think you've got a little drool there." He gestures at my chin. "Not that I blame you. She's fucking gorgeous. Man, do you see the rack on her?"

If only he knew.

At least the outfit I had delivered fits her, and her sexy cleavage is nicely protected behind the couture fitted jacket. Courtney sent her the perfect skirt suit. It's a rich, chocolate-brown color that complements her eyes and her skin tone. The fit is sublime too, and the expensive material hugs her body like a second skin. I look around, and every guy in the room is hanging off her every word, their eyes stuck to her sexy body. I shift in my seat as an unfamiliar territorial sensation sweeps over me.

When class ends, and everyone starts leaving, I realize I haven't heard a word she's said, nor have I taken any notes. I've been in a trance the entire time. I stand up, stretching my arms out over my head in an attempt to loosen my tightly strung body. Her gaze flicks up, and she spots me.

Although we're separated by a vast auditorium, and students are spilling out of their seats, making their way toward the exit, we may as well be in an empty lecture hell with no distance dividing us. Electricity ripples in the air as we stare at one another.

"I'd like to have a word with Kaden Kennedy," she says into her mic. "Please approach the desk."

Guess the cat's out of the bag now.

"What's that all about?" Duke asks, curiosity in his tone.

"I'll tell you later," I murmur, grabbing my backpack and making my way down to the front of the auditorium.

"Kaden." Her eyes meet mine, and there's confidence in her gaze that was missing this morning.

"Professor Garcia." My lips fight a smirk.

She rounds the desk. "Actually, it's Doctor Garcia," she admits. "But I prefer to keep that under wraps."

I stare at her in awe. "How is that even possible? You must have graduated in diapers."

Her lips curve into an amused grin. "It was something like that," she murmurs. "I trust my secret is safe with you?"

"Of course. I'll take your secrets to the grave." I shoot her a cocky grin.

Her expression turns serious. "Thank you for the suit." She gestures at herself. "It's ... spectacular, and it was extremely thoughtful of you."

I shrug. "It was nothing. Considering you called me by my full name, I'm assuming you've figured out it's my mom's company. All I did was call up her assistant and ask her to send you a suit ASAP."

"How did you know my size?"

"Lucky guess," I lie. I've grown up with a mom who is owner and CEO of one of the largest international fashion brands in the world. Every time

Mom meets a gorgeous girl, she asks her for her measurements and if she's interested in modeling. It's a running joke among me and my brothers, and we take bets on how long it'll take Mom to mention it. Plus, I've worked the last few summers in the office with her, so I know more about this stuff than the average guy. Not that you'll ever hear me confirming that out loud. That would do zilch for my street cred.

Grabbing her bag, she removes a checkbook. "How much do I owe you?"

I shake my head. "Nothing. It was a gift."

She levels me with a grave look. "It can't be a gift, Kaden. You're one of my students, and the last thing I need is someone suggesting I'm taking bribes for grades."

I scrub a hand over my jaw. "I hadn't thought of it like that, and I didn't know who you were when we met."

"Nor I you, but it doesn't change the fact this could look very bad for me. I really need this job, and my first day hasn't gotten off to a stellar start, so I'd be very grateful if you could work with me on this."

"Of course." I rush to reassure her. "I don't want you to lose your job." Not when you've just made this class the most exciting one ever. "I've no idea how much it retails for, but I'll find out."

She pulls a business card out of her wallet, handing it to me. "Have your mom's assistant email me an invoice, and I'll settle with her directly."

Our fingers brush as I take the card from her, sending another jolt through my body. Silence engulfs us, and she stares at me with a look I can't decipher.

Man, she's so beautiful.

And completely off-limits.

It's a crying shame.

"I'll do that." I pocket her card, breaking the spell. "I'd better go. I've got behavioral economics next, and I heard the prof's a real stickler for timekeeping."

She walks behind her desk, gathering up papers and books. "Of course. I don't want to keep you."

"Okay, well, bye." I scratch the back of my neck, awkward tension lingering in the air. I've only taken a few steps when she calls out to me.

"Thank you again, Kaden." I cast a glance over my shoulder at her. "That is honestly one of the nicest things anyone has ever done for me, and it's not something I'll forget in a hurry."

*And I won't forget you in a hurry.*

Little did I realize how prophetic I was in that moment.

# Chapter One
### Present Day – 3 Years Later

## Evelina

"I am going to murder that man in cold blood one of these days," I grumble, tossing my bag on my desk and slipping out of my jacket.

"Only if I don't beat you to it first," Renee agrees, flopping into the chair in front of my desk and kicking off her heels.

Hanging my jacket on the back of my chair, I rest my palms on top of my desk. "You know, when I first came to work here, I thought Harvard was more progressive than this, but they're no different from any other organization, and that has probably been my biggest disappointment to date." To be fair, it's the only issue I have with my career, because in every other way this job is my lifeline, my dream, my one true passion.

"Gender equality is still a desire rather than a right, and until the high level of disparity is fixed, until sociological and societal norms change, women like us, working in male-dominated environments, will always have to fight tooth and nail to be heard, to be given an equal footing, and forced to put up with sexist bullshit from assholes," Renee says, propping her feet up on the edge of the desk. "It sucks, but it is what it is, and Harvard certainly isn't the worst offender. Far from it. They are way more progressive than a lot of universities. The Gender Initiative and the various new diversity policies and measures are all wonderful steps in the right direction. The administration shows commitment, but they can't eradicate sexism or completely remove gender inequality."

"I know they're making policy changes and trying to stamp it out, but unless they're prepared to lobotomize the Jesses of this world, then I'm destined to put up with his sexist, macho bullshit for plenty more years to come. I'm really getting sick of it." I pull out my chair and sit down.

"Maybe you *should* consider reporting him."

"I have seriously thought about it, but I really don't see the point. He's too clever. All his comments, innuendos, and putdowns are subtle, and he'd just claim I misinterpreted his intentions."

"I'd back you up."

I reach across the desk, squeezing her hand. "I know you would, and I love you for that. But the two of us can't take on the rest of them. Naomi and Kristin won't say boo, they're too worried about tenure to risk rocking the boat, and we all know the guys will stick together." I slouch in my chair, massaging my throbbing temples. "And I'm entering into the fourth year of my five-year contract. I don't want to risk the possibility of tenure. This job means too much to me to lose it over a jerk like Jesse."

"Ah, I know. I felt the same when I was in your position." Renee's a few years older, and she's been here a bit longer than me too. She got tenure and a permanent professor position two years ago. "It's so wrong. He's been harassing you from the minute you stepped foot on campus, and all because he's jealous of your achievements, and he wants in your pants."

I cross my legs at the ankles, thinking of the number of times I've had to deflect my male colleague's advances. Jesse's an asshole with a superiority complex, but he's also ruled by his dick. He veers between hating my guts and resenting me as his main competition for tenure and lusting after me with little effort to disguise that fact.

A shiver tiptoes over my spine at the thought of his hands anywhere near me. I'd rather sear the flesh from my bones, excruciatingly slowly, than let him touch me.

Jesse is a handsome man, with no shortage of women to date, but he has the personality of a wet mop and the attention span of a goldfish. He's not the sharpest tool in the box either, and everyone knows he got his position thanks to his connections. Not that that seems to dent his ego in any way. The man takes arrogance to a whole new level, and there's nothing about him I find attractive.

Not one single thing.

Notwithstanding the amount of times I reject his advances, how often I call him out on his sexist bullshit, or all the ways he works to undermine and discredit me, he never gives up.

His love-hate battle is relentless, and I'm really getting tired of it.

The irony is all it'd take is one word to my husband, and he'd deal with Jesse.

Permanently.

But as much as I despise the man, I won't go there.

I won't have that on my conscience.

Especially not when Seth's demise still weighs heavy on my mind, even after ten years.

No. My hands are pretty much tied when it comes to Jesse.

And I'm done expending any more energy thinking or talking about him.

"What are you up to this weekend? Want to meet for coffee or lunch tomorrow?" I ask my best friend.

She props her elbows on the desk, and a dreamy expression washes across her face. "Oh my God! I totally forget to tell you! Lee has invited me to his parents' place this weekend, and I think he's finally going to do it."

Renee has invested seven years of her life with Lee, and she's spent the last four waiting, anxiously, for him to pop the question. I don't have the heart to tell her she has it so good right now, and that the reality is often the polar opposite of the dream.

Maybe I'm too cynical. Perhaps it will be different for my friend, and she'll live the dream. But I can't help feeling jaded, because my own experiences have been the complete opposite.

As a little girl, I was in love with the idea of love and addicted to big Hollywood romances and swoonworthy leading men who swept their women off their feet, riding happily into the sunset.

I had a rude awakening when I was fourteen and my parents shattered every dream I'd ever harbored. That was the moment I moved from adolescence to adulthood. The moment I realized there is no such thing as a fairytale ending.

The princess doesn't always get the prince.

Or even the frog.

And monsters do exist.

They don't hide in closets or under beds.

They walk around freely, always getting what they want, and challenging anyone who gets in their way.

I should know.

Because I'm married to one.

With every mile I drive, my anxiety ratchets up another notch, until I'm almost hyperventilating by the time I reach the ornate iron gates. It's the same every night I return home. My working week is my sanctuary. My escape. My breath of fresh air in the otherwise stifling environment of my so-called life. I delay the time when I need to return to my prison by working late, taking on additional projects, personally tutoring students, attending late night yoga classes with Renee, and occasionally having dinner or drinks with some of my colleagues.

I'm not close to many people, and that's by choice. Anyone I bring into my life could end up in danger, so I've learned to keep to myself and to hold others at arm's length.

I tried to avoid a friendship with Renee in the beginning, but she's persistent when she wants something, and she wouldn't take no for an answer. Now I couldn't imagine my life without her in it. She has no idea how much she has salvaged my sanity, and how highly I value her friendship. She doesn't know anything about Jeremy, and that's the only way this friendship can work. I made it clear at the outset that my husband and my marriage was off-limits. She took that with a pinch of salt initially, probing me for details, but I made it abundantly clear we couldn't be friends if she wasn't prepared to drop the twenty-questions routine.

She hasn't asked after him in years, and I'm grateful. I know she's curious, and she can tell I'm unhappy—hell, she isn't quiet about that—but she doesn't understand that I'm trapped and there's no way out.

The iron gates open inward, welcoming me home. I drive slowly up the impressive driveway, passing plush well-manicured lawns with tall trees and colorful flowerbeds, laughing inwardly at how deceiving the façade is.

The house looms into view in my windshield, like an imposing overlord. My husband had it built for his first wife just before they got married. Set over two levels, it's a drab gray stone building with narrow leaded windows that let in little natural light and creepy ivy covering half of one side of the house. The roofs are all at different angles, ending in triangular peaks. Ghastly turrets rest on all four corners of the house giving it a really dated feel.

This house has never felt like my home. It's dark and depressing on the outside, and inside it's a shrine to Jeremy's first wife, a constant reminder of all he misses and the innumerable ways I disappoint him. By all accounts, she was the love of his life, and he was devastated when she died giving birth to their first child. Neither his wife nor his son survived and, according to some gossip I've picked up over the years, their untimely deaths were the catalyst that led to his transformation from semi-legitimate businessman to criminal mastermind. They say grief can do strange things to a mind, and I can relate.

Because the minute I turned eighteen and was married off to this man, it felt like the real me died, and I've been in mourning ever since.

I turn off the engine and sit in my expensive Audi, giving myself a silent pep talk. I can't walk into that house until I've prepped myself for it. It's my usual nightly ritual, but Vincent still watches me from his position in the corner of the ten-car garage with a wary expression. His biceps bulge under his black shirt as he folds his arms around his chest, leveling a dark look my way. The gun belt at his waist holds two firearms, which I know he's not afraid to use. My body trembles as horrific images of a night I'd rather forget surge to the forefront of my mind. Shaking those thoughts away, I focus on steadying my breathing and forcing my limbs into action. But Vincent's sharp gaze pins me in place, making breathing difficult.

Most of Jeremy's men guard our home from the shadows, as discreetly as possible, but not Vincent. Wherever I turn, that man's brooding, menacing eyes seem to be there, watching, waiting, leering. I know better than to complain to Jeremy, but Vincent is one of the main reasons why I hate coming home and why I've taken to locking my bedroom door at night.

A powerful shudder rocks my body, and I squeeze my eyes shut, gulping over the painful lump in my throat. Mustering courage, I get out of the car, grab my bag, and walk toward the door, feeling Vincent's invasive stare with every step. But I won't give him the satisfaction of acknowledging him or letting him see how much he gets to me, so I plant a neutral expression on my face and push out into the corridor which leads to my home.

Camille, our housekeeper, has left my dinner on a plate in the kitchen, and I heat it up in the microwave while I pour a glass of chilled white wine. I'm planning on bringing it up to my bedroom when Jeremy steps into the kitchen.

"You're very late for a Friday night," he says by way of greeting.

"I had some assignments to grade and some coursework to prepare for next week." I close the refrigerator with my hip as the microwave pings.

"I've been waiting for you. I thought we could spend some time together." He rakes his eyes greedily over my body, and even though I'm wearing my favorite brown skirt suit, I may as well be naked.

My insides twist into knots, but I force a smile out. "Of course. Whatever you want."

The lustful expression on his face transforms in an instant. Leaning over the island unit, he stares at me with barely contained frustration. "Would it kill you to actually try?"

"Jeremy, I—"

He stalks around the island, taking the glass out of my hand and placing it on the marble countertop. Pulling my hand up to his cheek, he covers it with his much larger one. "Am I that repulsive to you?" he asks as I forcibly palm his face.

"No, Jeremy." And that's not really a lie. Jeremy is a handsome man and very youthful looking for his age. Apart from the tiny crinkles around his eyes and the few lines marring his forehead, he could pass for thirty-seven instead of forty-seven. With his chiseled jawline, light sandy-brown hair, and wide blue eyes, he is far from repulsive to look at.

"So, what is it then? I don't treat you right? Is there something you need I haven't given you?" His eyes bore a hole in the side of my skull.

*Yes. My freedom.*

I think it, but I don't say it. Because you don't ever get to walk away from this life. And I'm smart enough to know you never ask for that.

"I can't complain. I want for nothing."

He releases my hand, sighing as he claws his calloused hands through his thick hair. "Then why can't you love me? Why can't you be the wife I need you to be?"

I'm not sure what's brought all this to the surface now. It's not like he hasn't known this for years. I think he realized pretty quickly that his second marriage would in no way compare to his first. Living in the shadow of a ghost isn't easy, but that's only half the reason for my lack of investment in this marriage. Mainly it's because I had no choice and because I abhor the lifestyle he chooses to pursue.

I turn a blind eye, because I have to, but that doesn't mean I condone his illegal activities or that I've accepted them.

Because I haven't.

And I never will.

And it's that, along with the way this marriage was forced on me, that makes him so repulsive in my eyes.

"I'll try harder," I lie, hoping it will appease him.

He peers deep into my eyes. "Do you really mean that?"

I nod, keeping my eyes locked on his the entire time, wondering when exactly I became so skilled in the art of lying.

A softness creeps into his expression, and he hauls me against him, gripping the nape of my neck with his strong hand. "Good, because I'm sick of resorting to others for affection." It's the first time he's acknowledged his penchant for whores. I've always known, and it's never bothered me because it's kept him out of my bed, except for the weekly pity fuck.

But looking at him now, I see the determination in his eyes, and I know I'm not going to be so lucky going forward.

# *Chapter Two*

## Present Day – Senior Year of College

### *Kaden*

I grab a shower at the gym and quickly make my way through campus on foot, cursing as I spot the time. Tiffani hates being late, and she'll bust my balls if I'm not there to pick her up exactly when I promised I would. Not that my brother Keven will care if I'm late for his twenty-first birthday party.

He'd probably prefer if I didn't show up at all.

While we are back on speaking terms, things are still tense between us. They have been ever since the Ireland vacation and his blatant disregard of my privacy.

I hotfoot it off campus grounds, out along the busy Cambridge streets, jogging the last couple of miles until I reach my apartment building.

I purchased the penthouse apartment over the summer, and it's the first year I'm living off campus. Freshman year I shared a dorm with another newbie, and sophomore year I roomed with Kev. After our falling out, I took a single dorm last year, but it was way too cramped, and it felt like the right time to get my own place.

Best decision I ever made. I love having something that's solely mine, and the privacy and solitude suits me. Duke was angling for an invite, and I seriously considered asking him to move in, but I'm at a stage where I just want my own space. My apartment is only a short walk to Harvard and only a few blocks from my brother Kyler's place. I've yet to visit my cousin Faye's new apartment, but it's not far either. It should make it easier to hang with my family, but it doesn't. I hate that I'm not as close to Kev as I once was, and I hate that Ky feels caught in the middle, but I'm too fucking stubborn to admit I might have overreacted a little.

Back in my apartment, I grab a quick bite to eat, get changed, and then grab the keys to my Jeep and floor it out of there.

Tiffani is out on the sidewalk waiting for me, a customary scowl already planted on her face. I park at the curb and hop out. "I'm sorry I'm late. I got held up at the gym."

"There is always some excuse, Kade!" She shoves my arm away, frustration souring her tone as she yanks the door open, sliding into the car unaided.

I exhale heavily, already knowing I'm in for a long night. Not for the first time, I wonder why I'm doing this with her. Usually, when I reach this point, I break things off only for her to start a persistent campaign to win me back. Which usually involves pouncing on me when I'm drunk and horny and my defenses are lowered, and I end up back in a relationship with her.

Impatient, she presses on the horn, and I clench my hands into fists at my side.

This is the last time.

The last Kennedy family event she attends with me. The last time I'll be with her, I promise myself as I get back in the car.

The party is in full swing when we arrive at the Boston Merrion Hotel. Tiffani insists on going to the bathroom to check her makeup, so I wander into the ballroom by myself. Mom rushes me, enveloping me in her arms. "Sweetheart, I'm so glad you're here." She grips onto my biceps. "Every time I see you, I swear you get bigger and bigger."

"What're you benching now?" James asks, slapping a hand on my shoulder. It took my bio dad's passing for me to truly forgive Mom and James for keeping me in the dark about my parentage and for me to fully appreciate all that James has done for me. His blood might not flow in my veins, but he's my dad in every way that counts.

I was only starting to forgive them for lying to Kev and me for years, when we found out James wasn't Kyler's bio dad either, and I was enraged all over again. In some respects, it's no wonder I've ended up in this on-again, off-again scenario with Tiffani, because my head has been a fucking mess for years. But I've finally managed to put it behind me, and it's time to do the same with Tiff.

All the shit Ky went through helped me put things in perspective. Helped me realize what was important. Even though it was wrong to conceal the truth from us for so long, we all came to accept it was done out of love. James didn't know Kyler wasn't his son, and the revelation pushed the final nail in the coffin of my parent's marriage. While they haven't divorced yet, they are legally separated, and that's something none of us wanted to see.

I'm secretly harboring hope they'll patch things up, as I know my brothers are. For now, they seem to have an amicable friendship, and things at home are more settled than they have been in years.

"I'm benching two-two-five now, but don't tell Kev. He'll only get jealous."

Dad laughs. "I've no idea where you boys get your competitive streak from," he jokes. "None whatsoever."

Mom's smile fades a little as she looks over my shoulder, and I know she must've spotted Tiffani. My family has never warmed to her, which I feel is a bit harsh. Tiffani is a sweet girl, even if she's not the right sweet girl for me.

There's only one woman who has ever laid claim to my heart, and she can never be mine.

Shoving thoughts of Eva aside before I sink into depression, I stride to the door to greet Tiff. She's incredibly nervous, as she always is meeting my family. While they are never rude to her—in fact, Mom goes out of her way to be gracious and to include her—I think Tiff has a sixth sense about it. Or her upbringing renders her vulnerable amongst my family's wealth. Tiffani had to claw her way out of the rough neighborhood she grew up in, and she's one of the rare ones who snagged a free ride to Harvard. You don't get one of those without having plenty of brains up top. While she may present as a ditzy airhead to my family, that's not who she is. It's not her fault her nerves make her babble like an idiot when she's out of her comfort zone, and her insecurities lead to questionable decision-making at times.

I reach her side, tucking her under my arm protectively. We may not have a future, but I still care about the girl, and I hate to see her uncomfortable. "You look really pretty tonight, Tiff," I whisper in her ear, and her beaming smile lights up her gorgeous face. While she still favors tighter styles, which leave little to the imagination, I'd like to think my influence is notable these last couple of years. The dress she has on is figure-hugging, but it's tasteful and classy and she looks fantastic. Any man would be proud to have her on his arm, and if I wasn't already in love with someone else, perhaps things would be different between us.

"Tiffani," Mom singsongs, approaching with a forced smile. "How lovely to see you." She kisses both her cheeks, eyeing her up and down. "And you look stunning in that dress. If I'm not mistaken, it's Moschino?"

"Yes, Kaden bought it for me. I wanted to have something special for tonight."

"Well, you look a million dollars," Dad says, leaning in to kiss her cheek. "Come on in and join the others."

We join my brothers and their girlfriends at their table, and I procure a glass of wine for Tiff and a beer for myself. Kev is chatting with Faye's friend, Rachel, and another couple over near the door, and my younger brother Kal is chatting with Ky's best friend, Brad, by the bar. I urge Tiff to sit down beside Lana, Kal's fiancée, knowing she'll look after her.

"Hey, cuz." Faye smiles, leaning in to give me a quick hug. "Wow." She leans back, regarding me critically. "Hello, biceps. Someone's been working out. A lot."

I shrug. "I've really gotten into the gym this past year. It's a great stress reliever." I started going to the gym more regularly after we got back from Ireland. It took a while for me to realize it might be my subconscious at work.

"Stop ogling your cousin. It's gross," Ky jokes, coming up behind her and slipping his arm around her waist.

"Completely," Faye agrees, giggling. "I'm such a sicko." Angling her head, she leans back, twisting her face around and planting one on him.

They've been a couple for almost two years now, and they are as crazy in love as they were at the start. Maybe more so. I'm really happy for Ky, and he deserves every bit of happiness, because he had a few rocky years where he was miserable as sin. Then Faye came into his life, and things have been on the up for him ever since. Discovering James wasn't his biological father was a massive shock, but at least it meant Ky could be with Faye without any stigma. Even though dating your cousin isn't illegal in Massachusetts, most people frown on it, and it would've added unwanted pressure on their relationship.

At least they are free to love one another now.

I wish it was as easy for me.

I tip the bottle of beer into my mouth, draining half of it in one go.

No matter how hard I've tried, I can't evict Eva from my thoughts. God knows I've tried. I've tried so fucking hard, but she lives there. Like a part of her lives in my heart, and I don't know that it'll ever get any easier.

Tiff looks over at me in that precise moment, as if I'd spoken my thoughts out loud. She smiles adoringly at me, and I hate myself for my deception. While I didn't consciously get with Tiffani to try to forget Eva, it's what I've come to realize has happened, and it's not fair to her. I know she wants more from me, and every time I get back together with her, I've given her false hope. Tiffani deserves better than that, which is why this time when I end it I'll mean it.

"Kade." Kev's deep voice snaps me out of my mind. "Thanks for coming." I slap him on the back, but, like every interaction between us now-adays, it feels strained. "Wouldn't miss it for the world, bruh. Happy Birthday." I snatch the bag off the table, handing it to him. "Got you some stuff for running. Hope you don't have it already." He rips through the packaging and opens the box, eyes skimming over the Garmin Forerunner 1000 and LED headlamp set.

"This is the shit, man. Thanks."

I smile my first genuine smile in ages. "Cool. Glad you like it."

"I see Tiffani's here with you. I didn't realize she was still on the scene," he says, boxing up his gifts and placing them back in the bag. Faye swipes it out of his hand, depositing it on a table in the corner laden down with birthday presents.

"We have a complicated relationship." I'm not admitting the truth, not with Tiff sitting five feet away and because she deserves to be the first person to know our relationship is coming to a permanent end.

"Have you seen Eva?" he asks, like he always does, and instantly my good mood vanishes.

"Keep your fucking voice down," I hiss. "And, no, I haven't. As I'm sure you well know."

He folds his arms over his chest, stabbing me with a penetrating look. "I was only looking out for you, and I told you I wouldn't do it again, and I haven't."

"Well, I haven't seen her or even talked to her since Ireland. Happy?" I chug my beer, draining the rest of it in one swallow.

"You couldn't be more wrong, brother. You think I don't know how you're feeling? Well, I do, and I know that shit doesn't get any easier. It doesn't matter how much time passes."

I gulp as I stare at my brother. I know he gets it, but I didn't realize he was still hurting too. "What about Rachel?" I jerk my head in her direction. "She seems cool, and she's hot as sin." I also know Kev hooked up with her when we were on vacation in Ireland, although I'm not sure how far it went.

"She is, but we're just friends. I can't force what isn't there. I think you know that too." I nod, but I don't confirm it out loud. "Anyway, McConaughey is smitten with her, although I'm not sure he realizes it yet."

"Smitten with who?" Ky asks, rejoining the conversation, and totally jumping to the wrong conclusion if the frosty look on his face is any indication.

"Chill. We're not talking about Faye. Kev meant Rachel."

Ky's shoulders visibly relax. He rubs a hand behind his neck. "Sorry. Touchy subject."

A guy comes over to say hi to Kev, and he wanders off with him, leaving Ky and me talking alone. "Things aren't any better with Brad?" I inquire.

"Not really, and I'm wondering if I should've asked him to room with me again this year, but I feel bad for him. And he's still my friend, even if I'm struggling to be that for him. It's hard knowing he's lusting after my girl, and I can't help lashing out at him, even though it's not really fair."

"It's a shit situation, man, but it'll work out."

Ky quickly glances around, before lowering his voice. "I fucking hope so because this ring is burning a figurative hole in my pocket. I'm dying to propose to Faye, but I don't want anything overshadowing it. I need to resolve things with Brad before I move to make her mine forever."

"I was wondering why you hadn't asked her already, but I understand now." I look over at Brad, chatting to Kal by the bar. His eyes follow Rachel around the room. "Maybe Brad is finally moving on." I nod in Rachel's direction.

"I'm not so sure that's a good idea," he murmurs. "Rach seems to have her own demons, and all they do is fucking tear strips off one another."

I chuckle. "Verbal foreplay is the absolute best kind. My money's on them coupling up before the year is out."

"I hope you're right, dude, and not just because it'd solve my issue. He's been going through hell over all this crap with his family, and I feel like he's hanging by a thread at times. He needs the love of a good woman."

I bark out a laugh. "Christ, Kyler. Whatever the hell has Faye done to you?"

He grins. "I'm pussy-whipped and proud. Don't knock it till you've tried it." He looks adoringly at his girlfriend. Faye is currently locked deep in conversation with Melissa, Keaton's girlfriend, and oblivious to Kyler's loving stare. He looks up at me. "When you meet the one, you just know. I'd do anything for her, Kaden. *Anything*. Nothing or no one is taking her away from me again. Someday, you'll find that too."

What he doesn't know is that I already found it.

I already found my person.

But, unlike him, someone has already taken her from me.

And I'd do anything for her too.

But that means jack shit if I'm dead.

# Chapter Three
## Present Day

*Evelina*

As I glance around the prestigious hotel ballroom, I have to work hard to conceal my disdain. Most of the people here are work associates of my husband's, hiding criminal activities behind the façade of legitimate businesses. This annual charity fundraiser falls into the same category. Why they feel the need to legitimize themselves baffles me. Or maybe it's their way of sticking two fingers to the authorities.

Plenty of cops and federal agents have come sniffing over the years, but Jeremy has all his bases covered, and they can't pin anything on him. There was a time when I wondered if I could find evidence and turn him in myself, but he keeps me well away from the operational side of his business. All I know is he's involved in drugs and guns and probably plenty of other equally heinous activities.

"Evelina. How lovely to see you." Michael's snooty gold-digging new wife sidles up to me, skimming her gaze over my floor-length Chanel couture gown with a look that's half admiration and half envy. Michael Carlisle is Jeremy's right-hand man and a permanent fixture in our home and our lives. He's always pleasant to me, but I get the feeling he doesn't like me. Like most of this crowd.

"Jenna, you look fabulous." I lean in to kiss her cheek, playing the part of dutiful, blissfully ignorant wife to perfection. "That color really suits you."

She smooths a hand over her coiffed hair, smiling slyly at me. "Thank you. And you look wonderful too. My stylist was trying to push that one on me, but I always find silk so unforgiving on the hips."

She's such a bitch, but I'm used to this kind of reception by now. All the other wives are the epitome of the trophy wife. None of them work, and they spend their time gossiping over morning coffee and liquid lunches and spending their husband's ill-gotten gains. They can't understand why I want to work. Why I'm interested in building a career, or why I crave financial independence. I have absolutely nothing in common with these women, and it makes social occasions extremely unpleasant. I always get home feeling like I've lockjaw from all the forced smiling and fake conversation.

"True," I tell her, smiling sweetly, "but I'm happy with my body, and I don't care if the silk hugs my ample hips. I guess it takes a certain confidence to pull off a dress like this, and that's not something every woman possesses." I shrug, taking a healthy sip of my champagne as I watch her nostrils flare up. Take that and stick it up your bleached asshole. "Now, if you'll excuse me. I really must say hello to Daniel's new fiancée."

I stride away from Jenna with my head held high, ignoring the heated stares I pick up from several of the men as I walk by, making a beeline for the pretty blonde. I'd spotted her when we first arrived, but Jeremy had insisted on introducing me to some people before I had a chance to say hi. As I watch her now, nervously gulping back champagne, a pang of empathy hits me in the chest.

I remember how petrified I was in social situations when Jeremy and I first got married. There was no easing me into this lifestyle—it was full throttle from the very outset, and I'll never forget how terrifying it was. I was so out of my depth, and so innocent, and it took me years to figure out how to play the part to a T.

Looking at this girl is a lot like looking at a younger version of myself.

I step in front of her, smiling as I extend my hand. "Hello. I'm Eva. We haven't had a chance to speak yet, but I wanted to introduce myself. You're Daniel's fiancée?" Daniel is a relatively new business associate of my husbands. He's twenty-seven, like me, and I think he fancies himself as the next criminal overlord. Jeremy has taken him under his wing, like the son he never got the chance to know. I've only met him a couple of times, but I haven't warmed to him yet, if I ever will. There's something ruthless about the glint in his eye that has me on guard.

Her soft smile is blatantly grateful as she shakes my hand. "Yes, I'm Cheryl. It's really nice to meet you. Daniel told me all about you, and he worships the ground Jeremy walks on."

"I think it's a mutual bromance," I joke. "Jeremy has high hopes for your fiancé."

"I'm so excited for him," she gushes, and I can tell she means that genuinely. "The opportunity to set up his own law practice so soon after graduating is a dream come true for Daniel. He's so grateful for Jeremy's investment and his belief in him."

Ah. So that's what my husband is doing for Daniel. I wonder what happened to the last lawyer he had in his pocket. On second thought—I knock back my champagne—I'd rather not know.

"Have you two been together long?" I inquire.

She shakes her head. "Not really. It's been a bit of a whirlwind romance. I've only just moved back to Massachusetts. I used to live here when I was a teenager, but then we moved to Delaware when my dad was transferred with his company. I got a part-time job with a leading photography studio out here and decided to complete my final year of college at MassArt. Daniel came in one day to book some studio time, and it was pretty much love at first sight. That was three months ago, and we haven't spent a day apart since."

"That's very romantic." And tragically sad. She has no clue who Daniel really is or what he's setting himself up for. Once you get pulled into this world, there's no going back.

Ask my dad.

He'll tell you all about it.

She has a dreamy look in her eyes, one I know I'd have if I let myself look at the only man I've ever loved without this mask I hide behind. Kaden's gorgeous face looms large in my mind's eye, and I suck in a breath as acute pain slices a line straight across my chest.

"Are you okay?" Cheryl's worried expression pulls me out of my head.

"Fine." I shoot her a reassuring smile. "So, you're a photographer? That sounds exciting." I attempt to steer the conversation and distract my wandering mind.

Her entire face lights up like the glow from a thousand suns, and it only further highlights how stunning she is. Cheryl isn't wearing much makeup, but she doesn't need it. She has flawless porcelain skin that radiates inner beauty. Her trusting, big blue eyes are framed by long, thick lashes, and she has a dainty nose and plump lips. With her beautiful face and slender body, she looks like she'd be more at home in front of the camera, not behind it.

"Yes, or I aspire to be. My dream is to set up my own studio one day."

"Well, I hope it all works out for you."

"Do you work?" she asks, a little hesitantly.

I nod, and my smile is genuine. "I'm an assistant professor at the Harvard School of Arts and Sciences, assigned to the department of economics. This is my fourth year there, and I adore it."

"Oh, thank God," she blurts. Her cheeks flush a rosy pink color. "Sorry, I didn't mean to say that. It's just … none of the other women I've met tonight seem to work, and I've been feeling like I don't fit in, and it's just great to meet someone else who is focused on her career."

"Trust me. I totally understand. I've always felt like an outsider because I work, and it's difficult to find common ground sometimes. Not that they aren't lovely," I rush to add, in case anyone is listening in. "But it'll be nice to have another career-minded woman to catch up with at these events."

"Oh, gosh, me too!" Relief is evident in her tone.

I fish a business card out of my clutch, handing it to her. "Call me anytime, and if you have questions about *anything*, I'll try my best to help." That's as far as I can go in terms of warning her, but I vow there and then if I can do something to keep a sweet girl like Cheryl away from this lifestyle, I will.

She flips the business card over in her hand, and a nostalgic look washes over her face. "My childhood sweetheart goes to Harvard, or so I've been told," she muses. "I know it's a big campus, but do you know Ke—"

"Darling," Jeremy says, interrupting whatever Cheryl was about to say. "There you are. I've been looking for you."

He takes Cheryl's hand, lifting it to his mouth and planting a soft kiss on her skin. If there's one thing my husband is, it's undeniably charming. "We haven't had the pleasure of meeting, but Daniel has told me all about you. He's quite enamored with you, Cheryl."

Her voice betrays her nervousness when she speaks, trembling a little. "It's great to finally meet you, sir, Mr. Garcia. Daniel speaks very highly of you."

Jeremy smiles, circling his arm possessively around my waist. "He's a fine young gentleman, and you've got yourself a great catch."

Bile floods my mouth, and knots twist in my gut.

"I know. I'm very lucky."

Poor girl. I can tell she really means it. She has no clue what she's walking into.

*None.*

"I'm sorry to drag my wife away," Jeremy says, not sounding apologetic at all, "but I need her assistance with something. You should come over to the house one evening with Daniel for dinner."

"That would be lovely."

"We'll set something up. Enjoy the rest of your night, Cheryl."

I lean in and hug her. "It was great to meet you, and I look forward to seeing you again soon."

Jeremy pulls me away then, keeping a firm grip on my waist. "I had a feeling you'd like Daniel's fiancée, and I approve. The other men talk, and it doesn't look good that you don't mix well with their wives. This will give you a chance to redeem yourself."

I've never wanted to smash my fist in his face as badly as I do right now, but I rein my anger in, plastering a faux smile on my lips as we walk across the ballroom.

Jeremy stops at the door, leaning in to whisper in my ear. "Jenna has managed to get herself into a bit of a predicament, and I need you to go to the restroom and retrieve her. Bring her to the back entrance where Michael will meet you."

"Of course. I'll take care of it."

Predicament is code word for smashed, and it's not the first time Michael's new wife has made a spectacle of herself at one of these events. If I had to guess, I'd say she has an official drinking problem.

"Thank you, darling." Jeremy presses a quick kiss to my mouth, firmly slapping my ass as I slip out of the room.

I walk briskly along the corridor toward the bathroom, absorbed in thought, wondering how I can find a way to warn Cheryl without putting myself at risk, so I'm not paying attention to my surroundings. I slam into something solid, lose my balance, and tip back on my heels, falling backward toward the ground.

Warm, strong arms slide around my waist, holding me upright. "Eva?"

Little shivers dance over my skin at the sound of the familiar, deep voice. A voice like rich, molten chocolate, decadent and seductive, and dripping with temptation. It's a voice that haunts me in my dreams. I squeeze my eyes shut even as the musky scent of his cologne drifts around me, enveloping me in a haze of longing.

"Eva." He keeps his hand pressed on my lower back as I straighten up. "Look at me." Heat from his skin threads a web along my face as he tips my chin up with one finger. "Please open your eyes."

With my heart galloping in my chest and blood thrumming in my ears, I slowly blink my eyes open.

Beautiful blue eyes pin me in place, and the look on his face turns my limbs to Jell-O. It's just as well he's holding me up, because my knees feel like they're buckling underneath me. My hand has a mind of its own, sliding up his neck and cupping his face. "Kaden. My God. It's been so long, and I've missed you so much."

# *Chapter Four*

## Past – Sophomore Year of College

*Kaden*

I rap three times on her office door, shuffling anxiously on my feet as I wait for her to open it. Prickles of awareness sweep over my skin in expectation, and I wipe my clammy hands down the front of my jeans. It's the same every week since Eva agreed to personally tutor me. I'm addictively attracted to her, and the more time I spend in her company, the worse it's becoming.

I guess I must love torturing myself, because lusting after her from afar hasn't been enough for me. I had to go the extra mile—to torment myself week in, week out by enduring the pleasure-pain of our weekly studying sessions.

The door swings open, and she looms large in front of me—this tiny, little powerhouse of a woman who fills my world to the point where I see nothing or no one else. And I know this obsession is pointless—she's married and she's my professor, so nothing is going to happen—but I can't seem to help myself.

Since our first meeting, over a year ago, I have not been able to get this woman out of my head. It's the main reason why I changed my schedule, ensuring I was in one of her classes again this year.

"You're a little early, Mr. Kennedy. I'm just finishing up with another student, if you don't mind waiting out here for a few minutes."

"Of course not," I say, stepping back and dropping into one of the seats lined up against the wall. "Take your time."

I drum my fingers off my knee as I wait outside. The door swings open about five minutes later, and a tall, good-looking guy emerges, grinning like all his Sundays have come at once. "Don't forget to look up those sites I suggested," Eva tells him. "You'll find plenty of research material for your thesis there."

"Thank you so much, Professor. I'll definitely do that. And thanks for your time. It's been illuminating." His eyes trail a path over her body from head to toe, and he makes no attempt to disguise it. Zeroing in on her breasts, his eyes darken, and his tongue darts out, licking his lips. "It's always a pleasure," he murmurs, still not taking his eyes off her chest, and I'm two seconds away from flattening him into the ground. My shoulders cord into knots as I stand up, staring the guy down, my hands balling into fists at my side.

I mean, I know every guy on campus has a hard-on for Professor Garcia, and I've had my fair share of lustful thoughts about her over the last year, but that doesn't give any dude the right to objectify her in such a crude, blatant manner.

I'm embarrassed for the male race.

Eva's eyes narrow and her mouth turns down. Looking past the douche, she eyeballs me. "You can come in now, Mr. Kennedy, and I apologize for keeping you waiting."

I purposely shoulder check the guy as I brush past, and he smirks at me, whistling as he strolls off with his hands in his pockets like he hasn't a care in the world.

I step into her small office, and she slams the door shut with more force than necessary. Stalking to her desk, she drops into her chair with a heavy sigh, rubbing a tense spot between her brows.

"He was way out of line," I blurt. "And you should kick him off your tutoring program. The asshole doesn't deserve it."

She huffs out another exaggerated sigh. "I appreciate your concern, Kaden, but I can handle the likes of Todd. Unfortunately, it's something I'm all too familiar with around here."

I pull out a chair and sit down. "You have to put up with that kind of shit a lot?"

She props her elbows on her desk. "Not all the time, but it happens on occasion."

"You should report that. It's not right, and no one would dare objectify any of the male professors in the same way."

"I completely agree but I'm still relatively new here, and I can't afford to rock the boat."

She's shared some of her concerns regarding the tentative nature of her position with me previously, so I understand where she's coming from. While Eva's the consummate professional, and she's always focused on the agenda, I've come to love our casual chats at the end of each session, and it's given me greater insight into the woman at the center of my unhealthy obsession. I get the feeling she doesn't engage in chit-chat with any of her other students, although that could be my ego speaking. I like to think the fact we first met when there were no labels or restrictions means we're more relaxed around one another, which is why she feels comfortable talking with me.

Whatever the reason, I live for these sessions, starting a countdown to the next one as soon as one ends.

I tried hard to put her out of my mind when I first discovered she was my teacher, but forgetting a woman like Eva is no easy feat. It's ironic that I only need tutoring because I've fallen behind in her class thanks to zoning out so regularly. It's hard to concentrate when the woman occupying a starring role in my dreams hypnotizes me with that alluring voice of hers.

I had no idea when I approached her for tutoring that she'd volunteer to do it herself. She only takes on a handful of students to personally tutor during the year, and I couldn't help reading into that, which is ridiculous, because she's never given me any indication she feels even a tenth of what I feel for her.

She sighs again, exasperation bleeding into the air.

"There are so many things wrong with that statement." I'm fuming on her behalf, because she's suggesting the kind of assholery I just witnessed isn't anything unusual. The thought of any of those jerks treating her like that makes my blood boil.

Eva is the youngest professor on campus and she's damn smart. Her class is always full, and it's not just because every male wants to drool but because she makes a difficult subject interesting and easier to comprehend. She doesn't deserve to be treated like a piece of ass, no more than any woman does, but especially not someone with such intelligence and class.

"I know, and I wish I could do something about it, but this job means everything to me. I don't want to risk losing it."

"Do you want me to have a word with him?" That's code for punch his lights out, and I'm sure she knows it.

"Absolutely not." Her voice hardens. "And, like I said, I can handle it."

"Well, if there's anything I can do to help, you only need to ask."

Her features soften. "Thank you, Kaden. I appreciate that."

I pull a card out of my wallet, handing it to her. "Keep that in your purse and call me anytime. Honestly, it's no problem."

She places the card to one side of her desk, running the tip of her finger over the embossed lettering. "Are you working with your mother now?"

"I've worked with her the last couple of summers, and I help out with stuff when I have some downtime, but it's not anything regular. She wants me to focus on my studies. To get the best degree I can."

She nods. "Your mother sounds like a very smart woman."

"She is. She basically transformed an ailing business into a billion-dollar global brand. She's had to work her butt off for her success, but she deserves every bit of it."

Eva's eyes glimmer with warmth. "I'd love to meet her sometime. Kennedy Apparel would make a great case study."

I shift uncomfortably in my chair. "I can set up a meeting, no problem, but I'd rather you didn't use my mom's company for a case study. I try to blend in."

A look of understanding appears on her face, and she nods. "I understand, and I would never do anything to make you feel uncomfortable."

"Thank you."

Of course, she doesn't know that things are still strained with my mom. Especially since we've just discovered she lied to James for years about the fact my younger brother Kyler isn't his son. Ky's taken off to speak to the asshole sperm donor, and my nerves are strung real tight at the moment.

"Hey, is everything okay?" Concern underscores her tone, and compassion radiates in her gaze.

"No, not really." I surprise myself with my honest response and how eager I am to open up to this woman. Tiffani's been asking me the same thing for days, but I shut her down each and every time. She seems to have misconstrued our casual hook-ups for something else, and I'm having a hard time shaking her off. I'm not in the market for a girlfriend, but that seems to go in one ear and out the other.

Eva's eyes infiltrate mine, and I'm not sure what she sees reflected in my gaze, but she's on her feet, ushering me toward the small couch. "I'm a good listener, and I won't judge." She sits down, patting the space alongside her, and I find myself sinking onto the couch, our knees brushing in the process.

Without stopping to overthink it, I start talking. I spill my guts, unburdening all the shit that's been cluttering my head since I found out James isn't my bio dad. She doesn't interrupt me, but she takes my hand, squeezing it at certain key moments, and I cling to her touch as I relieve my soul.

Daylight is fading outside the window when I finally finish talking, and I'm physically and mentally exhausted. Slouching, I keep a firm grip on her hand, rubbing my thumb in lazy circles along the top of her skin. This is the first time she has ever initiated physical contact, and I'm not ready to let go of her yet. "Now you know it all. The Kennedys' dirty little secrets." My bitter laugh is harsh. "Everyone thinks we're perfect, and that money fixes everything, but isn't it incredible how different things look under the surface?"

She leans back on the couch, staring up at the ceiling. "Not really. Few things are as they seem. You'd be amazed at how often the perception is vastly different from reality." Something in her tone alerts me to the rawness of her observation.

"You sound like you're speaking from experience." I twist my head to look at her.

She turns around, so we're facing one another with our heads leaning on the back of the couch. My hand is still wrapped around hers, and the intimacy of the moment is suddenly clear. We just stare at one another, and the charge of static electricity I often feel in her company crackles in the small space between us. Conflict wars on her face, but I keep quiet, allowing her to process stuff in her own time. A small tear sneaks out of the corner of one eye, trickling down her cheek. Without stopping to question it, I lift my hand and smooth the tear away with my thumb.

She gulps, and the look of utter despair on her face is like a dagger straight through my heart. I want to grab whoever put that look there and end them. "Sometimes I wish I could return to my childhood," she says softly. "To live in that cocoon I created for myself, where everything was a fairy tale and the world was my oyster. Where doubts and fears and regret had no home. Where there was only hope and possibility."

"Sometimes I wish I could remove my brain and replace it with a new, shiny clean version. One without all the shit that keeps getting in the way," I admit.

She smiles sadly. "Yet here we are. The same people in the same bodies with the same lives. Wishful thinking is just that." Her eyes flit to where our fingers are entwined, and, as if she's only just noticed, she slides her hand out of mine, sitting upright and smoothing the wrinkles out of her pants. She glances out the window. "It's late, and I don't think your mind is in the right space for dissecting the finer points of empirical and mathematical reasoning." Her eyes are pained when she looks back at me. "I'll schedule an extra hour onto your session next week so we can catch up."

Nodding, I sit up straighter, swiveling a little so we're facing one another. I clear my throat. "The sentiment works both ways, you know." I gesture between us. "I'm a great listener too, and if you need to talk, I'm here for you."

Silence pervades the room. Her chest visibly inflates and deflates as she stares at me. So many conflicting emotions appear on her face. When she speaks, her voice is barely more than a whisper. "I wish I could talk to you, Kaden, but the words I want to say can never leave these lips, and there's no way I want to drag you into my shit."

"I don't—"

She places her hand over my mouth. "Don't say it. Please." Her hand drops away almost immediately, and I miss the warmth of her skin. "And I shouldn't have let things get so personal tonight. You're my student, Mr. Kennedy, and neither of us can ever lose sight of that fact."

I stand up abruptly, immensely pissed off at the world. And it's not like she needs to verbalize that shit. "I hear you loud and clear, *Doctor Garcia*." I'm an ass for taking my anger out on her, but her sudden coldness doesn't sit right with me.

It's not like we are doing anything wrong. All we are doing is talking. *And holding hands*. I curse at the unhelpful devil silently taunting me.

"I'm sorry," she blurts, burying her head in her hands, and my anger disappears as quickly as it arrived.

I crouch down in front of her. "I'm the one who should say sorry. I didn't mean to snap at you. I understand, Eva, and I don't want to make life more difficult for you, but I … I've come to care about you, and I don't like to see you in pain. I thought we were friends, and friends talk to one another."

"I wish we could be friends, Kaden, but that's not permitted either."

I wish for so much more, but I'd settle for friendship. I'll take any scraps she wants to throw my way.

I peer deep into her eyes, and I wish I could remove that dark cloud hovering over her. It's not the first time I've sensed how unhappy she is. Sometimes, this veil of sadness creeps over her, and she looks like the loneliest person on the planet. "If you can't talk to me, at least talk to one of your friends." I stand. She nods wearily, and I sense my outpouring has unlocked some hidden pain inside her. "Can I call someone for you?" I ignore the churning in my gut. "Your husband?"

She vehemently shakes her head. "No. I'll be fine." She offers me a fake smile. "I've more work to do before I head home. You should go. I'm sure that pretty girlfriend of yours is waiting for you."

I can't keep the surprise off my face. I've never mentioned Tiffani to her for obvious reasons and also because it isn't anything more than a casual friends who fuck kinda arrangement. At least not to me. "She's not my girlfriend. She's just a friend."

Her shoulders relax, and her lips tip up ever so slightly. I could be mistaken, but I think she's pleased about that fact.

*Is it possible she feels something for me too?*

As I exit her office, I warn myself not to get anymore invested.

Nothing can happen between me and Eva, no matter the connection between us, no matter how much I long for that.

But, usually, in a battle between the head and the heart, the heart wins out.

# Chapter Five

## Present Day

*Evelina*

I'm blaming the champagne and nostalgic thoughts for my unsafe outburst. With the way Kaden's holding me, and the emotional tornado brewing in his eyes, I can tell he misses me as much as I miss him.

That shouldn't make me happy.

But it does.

"Eva." He whispers my name like it's a precious commodity. "You have no idea how much I've missed you." He reels me in closer, and I should protest, should push him away, but I go willingly instead.

When it comes to Kaden Kennedy, I'm putty in his hands.

His strong arms are warm and comforting as they wrap around me. My eyes skim over him, drinking in every rock-solid, hard, toned line of his body. When I was with Kaden the last time, he still retained some boyish youthfulness, but looking at his broad shoulders, ripped upper torso, muscular arms, and the maturity on his face, there's no denying he's all man now.

And I think I want him even more than I always have.

He presses his mouth to my ear. "Not a day goes by where I don't think about you."

A delectable shiver cascades over my body as his warm breath and even warmer words sweep through me.

"Nor I you," I admit. Champagne has become my truth serum.

He leans back a little, still keeping a firm hold of my waist, and he starts a slow perusal from head to toe. No part of my body is immune from his gaze, and the affect is instant and potent. My core throbs with painful need, the like I haven't felt in years. From the moment I first met him, Kaden enraptured me, captivated me, and he became the forbidden fruit I had to avoid at all costs.

When he looks at me, I'm startled to see moisture brimming in his eyes. "You're so beautiful, Eva, even more so now."

"Kade." My voice is choked with emotion.

I want to beg him to steal me away. To run away with me and never come back.

But I'm not going to throw my sacrifice away after all this time.

"Are you safe?" he whispers, peering into my eyes, and those whispered words are exactly what I need to reclaim my sanity.

Shucking out of his embrace, I take a few steps back. "Of course, I'm safe." *Why would he ask me that?* I went to great lengths to keep that side of my life hidden from him. I guess it shouldn't come as too much of a surprise to assume he went digging into my life. I recall rumors around campus about his brother Keven and how he was apparently using his considerable IT skills for less than legitimate purposes. If Kade had his brother check into my background, I shudder to think what he knows.

"Eva, I know." His statement, and the look in his eyes, confirms it. His expression is a mix of concern and rage.

I shake my head, suddenly aware of my surroundings and how foolish it is to be talking to him in a corridor where anyone could spot me. For fuck's sake, Jeremy is only in the ballroom a few feet away. "Don't say it, Kaden. Not here. Not ever."

"Do you love him? That asshole you're married to?" Loaded anger is barely contained on his face.

Gulping nervously, I glance around again before moving in close to him. I stretch up on tiptoes, and he bends his head down lower so I can whisper in his ear. "Whatever you know, forget it. Pretend like you don't know. I didn't let you go for you to throw it all away. He's dangerous, Kaden, and if he knew what'd happened between us, he'd kill you."

"I'd like to see him try." He crosses his arms, and his powerful biceps flex and roll under the tight confines of his button-down shirt.

"Don't even think about it. You don't know exactly how ruthless he is. You need to put me out of your mind. There is no—"

"Baby!"

Kaden stiffens, closing his eyes momentarily and cursing under his breath.

"There you are! I've been looking everywhere for you." The familiar pretty redhead steps up beside him, looping her arm through his.

"I came out to take a piss and I bumped into Doctor Garcia. She used to teach one of my classes. We've just been catching up."

Technically it's not a lie, but he hasn't been wholly truthful either.

"Oh," she says, smiling curiously at me. "Are you here for Keven's twenty-first too?"

I force a return smile, but it's hard. She may not have been his girlfriend back in the day, but she clearly is now, and I hate the sharp pang of jealousy lancing me on all sides. I've seen them together around campus on occasion, but I always walk the other way to avoid any difficult conversations. I've tried to be happy for him. I didn't deliberately cut ties and want to see him wallow in the same cesspit of pain and grief as me, but it's hard to be magnanimous. To be grateful he's been able to move on.

Not when I'm still so irrevocably in love with him.

I never even got the opportunity to tell him that.

Because I knew if I returned his sentiment that he'd never leave me. And I couldn't risk his life like that.

I finally understand what it means to truly love someone, so much that you sacrifice your own happiness to set them free. Kaden would have walked over hot coals for me, and while it was tempting to hold onto him, to cling to some lingering fairytale notion in my head that said I can dance off into the sunset with my Prince Charming, I didn't want to bring him into this life I lead.

Because even if we ran away, we would constantly be on the move, always hiding, always wondering if today is the day my husband caught up to us.

The only way you leave this life behind is in a coffin.

And I love Kaden too much to risk his life.

So, I did what any woman in love should never have to do—I sliced my heart apart as I lied to him and pushed him away.

Straight into this woman's arms it would seem.

And I have no right to resent her. To want to rip her arm from his. To tell her he's mine and she has no claim over him.

This is what I wanted, I remind myself. And it's the only way it can be.

"No. I'm at a charity fundraiser with my husband and some of his work colleagues." I slant a cautionary look at Kaden. "And I actually need to check on one of my friends, so if you'll excuse me." I plant a fake smile on my face and step sideways. "It was great to see you again, Mr. Kennedy. Take care. Enjoy your brother's party."

His girlfriend slides her arm around his back, oblivious to the fact he hasn't taken his eyes off me for even a second. Swallowing over the messy ball of emotion in my throat, I turn around and walk as quickly as I can toward the bathroom.

As I round the corner, Vincent's dark beady eyes lock on mine, and an icy tremor whips up and down my spine. All the tiny goose bumps lift on my arms. Jeremy's trusted bodyguard has a habit of appearing out of nowhere, and the way he skulks around, always watching and listening, has scared me more times than I care to remember.

I feel physically ill as I ignore him, keeping my poker face on and pushing through the door into the restroom, acting as if I've done nothing wrong. At the same time, I'm frantically scouring my mind, replaying the conversation between Kaden and I to see how incriminating it was, in case Vincent overheard. He probably didn't, not from this distance, but I don't trust that man or his motives.

How could I have been so reckless?

Damn the cursed champagne for lowering my defenses. If I've done anything to place Kaden on Jeremy's radar, I'll never forgive myself.

After cleaning Jenna up and bringing her to a clearly enraged Michael, I return to the ballroom and beseech Jeremy to leave. I don't want to stay here a second longer, for fear Kaden will try to continue our conversation. Jeremy surprises me by agreeing, and twenty minutes later we are in the back of the limo heading for home.

I'm staring out the window, lost in thoughts of the past, when an arm wraps around my elbow, tugging me along the seat. Bile churns in my gut and travels up my throat, but I force it back down, smiling at my husband as he draws me into his side. "You look stunning tonight, darling." Planting his hand on my thigh, he rubs his thumb in deliberate circles over the thin silk of my dress.

"Thank you." My voice doesn't betray any of my apprehension. I've had almost ten years to perfect the right tone and the right look, and I have a whole slew of them to choose from.

"I've been like steel in my pants all night thinking about stripping that dress off you." Taking my hand, he plants it over his crotch, and I feel the hard truth. Lifting the hem of my dress, he slides his hand up my leg, quickly bunching the material around my waist. I glance nervously at the front of the car, and Vincent's dark, lust-filled eyes meet mine through the mirror. He lowers his gaze, watching my husband dig his fingers into the flesh of my thigh before cupping me through my flimsy lace panties.

"Can we put the screen up?" I ask, before leaning into his ear, hating these words before I've even spoken them. "Then I'll let you do whatever you want to me." I slick my palm along his hard length. "I'll ride your cock right here if you like, but not with an audience. Please."

He grips my face between his two hands, and his eyes are drenched with desire. He slams his mouth onto mine, demanding my lips open, and I take his tongue into my mouth, emitting practiced moans every few seconds which I know he likes. He pulls away, unzipping his pants as he instructs the driver to activate the privacy screen. Vincent glares at me through the mirror, and I wouldn't be surprised if he's got his hands down his pants right now. He's a disgusting, sick individual, and I pray Jeremy sees him for what he is one day and gets rid of him.

"Suck me off," my husband demands, grabbing my head and thrusting it at his naked cock. Closing my eyes, I zone off as I do as he commands, fighting to keep my tears at bay. Jeremy has never forced me into any-thing, but I've learned not to say no to him. If I did, I don't think it would end up in my favor, and I'm realistic enough to acknowledge that.

Jeremy figured out quite early on that I was not all that into sex—little realizing that it's only sex *with him* I'm not into—and he has satisfied his peculiar needs elsewhere, for the most part. He still expects sex from me on a weekly basis, and I let him into my bedroom when he requests it, but I've managed to survive all these years knowing I was getting off relatively lightly.

Since our chat the other night, I've been gravely concerned, and in this moment, I know I'm right to be worried. Things are changing, and that's not going to work to my advantage.

I suck him off and ride him to release, hating every single second of it, but I perform how he expects, and once inside the house, I kiss him goodnight, and head to my bedroom, relieved that I've gotten it over and done with.

I'm lying on my side in my bed, recalling every perfect line of Kaden's face and body when the knock comes at my door. Everything locks up inside me, and my stomach lurches to my toes.

*No! Not again.*

*Please just make him go away.*

On shaky limbs, I get up and let my husband into my bedroom. He's wearing black silk pajama pants that do nothing to hide the massive boner he's sporting. That man is insatiable. Putting a black case down on top of my bedside table, he sits on the side of the bed. "Come here." He pats his lap, and like the good little lapdog I am, I slide over, straddling him as my heart starts cracking in my chest. Grinding his hips against me, he tugs the straps of my nightgown down over my arms and buries his face between my naked breasts, moaning in a way that sours my stomach.

"I've been a patient man, Evelina. Some would say too patient." He grips my chin, almost painfully. "But I love you and I wanted you to be happy, so I have sat patiently by while you pursued your studies and your career. Now it's time you did something for me."

An ominous sense of dread tumbles over me. I have a terrible feeling I know where he's going with this.

"I've made no secret of my desire for a family, and I'm not getting any younger. I want a baby, Evelina. Several babies. And I'm not waiting any longer to start trying. From now on, you will open your legs for me when I tell you." I'm not sure what emotions he sees on my face, but he obviously feels the need to reassure me. "Don't worry. I know how to make it real good for you." An arrogant smirk crosses his face. "You'll be begging me to come to your bed every night."

I highly doubt that.

Reaching over, he opens the black box and all the blood drains from my face. "We're going to have fun, Evie. And I'm going to introduce you to things that'll have you screaming my name over and over again." His eyes skim over the myriad of toys and instruments of sexual torture, and he removes a few items before standing.

In one swift movement, he has my nightie fully off, and I'm completely bare before him. Pushing me back on the bed, he grips my wrists together, hoisting them over my head. "Don't worry, sweetheart," he says, noting the look of total fear on my face. "We'll start off nice and slow, but you will obey me. You will do exactly as I say."

I'm trembling all over and fighting tears.

He ties my hands to the bedpost, forcing my body down onto the mattress. "Open your legs really wide, and pull your knees up." I do as he requests, and, without any prior warning, he plunges something cold and hard into my back passage.

I can't help my natural reaction, and I cry out.

I didn't think the nightmare could get any scarier.

But it just did.

# *Chapter Six*
## Present Day

*Kaden*

"You can't break up with me!" Tiffani pleads the next afternoon. "I already told my mom I was going to your place for Thanksgiving break."

Interesting reaction.

Duke has always maintained Tiff is only with me for my money, but I've consistently refused to believe it. I like to think I can sniff a gold-digger a mile away. I'm not stupid—I know she likes the money, and the prestige of dating a Kennedy, but I've always felt Tiffani was with me because she liked me for me. Not for what I could give her.

Now I'm definitely second-guessing myself.

"That's not for two months, and why would you tell her that without even consulting me?"

"Because we're a couple and certain things are assumed when a couple have been going out as long as we have."

"Tiff. If you take all the breakups into the equation, we've actually not been dating that long." True fact. We've been off more than we've been on, and if I worked it out, I'm guessing our dating history would be three months max. Which is not the equivalent of a serious relationship. And, if I'm being honest, what we had was pretty superficial. It's not like either of us has taken the time to truly get to know one another, and that's another indicator of why this isn't meant to be. Tiff would know that too if she took the time to properly think about it.

In fact, the more I reflect on it, the more I realize my family and Duke are probably right. I don't think I know the real Tiffani at all.

"I know you need your space sometimes, baby," she purrs, sidling up to me. "But you don't need to break up with me to have some alone time. I can still be your girlfriend while you go do your thing."

My eyes widen in disbelief. "Are you seriously saying what I think you're saying?"

She slides her hand down my body, but I take hold of her wrist before she can touch my cock. "Don't."

She scowls, reluctantly moving her hand away. "Any other guy would be over the moon if his girlfriend gave him a free pass to score away from home."

I growl. "Any guy that agrees to that is a douche, and this isn't about sex, Tiff." I drag a hand through my hair, sighing. This is all my fault. I haven't been fair to her, keeping her on a string while I battle my forbidden feelings for Eva. "I shouldn't have let this go on as long as it has." I straighten up, pinning her with an earnest look. "You're gorgeous, Tiffani. You're sweet and great fun to be with, but you're not my forever girl. This has always been casual for me, and I knew deep down you wanted more, and I'm sorry that I didn't end this properly last year. Continuing to take you back was a shitty thing to do when I knew it was going nowhere. I didn't set out to hurt you, and I've enjoyed our time together, but it's over, Tiff. I mean it this time."

Tears fill her eyes, and I feel like a prize jerk. "No, you don't. You just need your space."

I shake my head sadly. "No, Tiff. It *is* over, and that means no following me around, no trying to get me in bed when I'm drunk. I don't want to reject you, but I will if you try any of the usual shit on me."

"I know you don't mean that." She shoots me a half cocky, half miserable expression. "You say that now, but you can't resist me."

Hell. This is a fucking nightmare. Maybe I should've done as Duke suggested and dump her via text, but that's too cold and impersonal, and only cowards take that way out. Honesty, I told Duke, is always the better strategy. With that in mind, I say what I need to say even if it's likely to hurt her, but I've little choice, because she's not listening to me. "I can, and I will. You can't wield sex to get what you want, Tiffani, because then you're little better than a whore."

My cheek stings from the impact of her slap. It's a low blow, and I deserved it. I don't blame her, even if I speak the truth, and she damn well knows it. "You fucking bastard. I hate you," she spits, tears rolling down her face.

"I'm sorry. I take it back. The last thing I want is to end up on a bad note. We had some good times, Tiff. Let's just try and remember that." I grab my bag and head toward the door, stopping at the last second. Turning around, I feel two contradictory emotions. Relief that I've finally cut her loose and sorrow that I've had to hurt her to free myself. "You deserve to be with someone who worships the ground you walk on, who cherishes you, and will love you forever. That's not me, and I care about you enough to want that for you. Hate me if you like, but, hopefully, one day you'll thank me."

I duck down as a pointy-tipped stiletto comes flying my way. "Get out! You sanctimonious prick! I hate you! And I never want to speak to you again."

Is it bad that as I walk away, with a new skip in my step, that I pray to God she sticks to her resolve?

The week passes by uneventfully with no Tiffani sightings, and she hasn't deluged my cell with the usual pleading texts and messages. Perhaps I finally got through to her. All week, my thoughts have been distracted by Eva. Seeing her in the flesh has reawakened all my dormant feelings, and just like the aftermath of our breakup, I'm suffering all over again. Now that I know who her husband is, I'm questioning why she ended things with me. It's not the first time. Since Kev brought the information to me, just after we returned from Ireland, I've been replaying our history with a different lens. A big part of me wondered if Eva did it to protect me.

After her blurted admission last night, I now know the truth.

She ended our affair because she was afraid her husband would do something to me.

There is little doubt in my mind.

And, instead of being afraid, I'm rejuvenated.

I nod my head at a few guys as I step into the gymnasium, dumping my bag in a locker and then sauntering into the workout area. Jumping on a treadmill, I continue to let my thoughts meander as I run, steadily building up pace until I'm sweating.

Maybe Eva was right not to tell me back then. My head wasn't in a good place, and I was stuck in that tricky space between being a man and a boy. I'm not sure I would've been able to deal with it. But I'm not the same. I've grown up. Faced my demons head-on. And I'm in a place where I want to fight for the life I want.

That includes both professional and personal interests.

Grabbing a towel, I mop at my clammy forehead, powering off the machine as I guzzle a whole bottle of water. As I make a beeline for the weights room, determination surges through my limbs. I know she isn't happy in her marriage, and after last weekend, I know she still wants me.

I saw it in her eyes.

In the way her body arched toward mine.

In the shivers that coursed through her limbs when my arms went around her.

I walked away without a fight last time because I thought she didn't want me and because I was too weak to battle societal norms.

But I've changed.

I love her, and she's who I'm supposed to be with.

I would stake my life on it, and I'm not going to rest until I find a way of making it work so we can be together.

"Bottoms up!" Duke says, carefully placing the tray down before sliding beers and shots across the table. The bar is teeming with students, as it usually is on a Friday night. A band is getting ready to play on stage, and the rowdy crowd is growing impatient. "A toast!" Duke adds when we all have a shot each. "To Kaden's freedom! Good riddance to the she-devil!"

I roll my eyes, knocking back my shot amid whoops and hollers.

Duke hops onto the stool alongside me. "The best way to move forward is to get under someone else, and there's some hot pussy in here tonight, man. Emily's been eye-fucking you all night."

"Not interested," I mutter before bringing the bottle of beer to my lips.

"What the fuck is wrong with you, dude?" He shakes his head in consternation. "Seriously, you need your head examined. You've ditched the she-witch, and girls are already lining up to take her place and you're *not interested*." His nasally tone brings a smirk to my face.

"That about sums it up." I chink my bottle against his. "Stop worrying about my sex life and concentrate on your own."

"No need, dude. The chicks love this bod."

He gestures at himself, puffing out his chest, and I burst out a laugh, prodding him in the fleshy stomach. "You need to start coming to the gym with me, dude. You'd get rid of that in no time."

"I'm rather proud of my beer gut, thank you very much. Chicks dig it."

"Well, they clearly dig something," I say, because Duke isn't spoofing. He has no shortage of pussy, and whatever he lacks in looks, he makes up for in charisma. In spades. If I ever need cheering up, Duke's my go-to guy because that dude is always up for a laugh. He has a serious side to him as well, something most people don't see, but we've been the best of buds from the first day we met on campus, and I know shit about him that no one else knows, and vice versa.

Although I told no one about Eva. I couldn't afford to risk her position by confiding in anyone.

Keven doesn't count because he took that decision out of my hands.

"And it ain't my money," Duke continues, "because you know I'm only into casual hook-ups."

Duke's dad owns a massively successful media corporation, and he's had to contend with the gold-diggers too. But Duke's savvy and smart, and he can weed them out straight off the bat. He hasn't had a single relationship in the three years I've known him, although he's slept his way through most of the sororities by now. Just as well, considering the Harvard president is threatening to ban frats and sorority houses next year.

"Spoken like a true playboy," I tease.

"If the shoe fits." He nudges my shoulder. "So, what you gonna do with all your free time now? You can't spend it at the gym because I'm pretty sure they frown upon dudes who try to sleep there."

"Funny. I do a two-hour workout a day. That's hardly excessive. Some of the guys spend most of their day there."

"If you work out any more, your arms will be bigger than your head. And your head's fucking huge, man."

"Like my cock."

"Like your ego."

"Asshole."

"Jerk face."

Smiling, I drain the rest of my beer, relishing the cool liquid as it slips down my throat. "I'll have more time to work on my business plan."

"The online golf site you mentioned to me before?"

I nod. "Yeah. I'm definitely going for it. Now that Mom's sold the business, there's nothing holding me back." The plan all along had been for me to study business in college and then join Mom at Kennedy Apparel where one day I'd become CEO. However, she was forced into selling it almost two years ago and, honestly, it was the best decision she ever made. I feel like I've only really had a proper mom since she turned her back on it and dedicated herself to me and my brothers. But I know she's itching to do something—she's not the type to sit around the house all day and do nothing. And now four of us are in college, and the triplets are in senior year of high school, she's going to have more free time on her hands.

"I thought you said your mom was thinking of starting something new?" he asks, finishing his beer and summoning the waitress. He gestures at the table, silently asking for another round.

"She is, but I've already told her I'm not interested. That I have my own idea."

"What'd she say?"

"She said to go for it, and to let her know if I needed any help. She was really cool about it, actually."

"You're lucky. I wish my dad was as reasonable."

I arch a brow. "I thought you wanted to work with him?"

He shrugs. "I do and I don't. Pros and cons, you know?"

"Yeah, bud. I do. You could come in with me on the venture? I'm going to need a partner." I was hoping Keven would come in on it, but we're not on great terms, and I haven't mentioned anything to him about it yet.

He levels me with a serious look. "I'm honored you would ask me. Genuinely. But golf's your passion, not mine."

"You wouldn't need to be passionate about it to help me set up and run the business."

"Agreed, but it would help. Besides, my dad would never go for it. He's been talking about me taking over from him since I was in diapers. Hell would freeze before he'd agree to let me do something else."

"You won't know till you ask. And I'm not saying that for me. My venture isn't right for you, but maybe you'll find something else that is? Or you'll come up with your own idea?"

"Nah. My future is pretty solid, and, most times, I'm cool with that." He smirks at something over my head. "Incoming. Double D's for the taking."

"Hey, Kade." I inwardly groan, recognizing her squeaky voice instantly. Cindy works at the coffee place, and she's been trying to get in my pants for years.

"Hi, Cindy. What's up?"

Propping her elbows on the table, she rests her head in her hands, giving both of us an up close and personal look at her rack. Hasn't she heard of leaving something to the imagination? Pushing her big tits in my face and calling me by my nickname won't endear her to me.

"I was wondering if you wanted to dance?" she asks, and I have to smother a laugh. The band has only just started up, like, this second, and she's over here asking me to dance. Got to give her kudos for the lady balls.

"Actually," I say, standing. "I was just leaving, but my buddy here would love to dance." I try to curtail my smirk. Drool is almost dripping off Duke's tongue, and the dude is panting in heat. He slaps me on the shoulder as I shuck my jacket on.

"Later, dude." Under his breath, he murmurs. "I owe you one."

Duke might think he's into this, but I'm betting he kills me in the morning.

The temps have dropped at night, and the cool air is a welcome balm against my heated cheeks as I walk the couple of miles home. I'm passing a quieter part of town, when a woman's cries echo through the still night air.

I freeze, alarm like a vise grip around my heart. I backtrack to the narrow lane I walked past, my heart racing when I spot the shadowy figures lurking at the back of the alleyway.

When she screams, there is no doubt in my mind.

I know that voice.

My feet pound the asphalt as I run toward the two men pinning Eva against the wall.

# *Chapter Seven*
## Present Day

*Evelina*

Blood rushes to my ears, and my heart is beating so fast and hard against my ribcage I'm worried I'm having a coronary. The two guys have me hemmed in against the wall, and I know exactly where this is heading. They're lucky I don't vomit all over them.

I should've let Renee call me a taxi like she wanted. But I needed to clear my head, and I thought walking for a bit would help cleanse my mind of all depressing thoughts. I was so consumed in self-pity that I didn't hear them creeping up on me until it was too late.

Now, I'm going to pay the price.

"Let me go," I plead, my voice shaking with fear. "You don't understand who I am. Who my husband is."

They both laugh. "Oh, trust me, we know exactly who you are," the smaller of the two says.

That puts an end to any thoughts this was a random attack. Inwardly, I curse Jeremy and his criminal leanings. "I won't tell my husband if you let me go now."

"And why would we want that?" the scarier one with the skin head and evil glint in his eye says.

"Your husband thinks he's fucking king and it's about time he was taken down a peg or two," the smaller man, with dirty blond hair, admits as he slides his hand under my skirt.

Bile rises up my throat, and I thrash about, trying to break free, but the other guy has my arms pinned firmly to the wall, holding me in place.

"Keep fighting, sweet cheeks," he drawls. "Only makes this more exciting."

On instinct, I gather saliva in my mouth and let a loogie loose.

It lands square on his face, coating his disgusting features in a layer of slime. He slaps me so hard my head whips around, my cheek grazing the coarse wall. Slamming my head into the concrete, he rips my blouse right up the middle, while the other guy rams two fingers inside me. Tears roll down my face unbidden, and I go to that new place in my head. The one I escape to when Jeremy is doing unspeakable things to my body.

I'm so focused on zoning out of reality that I don't hear the approaching footsteps until someone is on top of us. The blond guy is yanked backward, and I slump to the ground as both men drop their hold of me. The skinhead curses, throwing himself into the fray. Pulling my knees into my chest, I shiver as the sound of fighting carries on around me. I don't look up. I keep my eyes focused on the asphalt, watching as a gun slides along the dirty ground with a loud clang. I guess I still have some modicum of sanity because I crawl over and grab it, curling my fingers around the handle and pushing myself to my feet.

The alleyway is in almost complete darkness, so I can't make out the man fighting my attackers, but he's big and skillful with his hands, easily holding his own against the two thugs. The small blond asshole pulls a gun out of an ankle strap while my avenger is pummeling his fists into the other guy, slamming him into the wall as he rains savage blows down on him. Walking on shaky legs, I press the butt of the gun into the blond guy's temple before he has time to engage his own weapon and hurt my savior. "Don't even think about it." My voice quakes, but my hand is steady as I prod the gun into the side of his skull.

My avenger walks to my side, and his features become clear. I whimper at the sight of Kaden, and a layer of stress leaves my body.

Thank you, God. I don't know how he's here, but I'm so glad he is.

Sheltering me behind his strong body, Kaden takes the gun from me and the one the man is holding. "Take your buddy and get the fuck out of here," he says, his voice low and menacing. "And if you come near this woman again, I will personally hunt you down and make you pay."

He pushes him toward his buddy, who's moaning and groaning on the floor. The guy helps his buddy up, slinging his arm over his shoulder. "You're a dead man walking," he spits. "You better pray we don't come back for you."

Kaden pulls back the trigger, and it makes a distinct clicking sound as he points it at the man. "I can still shoot you, you piece of shit. And don't think I'm not tempted. Shut your mouth and fuck off."

I fist my hand in Kaden's shirt, pressing into his back, allowing his warmth and his presence to soothe my nerves. He says nothing, does nothing, as he silently watches the man drag his friend down the alley and out of sight. When he finally faces me, his features are contorted in rage, but he makes an effort to keep his tone calm as he speaks. "Are you okay?"

I'm mortified when a fresh bout of tears spills down my face. "I'm okay," I cry. "They didn't hurt me." His eyes dart to my ripped clothes and my bloody cheek. "Not really. You stopped them in time." I fling myself at him, wrapping my arms around his waist. "Thank you, Kade. You saved me."

A strangled sound rips from his throat as he circles his arms around me, holding me close to his chest. He doesn't say anything. He just holds me, and, gradually my breathing returns to normal, and the panic sluicing through my veins disappears. "We need to get out of here in case they come back. My apartment is only two blocks away. Come with me and let me clean you up." I can only nod, looking up at him through tear-stained eyes. "It's okay, Eva. You're safe now. I'm not going to let them hurt you again." Gently, he caresses my uninjured cheek. Then he removes his jacket, helping me into it. "Can you walk? Or do you want me to carry you?"

"I'm okay. I can walk."

He grips my hand, and I gratefully thread my fingers through his, letting him lead me down the alley. When we reach the end, he gestures to me to stand back while he pokes his head out, looking left and right. "The coast is clear. Come on."

He keeps a firm hold of my hand, and we walk briskly to his apartment. I'm practically jogging to keep pace with his longer strides, but I don't complain because I'm as keen as he is to get off the streets. He doesn't say one word, and judging by the waves of fury and frustration rolling off his body, I can tell he's trying to calm the raging storm inside.

Opening the door to his penthouse apartment, he steps aside to let me enter first. The lights switch on automatically the minute my foot hits the tiled floor of the small hallway. Kade closes and locks the door, taking my hand and silently leading me into the main living space.

I suck in a gasp as I take in the surroundings. Floor-to-ceiling windows rim the room on two sides, offering magnificent views of the city in the distance. On the ground level, there's a large pool and salubrious decked area complete with fire pit, stylish loungers, comfy outdoor seating, and several expensive-looking grills. "Make yourself at home while I grab my first aid kit," Kade says, striding off with purpose.

I walk to the plush cream leather couch, perching on the edge as I remove my shoes and carefully place them by my feet. The gorgeous hardwood floors are stained a deep walnut color, contrasting vividly with the understated cream and wood furniture and the cool duck's egg blue furnishings. A massive flat screen TV is mounted over a slick, modern gas fire, both adhered to the wall. A big, fluffy light blue and beige rug rests on the floor underneath.

It's not at all what I'd expected. This is about as far removed from a mancave as you can get. It's minimal and stylish, but there is still a warm, cozy ambiance and I see little personal touches all over his living space.

Kade reappears in the corner of the room, padding in bare feet to my side. He props his butt on the edge of the coffee table, placing a white medical kit down beside him along with some towels, a bowl of warm water, and some cotton pads. A pair of leggings, a tank, and a loose sweater rest alongside them. "Can I clean your wound?" he asks softly. "I'll be gentle."

I peer into his gorgeous blue eyes, nodding. "I trust you."

With great tenderness, he cleans the injury on my cheek, applying a salve with gentle fingertips. His touch against my sensitive skin is so familiar, his soft ministrations felt in every part of my body.

"Are you hurt anywhere else?" A muscle clenches in his taut jaw.

I shake my head.

"Are you sure?" His eyes probe mine.

"They didn't hurt me anywhere else. They tore my clothes, and they were going to ... but, yeah, you got there in time." I grip his hand, squeezing. "I can't thank you enough."

He grabs fistfuls of his hair, averting his eyes. "Don't, Eva." His chest heaves. "You shouldn't have been put in that situation." When he faces me again, a multitude of emotions is etched on his face. "What the hell were you doing walking the streets alone at this hour of night?"

I massage my throbbing temples, as the beginnings of a headache take root. "I know it was careless and thoughtless. I was in a bar celebrating my friend's engagement, and I just needed to clear my head." Little does he know my head was consumed with thoughts of him. I'm so happy for Renee and Lee, but I couldn't help feeling sorry for myself.

I'll never get to experience that kind of joy with the man I love.

Shaking those thoughts aside—because look what trouble I encountered the last time I zoned out thinking about Kaden—I focus on placating him. "I had every intention of hailing a taxi, but I wanted to walk for a bit first. I wasn't paying attention, and that's how they snuck up on me so easily."

"Where the fuck was your bodyguard?"

My eyes pop wide. "I don't have a bodyguard."

"Bullshit, Eva. I know who you're married to."

"It's the truth, Kaden. Yes, they guard our home, and when I'm out with my husband, we always have protection, but I don't need one, and I don't want one."

He looks incredulous. "Are you telling me your husband hasn't assigned a bodyguard to his *wife*? What the fuck?"

"I didn't want one, all right!" I snap. "It's a constant bone of contention between us, but I have little freedom as it is. This is one way to retain my independence, and I haven't needed one. Besides work, the yoga studio, the hair salon, and the odd night out, I don't tend to go many places."

He drags his hands through his hair. "Look, I don't want to fight with you." Air whooshes out of his mouth. "That just fucking terrified me, Eva.

What if I hadn't been passing and hadn't heard you scream?" Panic races across his face. "The thought of anything happening to you ..."

My heart expands in my chest at the look of blatant concern on his face. I'm such a selfish bitch, but it makes me so happy that he still cares.

Silence engulfs us for a couple minutes.

Bundling up the clothes, he hands them to me. "Why don't you go and get changed in the bathroom. Take a shower if you like. There are towels and shit in there."

I look at the clearly feminine clothing, scowling a little. "Are these your girlfriend's?"

He shakes his head. "No, they belong to my cousin Faye. She left a bag behind at my mom's house a few weeks ago. I took it with me, but I haven't had a chance to give it to her yet. She won't mind."

That makes me feel a lot better. I'm not sure I could've worn Kade's girlfriend's clothes.

"And I don't have a girlfriend. I ended things for good with Tiffani," he adds.

"Oh." I don't know what else to say. It's none of my business anyway. But try telling that to my stupid heart which is currently turning somersaults behind my ribcage.

"The bathroom is down that corridor and the second door on the left," Kade says, pointing with an outstretched arm.

"Thank you." I stand up, clutching the clothes to my chest as I take off in the direction he pointed.

I take a hot shower, allowing the water to erase the memory of those guys' hands on me. The clothes aren't a perfect fit, but they are soft and comfortable, and I'm feeling a million times better as I walk back out to the main room.

Delicious aromas of garlic and lemon float through the air, making my mouth water and my stomach rumble. Kade has changed into low-hanging sweats and a tight white T-shirt that leaves little to the imagination, clinging greedily to his massive pecs and his tightly rolled abs. I try to rein in my lust, but it's damn hard. Kade has never looked hotter. Combine that with his chivalrous rescue attempt and I'm a complete lost cause.

He glances over his shoulder, smiling when he sees me. "Feel better?"

"Much better, thank you." I rest my back against the counter as I join him at the stove. "That smells divine."

"I hope you still like prawns?"

He remembered. "Yep. I still consume them by the bucket load." I smile at him, watching as he takes two toasted garlic ciabattas from the oven and loads them with the steaming prawn and chili mix from the pan, adding some fresh herbs on top. "Wow. I didn't know you could cook."

He shrugs, jerking one shoulder as he gestures for me to follow him to the island unit. He places both plates on the marble countertop before pulling out a stool for me. Kade always had exemplary manners.

"Thank you." I sit down and pick up my fork, swirling it around in the air. "Gorgeous place you have here."

"Thanks. I only moved in over the summer, but it's great having my own place. My own space."

"You live here alone?" I ask, groaning as I taste the food he's made. An explosion of flavors hit my tongue, and I think I've fallen in love with him all over again.

"Yeah. My buddy wanted to move in, but I've always preferred my own company."

"I thought you lived with your brother?"

"Used to, but we stopped sharing a dorm a while back."

I sense he's being deliberately vague, but I don't push it. "And your girlfriend didn't want to move in?"

He almost chokes on his food. "Oh, she did, but it was never in the cards."

I want to ask why, but I'm being nosy enough as it is. Besides, I don't want him to think I'm asking for a reason. Because nothing can happen between us. Some things haven't changed. My current euphoric mood dissipates.

"It was never serious with Tiffani," he admits, without me asking. I look into his eyes, my heart brimming with emotion. "We were always breaking up and getting back together. It was never going anywhere."

"So why did you date her then?" I whisper.

He pauses momentarily before answering. "Because I was trying to distract myself from thinking about you."

Oh. Fuck.

I should feel sorry for the poor girl. I should criticize him for using her, because that's essentially what it sounds like, but I'm too hung up on the fact he was thinking about me.

When we first ended things, I figured he was probably hurting the same way I was, but, over time, I presumed he'd gotten over it, moved on.

To know he didn't, he hadn't, resurrects tons of warring emotions.

We stare at one another, and my chest aches with longing. His gaze flicks briefly to my mouth, and my tongue darts out, wetting my lips, as if it has a mind of its own. His gaze lifts, and his eyes ensnare me, capturing me in place and holding me prisoner. He reaches out, winding his hands through my damp hair. Kaden always had an obsession with my hair. And my hands. When we crossed that line, he was always touching one or the other.

I've missed this.

His touch and his devotion.

His obvious care.

"I still love you, Eva." He drills me with a sincere look. "And that's never going to change. You belong with me. It's the only truth that matters."

I want to tell him I love him too. That he's the only man I've ever loved. The only one I ever will.

But that will hurt him more in the long run, so I bite my tongue, forcing the words back into my mouth, safeguarding them in my heart where the truth lives.

"Leave him. We'll go abroad. I have the money and the resources to make it happen." Steely determination is etched on his face.

Tears pool in my eyes. "I wish it was that easy."

He leans in closer to me, hope flooding his eyes. "I know it wouldn't be easy, but it would be worth it to have you in my life. I can't live without you, Eva. You are all I see."

I lose the battle with my tears, and they roll silently down my face. "I'm not worthy of you, Kade. You deserve better than me. I can't take you away from your family and your friends. And it would never be over. He would never stop looking for me. And his enemies would seek me out too. You saw what happened tonight."

Alarm replaces the hope in his gaze. "What? Are you saying it wasn't a random attack?"

Shit. Why did I have to blurt that out? He won't let this go now. But I can't deny it now I've said it. I nod. "They wanted my husband to know. It was a message."

"Holy fuck, Eva." He grabs my hands, dropping his head onto them.

My chest tightens, and my lungs constrict, making breathing difficult.

He lifts his head up, pinning me with anguished eyes. "You need to tell him. Let him deal with those fuckers so they don't come back. If I'd known, I would've never—"

"No. Don't you dare say it," I cut in, fury rendering my tone. "You are not him, and I never want you to be. That is why it has to be like this. Why we can't ever be together."

I remove my hands from under his, sliding off the stool. "I can't drag you into this world, Kaden. I won't see you hurt because of me."

"Don't leave," he begs. "I'm not ready to let you go yet."

I cup his beautiful face. "I have to, because he'll start wondering where I am if I don't come home."

"Promise me you'll think about what I said. I can figure a way out of this." He turns his face into my palm, closing his eyes and emitting a sigh of contentment. "Just give me some time to work out how we can be together."

I shake my head sadly, ignoring my pleading heart. "I can't promise you that, Kaden, no more than I could promise you it two years ago."

I release his face, and, although it kills me to say this, I do what I have to.

I say what is necessary to protect the man I love.

"You need to forget me. Nothing has changed, Kaden, and it never will. I will never be yours."

# Chapter Eight
## Past – Sophomore Year of College

### Kaden

Eva's really distracted tonight. I watch her stare off into space for the umpteenth time, and I'm just about to ask her what's wrong when the door swings open, stopping me. A woman with cropped blonde hair sticks her head into the room. "Turn on the news, Eva! They've found a mass grave a couple miles from your house. The whole area is being cordoned off." She glances at me briefly before closing the door and departing.

Eva opens her laptop and pulls up the local TV station app. I round the desk, leaning over her as we both watch.

"A man out walking with his dog made the gruesome discovery a few hours ago," the reporter is saying, gesturing behind her to an area of woodland that is now teeming with cops, FBI, and medical personnel. Yellow police tape keeps the news crews and nosy bystanders away from the crime scene. "According to my source, twenty-one bodies have been recovered so far, but more extensive digging is taking place across this whole area." She sweeps her arms out to her sides. "And further bodies are likely to be found. While no official report has been issued yet, we have it on good authority that all the victims died from gunshot wounds. Police suspect this is the result of the recent acceleration of violence amongst those warring factions controlling the supply of illegal drugs in the Massachusetts area. This will come as a big blow to local authorities, coming so soon after the disastrous, failed drug raid on several warehouses at the docks last month."

Eva slams the laptop closed and walks to the sideboard resting against the far wall. She removes a bottle of whiskey, and I dart forward as it almost slips from her hand. Grabbing hold of it, I place the bottle on top of the sideboard. Removing two glasses, I pretend not to notice how her hands are shaking like she has Parkinson's.

I pour her a drink and she has it out of my hands before I can blink. She drains it in one go, and damn, if that isn't a major turn-on. Most women hate whiskey. Eva just knocked it back like a pro.

"Another." She holds out her glass, and I duly oblige, pouring one for myself too. I'm a few months shy of my twenty-first birthday, so technically I shouldn't be drinking, but I doubt Eva notices or cares. She's way too preoccupied to worry about something so minor.

She tosses the sharp, amber liquid down her throat with skill, barely flinching.

I refill her glass before she asks. "Do you want to talk about it?"

Drawing a large breath, she shakes her head. She sips her drink this time, staring off into space, and there's a dull glaze to her usual warm brown eyes. Seeing something so gruesome, so close to home, is bound to be shocking, but somehow her reaction seems more personal than that.

"I'm sorry, Kaden," she says after a little bit. "But I'll have to cut our session short tonight."

"That's okay," I assure her, as her tummy emits a large rumble. I smile. "I think someone's hungry."

That barely raises a smile. "I'm not sure I could eat now. Not even prawn, garlic, and chili masala."

I arch a brow, and her lips tug up at the corners a little. "Do you know Veda Restaurant?"

I rack my brains, shaking my head. "Can't say that I do."

"It's a small family-run restaurant off the beaten track. Everything is made from scratch and it's delicious. Their prawn chili masala is to die for. My friend Renee teases me mercilessly because every time we order takeout I get the exact same thing. It's just too good to turn down."

I have my cell out while she's talking, and I've already opened up the app. She frowns when I press the cell to my ear. "What are you ..." She trails off as the call is answered, listening with a funny look on her face while I place our order.

I hang up, sliding my cell into the back pocket of my jeans. "I hope you don't mind, but you're hungry, I'm hungry, and I don't have anything planned for tonight."

That's not one hundred percent true, but I can cancel my plans. I'd chew off both testicles if it meant I got to spend more time with her.

For once, she appears lost for words.

I grin. "I can hang out with you for a bit. Maybe we can stream a movie while we're waiting for dinner to arrive?"

Surprisingly, she nods, and I take her laptop over to the couch, plopping down and pulling up the site I need. She places my whiskey on the coffee table before sinking into the downy couch alongside me. I prop the laptop on my knees as I log into my account. "What do you like?"

"Something light and fluffy," she blurts. "Maybe a rom-com? If you don't mind?"

"No problem." We check various options before picking one, and then we settle down to watch it. Our takeout arrives a short while later, and I have to agree their prawn chili masala is divine.

I couldn't tell you anything about the movie. Although my eyes are glued to the screen, all I'm conscious of is the way Eva is curled into the couch with her shoes off and her legs tucked underneath her. The tips of her knees are brushing against my thigh, and I'm praying she hasn't noticed the semi I'm now sporting. I'm acutely aware of her every move, her every breath, and every giggle and snort coming from her mouth makes me feel like I'm on top of the world. Distracting her from her fears, if only for fleeting moments, boosts my male ego no end. Quiz me on any of her mannerisms and I'd ace that exam. Give me a pop quiz on the movie I've just watched, and I'd fail miserably.

But all good things have to come to an end, and when the credits roll and Eva yawns loudly, I know that's my cue. I help her lock up, insisting on walking her outside where a taxi awaits.

She turns to me with one foot on the floor of the back seat. "Thank you so much for tonight, Kaden. I really needed that, and it was very sweet of you."

I shove my hands in the pockets of my jeans. "It was my pleasure, and I had a good time."

She snorts. "You can admit *Legally Blonde* wasn't your kind of movie and I won't be offended. I know you only watched it for me."

"Don't be too charitable. I got to ogle a hot chick for a couple hours."

She laughs, and I love the sound, and the fact the worry lines have disappeared from her brow. "You've good taste, Mr. Kennedy. I'd nearly turn gay for Reese."

She winks before seating herself elegantly in the car.

I knew she'd jump to that conclusion, which is why I said it.

But I wasn't ogling Reese Witherspoon.

I only had eyes for one woman in that room, and it definitely wasn't the cute blonde on the screen.

As the car drives off, and Eva waves at me, I allow myself to acknowledge how completely fucked I am.

I'm not just in lust with my professor.

I think I'm falling in love with her.

Duke lets out a low whistle as Eva steps onto the podium. "Is it just me or is Prof Garcia looking even hotter these days?" He takes a quick look around the auditorium. "Nope, it's not just me." He snickers, and I elbow him in the ribs.

"Don't be an asshole. Not every dude is here to drool." I'm aware of how hypocritical my statement is, but I'm not just attracted to Eva's looks; her intelligence and quick wit are equally as appealing. "Did you not read the article she just had published in the *American Economic Review*?"

He snorts. "Is that a serious question?"

I roll my eyes. "Some of us actually came here to learn stuff."

"Most of us just came here to get laid."

I throw my hands in the air. "I give up." He grins. "It was a seriously impressive piece, and she's proven she's more than just a pretty face."

"You've got a real hard-on for the prof, don't you?" He quirks a brow. "I notice you jumping to her defense a lot."

"I feel frustrated on her behalf every time one of the guys talks shit about her." Especially since she confirmed she has to put up with that kind of crap a lot. "Yes, she's a beautiful woman, but her brain is equally as fascinating. Did you know she graduated high school at sixteen and was the youngest student to ever receive a PhD from Harvard? And that she's had ten articles published in leading journals since graduation and she presented a paper to the White House Council of Economic Advisers?"

"Whoa." He sits up straighter in his seat. "You're really a fully paid member of her fan club, aren't you?"

"She deserves our respect. That's all I'm saying." I'd like to say more, but to do so is risky. The last thing I want is Duke or any of the guys figuring out I've got real feelings for the woman, which is why I'm forced to quietly seethe every time the guys start talking about all the sleazy shit they'd like to do to her. I generally find some excuse to leave before I beat the ever-loving crap out of someone, but it's becoming increasingly harder to keep quiet when my natural instinct is to jump in and defend her.

Eva is a lot more than just the sum of her looks, and it's about time people around here started recognizing that.

Our Friday night study sessions have now morphed into Friday night movie-and-takeout sessions. There was no big discussion or decision made. From that point on, it was just accepted that that's what we'd be doing.

I'm in seventh heaven, and I'm no idiot. I'm not looking a gift horse in the mouth. If Eva wants to spend her Friday nights with me, I'm not going to complain.

Eva is all businesslike during the hour's tutoring, but she lowers her guard once study time is up, and as she gradually starts opening up to me, sharing more and more personal stuff, the harder I fall.

"I'm doing it," I tell her one particular Friday. She's tidying up her books, and I'm pulling up the restaurant's number on my cell. "I'm going where no man, or woman, has dared to go before." She looks up, sending me a quirky smile. "I'm breaking up with prawn chili masala in favor of more exotic delights." She laughs, and the sound sends blood rushing to my cock. I haven't screwed anyone in months, and that's how bad it's gotten—Eva laughs, and my dick springs to life. *Focus, douche*. I inwardly chastise myself as I scan the menu on my cell. "Wait for it. I'm going all out." My eyes meet hers, and we share a moment. Electricity sizzles in the room, and I know she's got to feel it too. Maybe I'm just a cocky punk, but I swear Eva is lusting after me too. "I'm going to order chicken makhanwala tonight."

"Wow." She kicks off her shoes and saunters toward the couch, her voluptuous hips sashaying sexily. My boner hardens, and I almost groan out loud. Eva moves her body in a way that's completely instinctual. Not like the girls who frequent the parties and bars around campus. The ones that scream "look at me" with their barely there outfits, tits and ass on full display, and the contrived efforts to come across sexy. None of them have even one-tenth of the sex appeal that Eva exudes in spades.

And that's without even trying.

I honestly think the woman has no clue how fucking stunning she is.

"Look at you," she mocks. "Being all brave and courageous." She tweaks my cheek. "I'm proud of you."

"Aw, shucks. You're embarrassing me," I joke. "Next I'll be blushing."

She barks out a laugh. "That, I'd love to see!"

I place our order and we settle back to watch our movie. This time, it's a high-octane legal drama, and I'm managing to keep my focus until Eva rests her head on my shoulder, and then my concentration flies out the window. Eva is very careful not to touch me, or get too close, so this is new and exciting. I'm stiff as a board—in more ways than one—as she snuggles into me.

I'm scarcely breathing. I want to slide my arm over her shoulder and tuck her in securely to my side, but I'm terrified to make a move in case I break whatever spell she's under.

When the takeout arrives, I actually feel like crying, because it forces her to move. She gets up, leisurely strolling to the door to pay for it. She insists on taking turns each week, refusing to let me cover it, even though I've more money than I know what to do with.

We eat quietly, still watching the movie, and I'm mourning the loss of her closeness.

"Well, traitor," she mumbles, in between mouthfuls. "What does betrayal taste like?"

I almost choke on my dinner.

She runs a hand up and down my back, handing me a glass of water. "Sorry, poor choice of words."

Now, I understand two things. One, she was talking about the food not where my mind went, and two, she's totally thought about me in the way I've been thinking about her.

"See for yourself," I say, holding up my fork.

Her eyes zoom in on my mouth, and I'm instantly rock-hard in my jeans again.

If there was a degree in turning men on, Eva would have a first-class honors award.

She opens her delectable mouth, and I feed her. Closing her eyes, she moans, and the sound is so orgasmic it's a miracle I don't come in my boxers. I'm painfully hard and straining against the crotch of my jeans.

She blinks her eyes open, and I feed her another forkful. She never takes her eyes off me as she slowly savors the food in her mouth, running her tongue around her lips after, in a way that makes me envious.

"What's the verdict?" I ask, my voice gruff with pent-up desire.

Her chest visibly heaves, and it takes ginormous willpower not to stare at the swell of her gorgeous tits. "It's delicious, and I'm not sure I'll be able to resist."

She reaches up, tracing the tip of her finger against my jawline. My Adam's apple bobs in my throat. *Are we still talking about food?*

"Then don't," I whisper, winding my hand into her hair. "You should always give in to your cravings." Feeling bolder, I grip the nape of her neck and move her in closer to me. Her gorgeous whiskey-colored eyes darken as she stares into my eyes. She cups my face more firmly, scrubbing a hand along the light layer of stubble on my chin and cheeks.

"Indulging my biggest craving could get me in a whole world of trouble," she whispers, still not removing the hold she has on my eyes.

"That depends on your definition of trouble, and sometimes the risk is worth it." I move my face closer to hers, and our noses brush. Her breath is warm and alluring as it gently fans over my face.

"Kaden." Torment floods her eyes, and I see the indecision as plainly as if it was written all over her face.

"Don't overthink it. Just go with your feelings." I gaze wistfully at her mouth. I want to be the one to bridge that gap, to devour her mouth like it's the oxygen I need to breathe, pouring months of longing into my kiss, but she's the one with everything to lose—her husband, her job. I'm pretty sure I could buy my way out of any trouble if I need to, so she has to be the one to make the move.

*Please be brave.*

*Please kiss me.*

"We shouldn't."

I don't know if she's trying to talk herself into it or out of it. "Do you want to?"

Tears well in her eyes. "So very much."

I mentally fist pump the air as I wrap my arm firmly around her back, pulling her upper body in flush to mine. "I want it. You want it." I peer deep into her eyes. "I don't think there's anything left to debate."

She zeroes in on my lips, and her head moves in a little until there's only a minuscule gap between our mouths. Blood is thrumming through my body, and my arousal is at an all-time high. I'm afraid to even take a breath. Afraid to move a muscle in case I throw her off and she changes her mind.

She sweeps her lips delicately against mine. It's brief and fleeting, but it's everything. Just as I move in for the kill, there's a firm rap at the door, and we break apart, almost comically fast.

"Eva!" A woman shouts through the door, her words slightly muffled. "Why is your door locked? Let me in."

Eva jumps up, a look of horror creeping across her face. I stand up and grip her forearms. "Get a hold of yourself. We haven't done anything wrong." She glances over her shoulder at the remnants of our takeout. "Go open the door and I'll clear this up," I say, already rounding up the empty cartons and soda cans.

I dump everything in the trashcan under her desk as she opens the door to her office. "Renee. I didn't realize you were still here," Eva says, and I detect the slight tremor in her voice.

I gather my backpack, strategically placing it to hide the protruding bulge in my jeans, and stroll toward the door where Eva is conversing with the same woman I've noticed her with before. From my research, I've discovered it's Professor March. She's cute with her blonde pixie cut and twinkling eyes, but she's not on Eva's scale of awesomeness, which is why her rep doesn't precede her in the same way Eva's does. "Thanks for the extra session, Professor Garcia. I think I'll ace the exam now." I smile cheerily at her like we weren't just seconds away from eating one another alive.

"You'd better," she jokes, playing along. "Or there'll be hell to pay." She pats me on the arm. "Good luck, Kaden. And I'll see you next week."

All week is spent in a hyped state of agitation. I go back and forth in my mind over Friday night, and I'm sorely tempted to stop by her office most every day, but I hold off because she hasn't made any move to contact me, and I'm not sure where things stand between us now.

When I show up in her office at the regular time Friday night, she acts as if nothing happened, and it fucking kills me. Especially when she walks to the door at the end of our session and flings it wide-open. "Okay, that will be all Mr. Kennedy until next week."

I stand up, staring at her. "That's it? You're shutting me out?"

She closes the door and pins me with a stern look. "I don't have a choice, and it's for the best."

"Says who? And you *always* have a choice."

She shakes her head, and the look of devastation on her face guts me. "I've never had a choice. I didn't choose this life. It chose me."

Her cryptic comment confuses me. "What? You don't want to work here?"

"No, I most definitely do, but that's the only aspect I've had a choice over."

Now I understand. Rumors around campus are that she married some old dude when she was eighteen. I'm sensing it's the truth and that it wasn't by choice, or maybe she was young and foolish and now she's wised up. "Divorce him," I blurt.

Her smile is sad. "I'm not discussing this with you, Kaden, and I've already crossed lines that shouldn't have been crossed." She folds her arms. "I'm glad Renee interrupted us last week before we both did something we'd regret."

"I wouldn't have regretted it," I spit out. "Not for a second."

Her features soften. "Perhaps you wouldn't, but I would. Once the excitement of fucking around with your teacher ends, you'll move on to the next girl, the next adventure, without a care in the world, and I'll be the one left devastated."

Anger simmers in my veins. "How dare you." I step up to her, peering into her eyes so she can see the truth radiating there. "How dare you put words in my mouth. How dare you suggest this is any less serious for me than it is for you. I care about you. *A lot*. I'm attracted to you. *A lot*. And I know you feel those things too. You can try to deny it, but I've seen it." Moving around her, I open the door. "The difference is, I would never have dismissed it so casually or cheapened your feelings. And maybe that's something to regret."

I don't stick around to hear her reply, if there is one. Exiting the room, I stomp down the corridor as fast as my legs will carry me.

# *Chapter Nine*
## Present Day

*Evelina*

Kaden calls a taxi, arranging for it to pick me up a couple blocks away, to be on the safe side. He insists on walking with me, and I don't put up a fight. After what happened earlier, I'm nervous to walk the streets alone. "Please think about what I said," he pleads with me again.

"We've already discussed this, Kade. No good can come from thinking thoughts like that. I'm really grateful for your help tonight. More than grateful. Honestly, there aren't words, but we can't fool ourselves into thinking this changes anything."

"Goddamn it, Eva." He tugs on my elbow, stalling me. "Why won't you fight for me?"

"This *is* me fighting for you!" I protest. "You have no idea how hard it was to let you go, but I did it for you!"

His expression softens. "I didn't fully understand back then, and I was a bit of a mess, but I've got my head screwed on now. I love you, and I'm not giving up this time. Not when I know who he is and what you're enduring."

"It's not so bad." I attempt to fudge the truth.

"Don't lie." He takes my arm, pushing the sleeve of my sweater up to my elbow. "Those marks don't lie, and don't pretend you got them tonight because the bruising is faded so I know they're at least a few days old." My wrists wouldn't bruise if I didn't strain against the binds so much, but I can't stand being tied up. Despite how much I beg Jeremy, he refuses to hear me. He's determined to knock me up and convinced he's making it pleasurable for me in the process, when the truth is the complete opposite.

Only a twisted pervert would mistake my anguished screams for cries of ecstasy.

I'm dying inside. Every day, a little bit more.

"It's not what you're thinking," I mumble, defeated.

He barks out a harsh laugh. "Oh, I think it's probably exactly what I'm thinking."

I look down at my feet. "We need to keep walking or I'll miss the cab." I feel the weight of Kaden's stare pressing down on me, but I keep my eyes affixed to the asphalt.

"I'm worried about you," he says, gently steering me forward, and we resume walking again.

"I'm not your responsibility," I softly reply.

"No. You're just the love of my life."

Oh, God. He's killing me. As surely as if he'd driven a stake straight through my heart.

I don't respond, because I can't tell him I feel the same, so it's best to stay quiet.

He sighs. "If you won't run away with me, at least let me help you stay safe," he adds a few minutes later.

"What do you mean?" I risk a look at him, and my heart melts on the spot.

"I train at the gym most nights. Meet me there. Let me teach you some self-defense techniques."

I open my mouth to immediately reject it, but he places two fingers to my lips. "Don't automatically turn me down without thinking about it. I'd rest easier at night knowing you are capable of defending yourself. Just promise me you'll think about it."

I find myself nodding, and I can almost see some of the tension leave his shoulders.

He watches me with those serious, intense eyes of his as I get into the taxi. Closing the door, he continues to eyeball me. As the taxi pulls away from the curb, I turn around and look at him, and we continue staring at one another until he's only a blip in the distance.

Back home, Jeremy is waiting up for me, and he's on guard the instant he spots the ugly gash on my cheek. "What happened?"

"I had too much to drink, and I tripped and fell on the sidewalk," I lie. "I ruined my clothes, so I went back to Renee's to get changed and cleaned up."

He frowns. "Evie, that's not like you." And he's right. It's not. I have an iron strong constitution when it comes to alcohol. I can count on one hand the number of times I've been drunk, and I can drink most men under the table.

"I think it's because I'm approaching my time of month. My tolerance must be less or something."

Jeremy pulls me into his side, more tenderly than normal. "Why don't you take a bath and I'll fix you some chamomile tea?"

I look up at him, shock splayed across my face. Jeremy is not the type to fuss over anyone. Except, perhaps, the first Mrs. Garcia, but he doesn't fuss over me, so this is a new development. He swats my butt, more gently than usual. "Go on. I'll bring your tea to your room."

The hot water soothes the aches and pains and helps relax me. After I'm dry, I dress in silk pajamas and crawl under my comforter. Jeremy appears in the doorway a second later dressed only in snug boxer briefs, carrying a tray with tea and some ginger cookies. Placing the tray on my bedside table, he closes my bedroom door and slides into bed alongside me, much to my dismay.

I was hoping my injury gave me a sexual pass for tonight, but that was clearly wishful thinking.

He obviously senses it, because he rubs a hand up and down my arm in a comforting gesture. "I know you're hurting, darling, so I won't prolong it tonight. I'll be quick and gentle."

The tea and cookies settle in my stomach like rat poison. So much for showing a nurturing side.

Since he decided we were going to try for a baby, he seems intent on impregnating me as fast as he can. His once weekly conjugal visits have now become nightly ones, and I'm beginning to really hate the feel of his hands roaming my body.

Thank God, I had the foresight to get a contraceptive implant a couple years ago. It was a precautionary measure when Kaden and I started sleeping together, and now I'm grateful for it and the fact Jeremy knows nothing about it. Although, I'm sure it's only a matter of time before it'll all come out. When I fail to get pregnant, I expect he'll send me to someone and the truth will be revealed.

He'll go crazy.

But I'll cross that bridge when I come to it.

For now, I want to delay the inevitable.

I'm deluding myself.

I know that.

But there's still a teeny, tiny part of me that harbors hope that I will someday escape his clutches. Add a child into the equation, and that becomes a definite impossibility. Jeremy would never let me take any child of his away, and I wouldn't be selfish enough to leave any child with him alone.

For now, I'm a certain kind of trapped.

But, maybe, just maybe, Kaden is right.

As Jeremy thrusts inside me, I go to that special place in my mind, imagining it's Kaden moving inside me, his hands exploring my body, and I allow myself to believe, if only for a few moments in time.

I believe in Kaden's determined words, and I imagine a full life with him, free of the shackles restraining me.

"This is gorgeous, Mrs. Hill," Jeremy tells my mom, tucking heartily into our regular monthly Sunday dinner of roast beef with all the sides. I enjoy visiting my parents about as much as I enjoy visiting my OB/GYN.

"How many times do I have to tell you to call me Isabel," she says, batting her eyelashes and patting his arm. In my head, I mimic her reply, because it's the same one I've heard over and over, like a broken record. "You make me sound so old." She giggles, a ridiculous shrill laugh that is unbecoming for a woman of her age. At least that is what my father has told her time and time again.

But my mom is a law unto herself.

She proved that when she made the deal with the devil, convincing my father there was no alternative.

There's never any question over who wears the pants in this household.

Jeremy groans as he bites into his beef, and I have a strong urge to kick him under the table. I'd think he did it on purpose, except I know my husband isn't the petty type. If Jeremy wants you to know something, you'll hear it. He is blunt to a fault.

"From the way you're devouring that meal, one would think you never get a home-cooked meal," she simpers, and I want to scratch her eyes out. Although she is deliberately riling me up, I can't resist going there. It embarrasses her no end when I retaliate—it's unladylike and uncouth, she's often told me.

"Jeremy gets a lovely home-cooked meal every night. Camille is a wonderful cook." I shoot her a forced smile as I pop an overdone green bean in my mouth. "And she always serves her green beans al dente. I can send her over to you for a demonstration, if you like."

"Evie." Jeremy's voice is like steel as he slants a cautionary look my way. "Don't be rude to your mother."

"Sorry, Isabel." I don't even attempt to sound genuinely apologetic, and tension slices through the air like a knife gliding through soft butter.

My father clears his throat. "Any update on tenure yet, sweetheart?" he asks me. Predictably, my mother scowls, and Jeremy looks bored.

"Not yet. Competition is tough, and places are limited. Jesse Roberts is looking for tenure too, and he's very well connected. This is a crucial year for me if I'm to stand any chance against him."

"You'll get it," Dad says, smiling proudly. "Harvard recognizes quality when they see it, and they'd be fools to risk losing you."

"It's a moot point," Jeremy cuts in, dabbing the side of his mouth with his napkin. "Because once Evie is pregnant, she'll be giving up work to look after our children."

My fork clangs to the table, and my mouth hangs open in shock. "What?"

Jeremy drills me a serious look. "I'm not having some stranger rear my children. Your place will be at home."

"I never agreed to that," I hiss.

"It was an unspoken condition of our marriage."

"I didn't agree to that either," I blurt, too enraged to curtail my feelings.

"Evelina!" Mom's shocked tone bounces off the cream walls. "Apologize to your husband right this second."

I stand up. "Or what, Isabel? You'll put me over your knee and scold me with the wooden spoon like you did when I was naughty as a child?"

I begin clearing the dinner plates. My father locks eyes with mine as I lift his plate, his regret and anguish plainly evident. His eyes flit to my wrists and the yellowed marks peeking out from under the cuffs of my blouse. Sadness mixes with frustration and anger as he gulps, knotting his napkin on his lap.

He may have inadvertently got me into this situation, but he's not the one I blame.

All fingers point to the woman who birthed me. I refuse to call her mother because she relinquished that title the day she traded my future away.

When Dad realized who he was working for, and what he'd gotten mixed up in, he tried to get out, but the guy in charge before Jeremy—his father—made sure he'd be tied to them for life.

I still remember the night he came to our house. I had just turned twelve, and I woke up, roused by the shouting from downstairs. I'd been scared, but not scared enough to stay in bed. Creeping out onto the landing, I had hovered at the top of the stairs listening to the raised voices arguing below. Then the kitchen door opened, and the argument had moved into the hall. "Get out," my dad told the strange man. "I will never agree to such a thing."

"Jack," Mom pleaded with him. "Let's discuss this on our own, and you can call Robert tomorrow."

"You listen to your little lady," a deep, unfamiliar voice said. "She understands the situation. Decide carefully, Jack. Your family's future depends on it."

The man strode to the front door and opened it, but he stopped, as if he'd heard some silent calling card. Whipping his head around, he stared straight at me.

Even as a child, the sly smile he threw my way sent shivers down my spine.

His premature demise was a welcome reprieve. He died four months before Jeremy and I were married, so at least I didn't have to suffer him as a father-in-law. Jeremy's mother died when he was young, before she'd had the chance to give him any siblings, and the lack of in-laws to contend with is the only small blessing I've received.

"Evelina!" Isabel snaps, yanking me from my mind. "I need your help with dessert."

Calmly, I carry the dirty dinner plates to the kitchen, loading them into the dishwasher.

"What the hell has gotten into you?" she demands once we're in the kitchen and the door is firmly closed.

"I'm sure I don't know what you mean."

"You shouldn't goad your husband like that or speak back to your elders in front of him." She removes the chocolate cheesecake I made from the fridge, placing it on the counter.

"He's not fucking God, Isabel!"

She raises her hand to slap me, but I grab hold of her wrist. "Hit me and I'll hit back. I'm not some vulnerable little child you can whack with a spoon when you feel like it."

"That was for your own good, and you know it."

"Yeah," I snort. "Fat lot of good it did." I yank the cupboard door open, removing small plates.

"After everything your father and I have done for you." She mutters under her breath, shaking her head as she starts cutting through the decadent dessert.

"Are you kidding? After everything you've done? You've trapped me in a loveless marriage to a criminal who now wants to chain me pregnant and barefoot in the kitchen. Thanks a bunch, *Mother*. I definitely owe you for that."

This time I don't see the slap coming in time to stop it. My head jerks back with the force of the impact. Stinging pain glances across my cheek. She would have to hit the one that's already sore. I'm tempted to follow through on my threat, and hit her back, but then I'd be no better than her. And I pride myself on the fact I'm nothing like her.

"You ungrateful little madam! That man is a good man, and he's given you a great life. Plenty of women would kill to be in your place."

"I'd happily trade places!" I hiss, deliberately keeping my tone low in case anything filters back. "And how can you call him a good man? He sells drugs and guns for a living, and that's only the stuff I know about."

"He is good to you and that's all that counts."

I shake my head, practically throwing the cake onto the plates. "How can you live with yourself? With all these lies you tell yourself? How can you look in the mirror knowing you forced me into marrying someone I didn't love?"

"Love," she scoffs. "You always had your head in the clouds. I blame your father and all those movies he took you to. Love doesn't exist, Evelina. Survival is all that counts. And your father and I ensured that the day we made that deal. It was that or we all died." She shoves two plates at me, taking the other two and heading toward the door. "It's time you grew up and faced things like a mature adult. Whether you approved of our decision or not, you want for nothing. Your children will want for nothing. Maybe when you're a mother yourself, you'll finally see what's important in life."

She flings open the door, casting one last derogatory glance over her shoulder at me before she exits the room. "And it's not love."

# *Chapter Ten*
## Present – Senior Year of College

*Kaden*

I have renewed vigor in my step as I walk toward the gym tonight. Since Eva texted last night to say she'd accept my offer to train her in self-defense, I've been on a countdown, dying to get up close and personal with her again. I'm glad she agreed, because she needs to know how to defend herself. And it gives me the opportunity to work on eliminating the barrier she's still keeping between us. I understand her reasoning now—it all makes sense, and I'm not walking away from her this time.

"Yo, Kennedy." Dylan Barnes shouts out as I walk through the doors of the gym. Dylan co-owns this place with his partner Gary and I've gotten to know both of them since I joined.

I stride toward him, and we knuckle touch. "'Sup, dude?"

"Heard you and Tiff broke up again."

"Yeah." I shrug, not wanting to dwell on it. "She's cool, but it ran its course, and we're totally done this time."

"Hmm." He scrubs a hand over his jaw. "Guess you won't be pleased to hear she's in the office waiting for you then."

I groan. "Ah, shit, man. I actually thought she'd gotten the message this time."

"Want me to get rid of her for you?"

I shake my head. "Nah. I'll talk to her myself, but can you do me a favor?" I lower my voice. "I've agreed to provide some self-defense lessons to one of my ex-teachers. She's due to arrive shortly. Can you show her to the ladies' locker room and tell her I'll be with her as soon as I can?"

"No probs." He shoves a clipboard at me. "Just add her name to the guest list and I'll look after her."

I quickly write Eva's name down.

"Holy shit, Kennedy. You're coaching Professor Garcia?" He whistles low on his breath. "Better hope word doesn't get out." He chortles. "Or maybe I should leak it myself. I bet new memberships would go through the roof."

My jaw locks up, and I glare at him. "You better fucking not!"

He steps back, holding his palms up. "Whoa! Calm the fuck down. I'm only messing around."

I force myself to cool it, rubbing a hand along the back of my neck. "There's a reason she needs these sessions, and she's notoriously private. I don't want anything to get in the way."

His expression turns more serious, and he nods slowly. "Yeah, I've heard some of the rumors going around. Her old man's not to be messed with."

"Something like that," I mutter, not wanting to create more gossip. "Just keep this on the down low."

"Done, dude." He slaps me on the back while I go to get rid of Tiffani.

"But I miss you, babe." Tiffani pouts, getting up from the couch in Dylan's office and crossing the room toward me.

"It hasn't been that long." I hold out an arm, stalling her forward trajectory.

"Feels like eternity to me."

I sigh. "I'm sorry, Tiffani. I don't know what you want me to say. I haven't changed my mind, and I'm not going to."

"Don't make me beg." She pouts again, and her lower lip wobbles.

"Don't go there, Tiff. It won't make any difference. We're done. It's time to move on and date other people." I don't know how I can be any blunter without hurting her feelings. "And you can't come here again. I don't want to tell Dylan to ban you, but if you show up again you won't leave me much choice."

A dark shadow descends upon her face. Yanking her bag off the arm of the couch, she angrily slides the strap over her shoulder. "You're making a big mistake, Kaden."

"I'm sorry you feel that way." I walk to the door and open it. She shoves past, sending me a hate-filled look. I shake my head as I close Dylan's door and turn to go after her. I want to make sure she leaves the premises promptly.

"Oof!"

I look up in time to see Tiffani run straight into Eva. Fucckkk!

"What are you doing here?" Tiff demands, frowning at Eva.

"She's a new member," Dylan pipes up, lying smoothly, and I could kiss him, if I was that way inclined. "I'm just giving the obligatory tour, so, if you'll excuse me." Dylan gently takes Eva's arm, steering her away from Tiffani.

"Mr. Kennedy." Eva smiles and nods at me in passing, barely giving me any attention, and I've got to give her credit for playing it perfectly.

Tiffani has narrowed her eyes, and she's slanting daggers in Eva's back as they walk off.

"Let me show you to the door." I place my hand very lightly on her back, nudging her toward the front entrance.

"Take your hand off me!" she hisses, slapping my arm away. "I'm well capable of finding the exit by myself."

"Suit yourself." I stop at the reception desk, watching her stomp outside.

"She's a piece of work," Dylan says, coming up behind me.

"She's not so bad. She's just upset."

"What do you want me to do if she shows up here again?"

"Don't let her in, and if she wants to take out membership, tell her you're full." I eyeball him. "Under no circumstances do I want her work-ing out here." I feel confident making demands because I helped Dylan and Gary get a great deal on equipment when they first took over the gym, saving them thousands in the process, and I've never asked for any favors in return. But I need this one now.

Dylan slaps me on the back. "Consider it done." He jerks his head to the side. "Eva is getting changed, and she said she'd meet you in the main room in a few minutes."

"Thanks, man. I owe you."

I'm limbering up, doing a few stretches, when Eva walks out onto the floor. She looks even tinier than normal in her sneakers. She's wearing black yoga pants that mold to her envious curves and a black-and-white sports tank top that hugs her rack to perfection. Her hair is slicked back into a high ponytail, and she isn't wearing a lick of makeup, but she's still the most stunning woman I've ever seen. As my dick springs to life in my sweats, I wonder why I thought this would be a good idea. I'll probably spend the entire session rock hard and struggling to hide that fact.

I straighten up, discreetly adjusting myself in my pants. "Hey, Eva."

"Hi, Kade." Her smile is a little shaky, and as she glances around, noting the mostly male members, I sense her nervousness.

"Don't be nervous." I rush to reassure her. "These guys won't pay us any attention. These dudes are hard-core and they have no interest in anyone else. We can do our stuff without prying eyes."

"Okay." Her smile is a little brighter.

I frown at the discoloration on her cheek. The gash has scabbed over, but the bruising looks fresh. "Did something else happen?"

Anger flashes briefly at the back of her eyes, and she grits her teeth. "Nope. Can we get started?"

Letting that obvious deflection pass, I nod. "Come this way." With a one-shouldered shrug, I lead the way over to the side of the room where the padded mats are laid out. "I thought we could start with some stretches and then a couple of basic moves once you're warmed up."

"Sounds good."

We spend ten minutes limbering up, with Eva diligently copying my every move. "You're very flexible," I say. "And you mentioned yoga the other night. I assume you go regularly?"

She nods, leaning forward with one knee bent as she stretches her other leg out behind her. "I've been going twice a week religiously for years. Helps keep my body and mind in check."

"My cousin and her friend attend the yoga classes on campus. Is that where you go?"

She shakes her head, straightening up as I do, swinging her arms from side to side and loosening her muscles. "I go to a studio on John F. Kennedy Street with Renee."

I nod. "Oh, yeah. I know the place. It's on my walk home."

"Have you ever attended a class?"

"Nope, although I did consider it. Yoga's definitely becoming more popular with guys."

"A lot of professional sports teams have full-time yoga instructors on payroll, and it's not just about the physical benefits. It's a total mind-body workout, and I find it super helpful whenever I'm stressed."

"Maybe I'll sign up for a class." My lips tip up at the corners.

"That would be interesting," she murmurs, fighting a smile of her own. "Do you still play golf?"

"Not as much as I'd like to. My course load is heavy this year, and I'm in the early-stage process of establishing my own online golf business. It's what I plan to do after I graduate."

A look of admiration ghosts over her face. "Wow, that's fantastic, Kaden." Her radiant smile is doing funny things to my insides. "I'm really proud of you, and I know you'll make it a great success."

"Thank you. I hope so."

"You always had plenty of drive and determination, and I believe that's half the battle."

I want to scoop her up into my arms and hug the shit out of her. She has no idea how much her words of encouragement mean, but I'm conscious we're just standing in the middle of the gym talking, and we're starting to garner attention.

"Thanks for the compliment, but we should probably focus on why we're here." I crick my neck from side to side and cross my arms over my chest. Her eyes follow the movement, and that does wonders for my ego. Smothering another grin, I clear my throat. "I think that warmup will suffice. Let's get started on the good stuff." I wink, purposely trying to keep this lighthearted.

"Turn around," I instruct, and she obliges. I move up behind her, and her body tenses a little. "I'm going to try and grab you from behind, and I just want you to react instinctively."

I lunge for her, wrapping my arms around her waist from behind and she immediately starts squirming, trying to wriggle out of my grasp, but I tighten my arms and pull her back, and she gives up fighting after a couple of minutes.

I let go and twist her around to face me. "That's the way a lot of people would react if attacked from behind, and your instincts are good, but you'll only have a short window to take back control, and being as aggressive as possible is crucial." She's watching and listening intently, a serious expression on her face. "We're going to try the same maneuver again, only this time I want you to drop as low to the ground as you can and wriggle aggressively, trying to get out of my hold."

She nods and turns back around, and I reach for her again, but she isn't fast enough, and my arms lock firmly around her, easily restraining her. We try another few times, and I admire Eva's tenaciousness. She never complains. Never criticizes herself. She just focuses, determined to lower her center of gravity and evade the attack.

On the tenth attempt, she drops instantly to the ground, wriggling as I struggle to hold onto her. "Good! Now reach back with your leg and aim for a groin kick."

She does as I suggest, but she loses her balance, and I'm bent awkwardly over her, so I lose my balance too, and we tumble to the ground. At the last second, I clasp her hips firmly and twist her around, sliding underneath her to take the brunt of the fall. She lands on top of me as my back flattens to the ground.

Suddenly conscious of how perfectly our bodies are aligned, I tense up, every muscle in my body becoming rigidly stiff.

Especially the muscle in my pants.

Fuck.

There's no way she's not feeling the hardness against her lower belly. Her breathing becomes heavy, and she's gone still and quiet. It's as if our surroundings have faded away and there's only the two of us in the room. I'm aware of every exaggerated breath trickling out of those plump lips and how she leans into me, ever so subtly, but it's there—the desire to get closer. And I'd love to capitalize on that, but we're *not* in our own little universe. We're in a busy gym with too many eyeballs in the vicinity, and we need to get up, but there's no hiding the massive erection I'm sporting.

"Eva." My voice is low but ragged. "I need you to get up and grab my bag for me. Okay?"

She clears her throat. "Sure." Her voice sounds as strained as mine.

Asking her to move kills me. I'd quite happily stay in this position, but I have to do it. The longer we stay pressed against one another without moving, the more attention we're likely to attract. She stands, and I jump up, turning around in an attempt to hide my monster boner. She hands me the sports bag, and I sling it crossways over one shoulder, strategically covering my groin. I turn to face her, and the depth of emotion on her face almost undoes me.

She coughs, clearing her throat again. "I guess we should call it a night."

I nod. "Yeah. After you've changed, wait for me in the reception area, and I'll walk you to your car." I'm expecting her to argue but she doesn't.

"Okay."

We walk side by side to the changing rooms, neither of us speaking. Tension lingers in the air, and my fingers twitch with the craving to touch her. The feel of her curves under my hands has reignited my desire for her, and I know I'll be rubbing one out when I get home.

Or two or ten.

We reach the changing area, and I place my hand on the door to the men's room. "Kade." Her soft voice does strange things to my body. I turn around, and a knowing smile graces her mouth. She stretches up on tiptoe, and I meet her halfway, bending down. Pressing her mouth to my ear, she whispers, "If it's any consolation, if I was a guy, I'd have a raging hard-on for you right now."

I jerk my head back in surprise, and she laughs at the expression on my face.

"I don't want you to go," I blurt, grasping this opportunity with both hands. "Let's order some takeout and go back to my place."

Her smile falters, and she glances around, making sure no one is paying attention. "I'm not sure that's such a good idea."

"Who cares?" I pin her with a penetrating look. "All that matters is whether you want to or not?"

She averts her eyes, sighing as she rubs a hand across her chest. When she lifts her head a few minutes later, I note determination on her face. "Okay. But we go in separate cars, and I'll be parking a couple of blocks away."

"Fine. You still have my number?"

"I know your number."

"Hit me up once you're parked, and I'll come get you."

She gulps, and a look of fear skitters over her face. I'm afraid she's already going to change her mind, and it'd crush me. "I just want to talk to you, Eva. It's only dinner and conversation. I'm not expecting anything else." That's no word of a lie. It *is* all I expect. But if you asked me what I *want*, what I *hope* and *pray* and *wish* for, the answer would be completely different.

A smile ghosts over her lips as she pushes the door to the ladies' locker room open. Holding the door open, she sends me a seductive grin. "Maybe I am."

Hot damn.

With those awesome parting words drifting in and out of my ears, she skips into the room, leaving me standing in the corridor like a schmuck with a goofy grin on my face and my jaw hanging open.

# Chapter Eleven

## Past

*Evelina*

It's been two months since the night Kaden and I almost kissed, and I can't get him out of my head. It's wrong on so many different levels, but his soul speaks to mine in a way I can't explain. If we had met in a different lifetime, there's little doubt we'd be together. We just clicked from the moment we met. He gets me, and I get him, and being with him is as natural as breathing.

The age gap is almost five years between us, and for most that would probably be the biggest turn-off, but it's the last thing I have an issue with. I hardly ever remember he's younger than me. Kaden is very mature for his age. He's had to grow up a lot these last couple of years thanks to all the stuff going on in his family, and it's clear he's well-educated and well-read, and we've had some interesting conversations. He's also passionate about enterprise, with a real fire in his belly. He exudes this calm, cool confidence that is extremely attractive. But he doesn't take himself too seriously either, and I laugh so much in his company. He reminds me what it feels like to be young. I feel like I skipped a whole phase in my life. That my world came to an end at fourteen, and I've only just begun living again.

But I had to put a stop to it.

Because there's no future in it, so why start something?

Try telling that to my foolish, lovesick heart though.

Acting impersonal and professional during our weekly tutoring sessions is slowly killing me inside. Each week, another layer tears off my heart. Very soon, there'll be nothing left but a bloody pulp in my chest.

Everything about Kaden sucks me in. His voice. His smell. His powerful presence. That deep, intense, hypnotic gaze of his—the one that seems to delve deep into my soul, to drag the truth I'm hiding straight from the very heart of me.

I shake my head, laughing at myself as I finish styling my hair. I sound like a Mills and Boon novel. And it's unusual for me to indulge that long-forgotten romantic side of me.

"Where did you say you were off to tonight?" Jeremy asks, popping his head into my room unannounced.

I jump at the unexpected intrusion, dropping my makeup bag on the floor. I sink to my knees, hastily grabbing the errant contents and stuffing them back inside. I'm all flustered when I straighten up. "I'm going to that new bar on Garden Street with Renee and a few of my work colleagues. Renee just got tenure so we're celebrating."

He casts an approving eye over my conservative black and green dress. With a high collarbone, knee-length hem, and small cap sleeves, it's a sophisticated style that covers my curves from straying eyes. "You look beautiful, Evie."

"Thank you."

He steps into the room, and my heart stutters at the thought of what he might want. We have a pretty solid, unspoken agreement. He visits my bedroom every Friday night, and I put out like a good, dutiful wife. The rest of the time, we are like passing ships in the night, coming and going at different hours. Jeremy is gone a lot. Overseas "business" trips, but unlike most wives, I relish the time apart. I feel a little guilty on occasion for my lack of investment in this marriage until I remember I was forced into it at eighteen, and then any sympathy I have for my husband evaporates. He should know not to expect much when your bride was coerced into marrying you.

Still, I'm savvy enough to know it could be a lot worse.

Jeremy doesn't demand too much of me—he seems to have accepted the loveless state of our marriage, and he has been reluctantly supportive of my studies and my career.

He pecks me on the cheek. "I'll send Vincent out with you tonight."

"That will *not* be necessary." I fold my arms in a stern manner. "Please let's not argue about this again, especially not when we're both getting ready to go out."

"Evie. It's for your own protection."

"And you've been saying that for years, and I've gone without a personal bodyguard and I'm perfectly fine. Please, Jeremy. Just trust me. I can handle myself. I'll be getting a taxi there and back and nothing will happen to me."

He brushes a lock of my hair over my shoulder. "You're so stubborn."

"I like to call it independent."

He chuckles. "You'll be the death of me one of these days."

*I wish.*

I'm shocked at my own thoughts. Irrespective of how trapped I feel, I could never wish him ill. It was a random selfish thought. One that deserves no more time spent on it.

I won the argument and I'm out sans Vincent. Thank God. He's a new guy Jeremy hired a couple of months ago, and the way his eyes follow me around the house creeps me out.

"We're dancing!" Renee decides, grabbing hold of my hand and pulling me out into the middle of the packed dance floor. We left the bar after a couple of hours and headed to a nearby club. I think Renee was shocked I readily agreed to attend, but I missed out on all this when I was in college, and I seize every opportunity that comes my way now. Being married at eighteen and wearing the hated "child prodigy" label made me stick out like a sore thumb when I was a Harvard student. No one wanted to hang around with me, and Jeremy made it clear I would not be falling drunk out of frat houses or socializing with any single males. After the Seth experience, I had no desire to involve anyone else in my fucked-up life, so it was a moot point, but there would've been no easy way to explain that to Jeremy. So, I just put up and shut up instead.

Nights like these are precious, so I try and make the most of them. Jeremy's traveled upstate and he won't be home till Monday night, so I'm free to do as I please. I've no doubt his bodyguards will report the time

I arrive home, so I can't go too crazy, but I can let my hair down without fear of repercussion.

Sometimes it feels like I'm married to my dad.

Renee's two sheets to the wind already, dancing like a crazy woman in the middle of the dance floor, and all I can do is laugh. "Come on, Eva," she encourages, shimmying her hips from side to side, her words slurring a little. "Let go! You've got the killer curves and the killer dress. All you're missing are the killer moves."

She winks, and I laugh again, rotating my hips in time to the music. She throws her hands in the air, whooping and hollering, and a surge of emotion sweeps over me. Pulling Renee into a hug, I press my mouth to her ear. "I'm so proud of you, bestie. And no one deserves it more."

"Aw. I love you, Eva. And it'll be your turn soon enough. Everyone knows you're the most dedicated assistant prof there is." She squeezes me tight. "It's you and me against the Harvard dicks, babe."

I throw back my head, laughing as I let the lure of the music take full control of my body. I rock my hips in time to the beat, flinging my hair over my shoulders and closing my eyes as rhythmic waves crash over me. My moves are fluid, and I'm thankful I changed out of that boring dress the minute I hit the bar, switching it for a short lacy black dress with thin straps that crisscross over my shoulders and halfway down my back. The hem stops mid-thigh, and combined with the seven-inch heels I'm wearing, it makes my legs appear longer and thinner.

Jeremy would stroke out if he saw me dressed like this.

Perhaps it's the dress, or the sultry music, or the copious cocktails I've consumed, but I'm feeling sexy and dangerously reckless, which should be a worrying combination. But I'm too high on the illusion of freedom to care.

"Woo-hoo!" Renee grabs my hand, twirling me around, and I'm laughing so hard I don't notice him at first.

But it doesn't take long, because Kaden Kennedy owns every room he steps into, his commanding presence filling the space without even trying. All the tiny hairs lift on the back of my neck as my eyes lock on his. He's standing at the end of the bar, his gaze fixated on me, and he's making zero attempt to disguise it.

I wonder how long he's been watching.

Saliva pools in my mouth, and my panties are instantly soaked as I drink him in. He's wearing dark denim jeans that emphasize his long legs and a slim-fitting white Henley with the top two buttons undone. The shirt looks like it's spray-painted on his body, molding to his ripped abs and broad shoulders. His hair is styled back off his face, highlighting his exquisite bone structure and the five o'clock shadow on his chin. Even from here, his captivating blue eyes and masculine jawline draw me in. I've never been so physically attracted to any guy before, and it's hard to deny my feelings when he's looking at me like he wants to eat me alive.

Powerful need pulses through my body, and I'm walking toward him before I've consciously processed the motion. His eyes rake me up and down as I approach, and the potent lust-filled look on his face is unmistakable. I'm about ten feet away when a gorgeous blonde plants herself in front of him, running her hands up his chest and circling them around his neck.

Jealousy jumps up and bites me, and I'm having a hard time ignoring the devil on my shoulder, the one taunting me to claim what's mine.

I make a last-minute detour, veering toward the bathroom instead. My heart is beating wildly against my ribcage, and blood is thrumming through my veins. *What the hell was I thinking back there?* Anyone could've noticed me making a beeline for Kaden across the dance floor. One look at both our faces would've given the game away. My hands are shaking as I push through the door out into the corridor leading to the restrooms. Nausea swims up my throat at the thought of that girl with her hands all over him. I stop, resting my forehead against the wall. *What the hell is wrong with me?* He isn't mine, and I shouldn't be having these thoughts.

I'm married, for God's sake, and he's my student.

He's as off-limits as they come.

Perhaps that's why I want him so badly.

Isn't it true what they say? You always want the things you can't have.

The door crashes open, and I stop breathing. "Eva."

Oh, God. Please give me strength to do the right thing. I hurriedly compose myself before I turn around to face him. "Kaden."

"We need to talk."

"I don't think that's a good idea."

"Well, tough," he says, walking around me and pushing the door to the wheelchair-accessible toilet open. "In here, quick."

Against my better judgment, I duck under his arm and step inside the small stall. He locks the door and then leans back against it, running a hand through his hair. Strands come loose, falling over his forehead in a casual way that is completely sexy.

"I can't stop thinking about you," he admits candidly, and butterflies take up residence in my chest. "And I miss our chats. You're one of the few people I'm comfortable talking to. It's so easy to just be myself when I'm with you." His expression is deadly serious as he eyeballs me, but there's a soft layer underneath it. "I guess I just miss everything about you. And judging by the way you were looking at me out there, I'd say you're the same." I chew on the inside of my mouth, hugely conflicted. "And you look beautiful by the way, and too damn sexy for that crowd."

I thrill at his bold statement, and I know I'm fighting a losing battle even as words to the contrary slip from my mouth. "This can't happen, Kaden."

"Why not?"

"You know why." I start pacing the small space. "I'm married, and you're my student. Starting something could get both of us into big trouble."

"The things truly worth fighting for in life come with the biggest risks." He pushes off the door, cautiously approaching me. I'm acutely aware of every delectable inch of him as he approaches, and I'm struggling to hold on to my willpower. "And you don't need to worry about me." Tentatively, he reaches out, caressing my cheek. "If it blew up in our faces, I would be okay. The biggest risk is on your end, and it's the main reason I haven't said anything these last couple of months. I'd come to the conclusion you weren't feeling it the way I was, but I see it written all over your face. I know you want me as much as I want you."

I take a step back, needing to clear my head. "Wow, you're awfully sure of yourself."

"Tell me I'm wrong and I'll walk away. I'll leave you alone and never mention this again."

I gulp over the sudden panic in my throat. I don't want him to leave. Screw it. I throw caution to the wind. "I can't tell you that."

A massive smile coasts over his mouth. "Thank you for being honest." His smile turns more serious. "And I meant what I said. You have the most to lose so this is your call. I won't think any worse of you if you decide you can't take the risk. I'd hate myself if you got into trouble because of me."

I step forward, placing my hands lightly on his chest as I stare up at him. "I'm not sure I have much of a choice anymore. I've tried staying away from you, and it's slowly killing me inside."

He grips my face more firmly. "Tell me about it." His warm breath intoxicates me as he leans in closer. "If we do this, I'm not holding back. I'm on the verge of fucking exploding. I need you, Eva. I need you now." He probes my eyes. "How much have you been drinking?"

I grab hold of his shirt, pulling him even closer. "I've had a few cocktails, but I'm not drunk. Not even close to it. I can handle my liquor." I drag my fingers up and down the exposed column of his neck, enjoying how he trembles at my touch. "I appreciate you ensuring I'm sober enough to make this decision, and I assure you I am. You're not the only one hurting, Kaden." I lower my voice. "I want you so badly, but this works both ways. My husband is a dangerous man, and if he ever finds out, he will come after you."

He pulls my hand up to his mouth, pressing a kiss to my palm. "We'll be careful and make sure he doesn't find out, and if he does, I know people. I can make sure I'm protected. Like I said, my worry is for you. I don't want you to lose your job."

"Me neither, but I don't think I can stop this anymore."

He presses his forehead to mine, pulling me in flush with his body. "Thank God, because I'm about to die of the worst case of blue balls known to mankind."

I laugh, but there's a layer of excited anticipation behind it. I slide my hand down between us, cupping his very hard, very impressive erection. He hisses, thrusting into my palm as I rub up and down his length through the denim. "We can't be gone too long," I whisper, popping the top button of his jeans. I look up at him, and the heated look in his eyes floods my body with arousal. My nipples are hard and straining against my bra, my panties soaked. "Fuck me hard and fast, Kaden. No more thinking of right or wrong. Just do it."

His mouth crashes down on mine, and I lose all rational thought. He isn't gentle, and I'm loving it. His tongue prods at my lips, and I open for him, welcoming him into my mouth. The kiss turns frenzied very quickly, and we're devouring one another as months of pent-up frustration is finally released. I yank his jeans down and slip my hand into his boxer briefs, moaning into his mouth as I grasp his velvety soft, hot length and start stroking. He's thick and firm and my core pulses in achy need. His hands are roaming my body, exploring with an urgency I appreciate. He pulls the straps of my dress and bra down, and cool air floats across my breasts, hardening my nipples further.

He rips his mouth off mine momentarily to take his fill. Grabbing both of my breasts, he fondles the sensitive skin, emitting a slew of expletives as he looks and touches. "Fuck, Eva. You've no idea how often I jerk off to thoughts of your naked body, but my imagination did not do you justice at all." Dropping his head, he sucks one nipple into his mouth, and I cry out, stroking him quicker and rubbing my thumb across the tip of his cock. Precum slicks across my skin, and he pulls back, removing my hand. "If you continue doing that, this will be over in seconds. I need to fill you up. I want to feel what it's like moving inside you."

He frantically pushes my dress up to my hips and tugs my lace thong down in one swift move. "Jesus Christ," he says, pushing one finger inside me. "You're fucking drenched, Eva."

"I need you now, Kaden." My voice drips with need, and I scarcely even sound like myself.

He adds a second finger, pumping in and out of me in languid strokes. I rest my head back against the wall, writhing with uncontrollable lust, greedily riding his fingers as he fucks me. No guy has ever gotten me this aroused, and the need to feel him inside me is almost overpowering. "Kade!"

He chuckles, removing his fingers and pulling me forward. His mouth collides with mine in a hungry kiss. "Tell me you want this, Eva," he whispers in between drugging kisses. "Tell me you want my cock inside you. I need to hear you say the words."

"I want that. So badly. Right now, Kade."

He flips me around, and I press my palms to the wall. He spreads my legs wider, and I hear the rip of paper as he sheaths himself. "I love this ass," he says, pressing a tender kiss to each of my cheeks. Lining himself at my entrance, he thrusts inside me in one fluid move. I bite back my scream, moaning quietly as he fucks me hard, slamming in and out of me, making stars appear before my eyes. Pressure is building inside me already, and my body is alive in a way I've never experienced before. The depth of pleasure coursing through my veins is new and like a drug I think I could easily become addicted to.

Keeping one hand on my hip to steady me, he moves his other hand around, cupping my breast first and tweaking the overly sensitized nipple. I push my tit into his hand, and he kneads my flesh harder. Blood rushes to my pussy, and I'm rocking back against him, demanding he move faster and harder. When his hand moves lower, he teases my clit with soft, featherlike brushes of his fingers while continuing to thrust into me like a wild, out of control animal. "Fuck, Eva. You feel incredible." He leans over me, covering my back with his body. Slowly, he pushes my hair to one side, sucking on my neck, right where my pulse throbs for him. "I won't ever get enough of you. This is only the start," he whispers before easing back. Then he thrusts long and deep before pinching my clit, and I detonate on the spot, exploding from inside in a colorful burst of pleasure that consumes me from my head to my toes. My entire body is shaking and trembling as the strongest orgasm rocks my world. He grunts, his thrusts becoming more urgent as he slams into me. Then he's coming, burying his shouts in my back as he presses his face into the exposed skin on my upper spine.

We don't move for a couple of minutes. We stay wrapped around one another like that as we both fight to get our breathing under control. Gradually, he eases out of me, disposing of the condom while I fix my dress. Water softly trickles out of the faucet and then he's on his knees in front of me. "Allow me."

My eyes glisten as I watch him cleaning me up. Then he slides my damp panties back up my legs, helping me smooth my dress into place. Leaning down, he kisses me softly, and then he reels me into his arms. I go willingly, circling my arms around his waist and nestling my head against his chest. I close my eyes, committing everything to memory.

"Tell me we're still doing this. Tell me you're not backing out, because one taste isn't enough."

Opening my eyes, I peer up at him. "We're doing it. I won't be able to keep my hands off you after this."

He presses his forehead to mine. "You don't know how long I've wanted to hear you say that."

"Probably as long as I've wanted to say it," I truthfully admit.

He kisses me again, slow and tenderly, and I'm feeling cherished and adored, but the worries are there too, simmering under the surface, wondering what exactly I've gotten us into.

I'll come to remember that moment with a myriad of conflicting emotions.

Because that was the moment that really set everything into motion.

# Chapter Twelve

## Present Day

*Kaden*

I intercept the takeout guy in the lobby and return to the apartment to find Eva unloading plates, silverware, and glasses. I smile at how natural it is to have her moving about my kitchen like she lives here. Back at the gym, I knew she was hesitant to do this, and I'm surprised I convinced her to agree. At any second, I expect her to bolt for the door, but as the minutes roll by, she seems to relax more.

She laughs when I unload the takeout.

"What?" I arch a brow as I place the cartons on the marble countertop, stuffing the empty bag in the trash.

"I think someone's determined to bring me on a trip down nostalgia lane." A broad smile plays across her lips as she starts dishing out the food.

"It's your favorite. What else was I gonna order?"

I grab a bottle of chilled sparkling water from the refrigerator and pour two glasses.

She moans at the back of her throat as she tastes the first mouthful of prawn chili masala and she may as well have her mouth wrapped around my dick. My cock turns rock hard in an instant. Eva is the only woman with the ability to turn me on in less than a second flat.

"How is this so good?" she asks after she's chewed her food. "I mean, I must've eaten this dish hundreds of times, and each time is like tasting it for the first time."

That perfectly describes how it feels making love to her, and that thought does nothing to quell the raging boner in my pants. Once Eva and I crossed that barrier the first time, we were insatiable for one another. It's a wonder my dick didn't break from overuse during our month-long affair. I couldn't get enough of her, and the feeling was definitely mutual. I look away as remembered pain resurfaces. It's been almost two years, and the heartache is as fresh as ever. One part of me wonders why I'm risking it all again, but the bigger part of me knows why and tells the cautious part to shut the fuck up.

"Hey, are you okay?" she asks, noticing my melancholy.

"Yeah." I flick my lip between my teeth. "No." I swivel in my stool, facing her as I pin her with a grave look. "Why did we stop, Eva? We were so good together."

She puts her fork down. "You know why we did. I was terrified he'd find out, and I didn't want anything to happen to you."

"Why did you marry him, Eva? It's obvious you're not happy, and I understand now why you can't leave, but I don't get how you married the asshole in the first place."

"That's a long story," she says, taking a healthy sip of her water.

"You don't want to tell me?"

She bites on the corner of her lip, and it's distracting as hell. "No, that's not it ... it's just not a happy story, and every time I think about it, I get mad all over again."

"You can tell me another time," I relent, because I hate seeing that miserable look on her face.

She places her hand over mine. "No. I want you to know. I want you to understand."

I stare at her beautiful hand, admiring the slim elegant fingers, remembering how good her touch felt. Shaking those thoughts aside, before my boner explodes out of my pants, I clear my throat. "Let's eat and then you can tell me," I suggest.

She looks at me for the longest moment, and then she nods. We eat silently, and after a few minutes she pushes her plate away. "I've had enough. Let's talk, but I'll need something stronger than water for this conversation."

"How about wine?" I don't feel comfortable offering her whiskey. I've seen how quickly she can put the stuff away, and I'm conscious she still has to drive home. I know she can handle her liquor better than most guys, but I don't want to be up all night worrying about whether she got home safely or not.

"Perfect. Thank you."

I bring the plates to the sink as Eva crosses to the fridge. I retrieve two wine glasses and hand them to her.

Once we are seated side by side on the couch with our wine, I wait patiently for her to start.

"Are you sure you want to hear this?" she whispers.

"Yes. You don't need to shut me out, Eva. Even if all we are is friends, I would still rather know."

She nods, gingerly sipping her wine. Kicking off her shoes, she pulls her knees up to her chest, resting her back against the arm of the couch as she faces me. Did I mention how much I love how comfortable she is here?

"When I was little, I was in love with love. I was definitely one of those girls who had her wedding day all planned out, right down to the tiniest little detail." She smiles, but it's tinged with sadness. "I used to fall asleep at night dreaming of my very own Prince Charming." Her smile fades. "I think I was obsessed because I wasn't surrounded by that kind of love. My parents never openly showed one another affection, and I knew, even as a little girl, that they didn't have this big love affair." She takes another sip of her wine. "Well, I was determined I was going to have it all, but I didn't know fate was about to take a sledgehammer to my dreams." She gulps back her wine, as I sit up straighter in my chair, sensing how difficult this is for her.

"My father is an accountant, and a really good one at that. He graduated Harvard top of his class, and within six years, he had set up his own practice." Pride suffuses her words, and it's obvious where she got her intelligence and her drive from. "He married my mother a year later, and then I came along a year after that. A few months before my twelfth birthday, he obtained a new prestigious client. I remember how excited my mother was." She rolls her eyes, and a look of disgust appears on her face. "She was already planning how to spend the extra cash before he'd even earned it." She puts her wine down on the coffee table. "I didn't know most of this stuff back then, and I only found out years later when I put my father on the spot and made him tell me, but the new corporation he had taken on as a client was not what it appeared to be. On the surface, it was a respectable highly profitable organization, but it was a front for a multi-billion-dollar drugs and guns operation."

And the rest. I think it, but I don't say it. If Eva isn't aware of all the pies her husband has his hands in, then I'm not going to enlighten her. The less she knows, the better.

I'm sensing where she's going with this, and I don't like it one bit.

She eyeballs me. "My father is an honest man, or, well, he used to be." She sighs heavily. "When he realized what he'd gotten mixed up in, he tried to sever the contract and end the arrangement."

"But you don't walk away from those kinds of deals," I supply, and she nods.

"He found that out to his detriment. Jeremy's father was in charge back then, and he visited our house one night. I woke up to arguing downstairs. I will never forget the look that man gave me as he was leaving that night." She visibly shivers. "It scared the hell out of me but not as badly as what I eventually discovered he had come to demand."

"Your father was blackmailed into agreeing you would marry his son?" I guess, hating the words as they leave my mouth.

She bobs her head, gulping, and her face turns pale. "He told my father in no uncertain terms that he didn't trust him and he needed to ensure my father remained working for the firm and that he had enough invested not to go to the authorities."

"Jesus." I scrub a hand over my jaw, sitting up and putting my glass down on the table alongside Eva's. I rest my head in my hands.

"My dad told him to fuck off at first, and Jeremy's dad told him he'd be sealing all our fates if he continued being so stubborn. He gave him one week to come to his senses." She rubs a spot between her brows. "In the end, it was my mother who talked him around. When my dad told her he wanted to flee the country, she refused to leave and said she'd stop him from taking me too. She told him there was no option but to accept the offer, and she made out like it wasn't the end of the world." Her tone turns biting. "According to her, I have the dream life because my husband is wealthy, I want for nothing, and my kids will want for nothing."

My stomach twists into painful knots at the mention of kids.

She looks up at the ceiling, and a horrid tension settles in the air. When she looks back at me, devastation is clear to see. "I was fourteen when they told me I'd be marrying Jeremy the day I turned eighteen. I was horrified."

Tears pool in her eyes. "Especially after he came to visit me, and I realized how old he was. I was fourteen and he was thirty-four." Anger blazes a path across her face. "Who agrees to pledge their daughter to a man when she's still a little kid, especially one twenty years older? It absolutely destroyed me." She shakes her head repeatedly. "Obviously, I was too young to understand what was going on. I could see my father was really upset over it, but my mother actually seemed pleased by it."

"I'm sensing you don't have a great relationship with your mother."

She snorts. "You'd be correct. I have nothing but disdain for that woman."

"I'm sorry."

She shoots me a sad smile. "I know family means everything to you, but it means next to nothing to me. I have love in my heart for my father, but some days I'm consumed with hatred for him. Why didn't he just take me and run? Why didn't he leave that stupid bitch here? Hell, Jeremy probably would've married her, and my mother would have zero issue with that. You should see the way she flirts and fawns over him when we go to dinner at their place. It sickens my stomach."

"Shit, Eva. That's horrific." I don't admit to a certain amount of relief. When Kev first informed me exactly who Jeremy Garcia was, I couldn't fathom how Eva could marry such a man. Now I know it wasn't by choice, and it reaffirms what I've always thought about her character. To know she didn't willingly or knowingly tie herself to that gangster only makes me more determined to extract her from the situation.

"You've no idea. I spent my teenage years seething and rebelling against it. Jeremy came to visit every Sunday from that point on, and I barely spoke to him. Mother took the wooden spoon to me after most visits, but it was worth it. I silently hoped Jeremy would decide he didn't want me if he thought I was a brat. But then I took it a step too far."

Her lower lip trembles, and tears well in her eyes again. I move closer to her on the couch, opening my arms in invitation. She doesn't hesitate, crawling over and lying back against me. My arms encircle her waist from behind as she leans into me. "You don't have to tell me if it's too difficult," I say, hugging her tightly.

"I want to tell you. I *need* to tell you."

I wait patiently for her to compose herself.

"When I was fifteen, Jeremy was permitted to kiss me." My stomach heaves in agony at the thought. It's so wrong, and while I understand her parents were probably terrified, surely they could have laid more solid ground rules? "And mother let him come up to my bedroom for twenty minutes after every Sunday dinner." She shivers in my arms, and I hold her closer. "I tried fighting him off but that didn't work. He didn't do anything but kiss me for the first year, but he explained about sex and told me I was not allowed to let any other boy touch me. He wanted me a virgin on our wedding day."

Bile travels up my throat, and I clamp my mouth shut.

"After I turned sixteen, he progressed things. He fucked me with his fingers and his mouth, but never his cock. He was practically salivating at the prospect of a virgin wife, not that it stopped him from teaching me how to give head and ensuring he fucked my mouth every Sunday in my bedroom while my parents watched TV downstairs."

She shudders, and I work overtime to contain my blossoming rage.

"But he gravely underestimated how much I loathed him," she continues. "How much I wanted to make him renege on the wedding. And how stupid it was to educate me in all things sex-related." She twists her head around, looking up at me. "He used to make me watch porn with him and, later, a few months before we were married, he brought me to his house and made me watch while this other girl fucked him every which way from Sunday. It was all part of my 'education.'" She makes air quotes with her fingers.

The more I hear about this man, the more scared I am for her. And now my mind is going to all kinds of nasty places. I'm sorely tempted to kidnap her and make a run for it myself.

"What did you do?" I ask, running my hands up and down her arms.

She twists around, repositioning herself so she's half lying across my lap. "I started fooling around with this guy in school. We were both seniors, but I was only barely sixteen and he was nearly eighteen." Eva had told me before that she graduated high school early and went straight on to Harvard, so that's not a huge shock to me. "I told him my parents didn't let me date," she explains, "so we met in secret. I used to lie and tell my parents I had after-school activities. Instead, I would sneak off with Seth, and we'd hide out in his sister's tree house, making out like demons."

She worries her lip between her teeth. "I did like him, but I wasn't in love with him or anything even close to it. I was turned on by how illicit it was and the knowledge of how much my parents and Jeremy would hate me if they knew what we were doing." A lone tear sneaks out of the corner of her eye, rolling down her face. "I didn't stop to think about consequences, and I didn't know who Jeremy was then. I had no idea the kinds of things he does or how dangerous he was."

I hold her against me, smoothing a hand up and down her back. "He found out?"

She nods. "I gave Seth my virginity, but I never told anyone. Shortly after that, I graduated high school and started at Harvard. Finding time to be together was more challenging, and I started pulling away when Seth began pressuring me to go public. When I turned seventeen, Jeremy put an engagement announcement in the newspaper, and the whole town was talking about it. Seth was really upset. He told me he loved me and he couldn't believe I was going to marry some old dude. He said he felt used and he never wanted to see me again."

A sob rings through the air, and I hold her tighter, pressing a kiss to the top of her head. I know this story doesn't have a happy ending, and now I understand why she wanted to tell it to me.

"Jeremy was livid the night of our wedding night when he realized my hymen was no longer intact." She shivers again. "He dragged me out of bed in the middle of the night and drove to my parent's house. He started screaming at them, but, of course, they were oblivious. He got it out of me, and I confessed about Seth." She's full on crying now, and I want to murder that piece of shit she's married to.

I reach behind me, grab a box of tissues, and hand them to her. She sniffs, dabbing at her eyes and blowing her nose. The tears subside, making way for anger. She peers deep into my eyes as she finishes the sorry tale. "Seth died two weeks later. He was coming home late one Saturday night, and his truck careered off the road, straight into a tree. It caught fire immediately, and he died on the spot. Or at least, that was the official verdict, but I know it's not the truth." She cups my face and worry races across her eyes. "Without needing proof, I know Jeremy arranged his death. Jeremy killed Seth because I had sex with him. Imagine what he would do to you?"

"We're not kids, Eva, and I have considerable resources at my disposal. I'm not an idiot. I know your husband is a dangerous man, but I can take care of myself. I can take care of *you*." I brush moist strands of her hair back off her face. "And he never found out about our affair. I wouldn't be here if he knew."

"No, you wouldn't," she agrees. "And it's why I had to call a halt to it."

I wind my hand around the nape of her neck. "I'm not going to let him scare me away. Especially after what you've just told me."

"I didn't tell you so it would strengthen your resolve!" she shrieks.

"I know why you told me, and I'm glad you did. It just proves the need to take extra-precautionary measures."

"Kade, you're not listening to me. We can't start this up again, because we may not be so lucky the second time around. Jeremy killed the teenage boy I gave my virginity to. Imagine what he would do to the man I love?"

Her words are both a balm and a bomb to my soul. She has never admitted her feelings for me out loud, and I wish I could take this moment and cherish it, but it's not a happy moment, not with what I fear she's going to say next. She grips my face, almost painfully. "You would be pleading for death after he finished with you." Her panicked eyes lock on mine. "And once you were dealt with, he'd mete out the same form of justice on me." She gulps, and tears slide down her face. "Is that what you want for us?"

I press my forehead to hers. "I understand your fears and I share them, but it doesn't mean that's the only way our story ends."

She pulls back and stands up. "No, Kade. That *is* the way our story ends, which is why it should never have started in the first place."

110

# *Chapter Thirteen*

## Present Day

*Evelina*

I left Kade's place with a lump of mincemeat in my chest, right in the place where my heart should be. I ugly cry the whole way home, furiously swiping at the hot tears that blur my vision and pierce my soul. Stopping at the side of the road a few miles from my house, I apply makeup in an effort to disguise my blotchy skin.

An hour later, when Jeremy has me blindfolded, naked, and on all fours, with the restraint locked around my neck, I almost welcome the cold, clinical way he fucks me, hiding behind the mask while I quietly self-destruct on the inside.

The rest of the week drags. Jesse is being an ass at work, but it's the least of my worries. Kaden has tried to talk to me during our self-defense lessons, but I've shut him down. I can't afford to indulge hope, and I meant what I said—I can't involve him, because I love him too much to risk his life. But he's unrelenting, and I'm seriously thinking of canceling my sessions except I'm genuinely scared that those guys who attacked me will make a reappearance. Kade is teaching me some simple, but effective, moves, and I don't want to stop until I'm fully confident I can defend myself.

I deliberately didn't tell Jeremy about the incident because I'm afraid he would retrace my movements and find out about Kade's involvement. I could lie and say something scared my attackers and they fled, but it's a flimsy excuse and he'd know it. Nothing can lead him to Kade, so it was best to keep quiet about it.

"Hello!" Jesse waves his hands in front of my face. "Earth to Eva! Is anyone home?"

I slap his hands away. "What do you want, Jesse, and it's Evelina to you."

He smirks, perching his ass on the corner of my desk. I make a mental note to wipe it down the instant he leaves my office.

"I asked if you wanted to come to that conference with me the weekend after next?"

I look at him like he's sprouted ten heads. "Excuse me? Why the hell do you think I'd want to go anywhere with you?"

He snorts. "Are you this prickly at home? Or is that something you reserve especially for me?"

An exhausted sigh escapes my lips. "Was there a point to your visit, Jesse? I'm busy."

"You're so uptight, Eva. You need to get laid or drunk or sign up for a personality transplant."

"Get out." I point at the door. "Or I'll call security."

He jumps down, rounding my desk and leaning over me from behind. Planting his hands on the table, he semi-cages me in.

"Get away from me."

"I've got some free time on my hands. I'd be happy to oblige. Just lean over the desk, and I'll give you a quick fuck. It'll do wonders for your stress levels."

I don't need to look over my shoulder to know he's staring down my top. I shove my chair back, uncaring that it crashes into him, most likely flattening his balls. Perhaps that'll help cool his ardor.

He yells, falling back and clutching the edge of the desk for support. "What the fuck? I'm going to report you for that."

"Try it ass face," Renee says from the open doorway. "And I'll report you for sexual harassment. I heard every word." She steps into the room, folding her arms as she stares him down.

Jesse hobbles away, pausing in the doorway to send me a hateful look. "I was only trying to do you a solid with the conference, but screw you, bitch. I'll enjoy laughing in your face when I secure tenure and you don't."

Renee slams the door closed behind him, and I slouch in my chair, locking my hands behind my head. "Did you really hear it all?"

"Nope," she says, sinking into the couch. "I just caught the tail end, but that asshole's predictable. I knew it wasn't a huge stretch, and I was right."

"What's this conference about, and why haven't I heard of it? Should I be there?"

She grins. "He's such an idiot to boot. You attended the same one two years ago, but he clearly doesn't realize that. Remember the Digital Strategy Innovation Summit? There's little point attending again, but if it was me, I'd email the organizers and see if they'd send any updates."

I get a little flustered, realizing which conference she's referencing. The department only sent me that time, and none of my colleagues have any clue I never actually attended. I got the slides and session notes emailed to me, and I gleaned what I needed to from them, so no one was any the wiser. "That's a good idea," I say, pretending to make a note of it. "I'll do that."

"So, I wanted to ask you something," she says, sitting bolt upright and clasping her hands nervously in her lap.

"Sure. What is it?"

"Would you be my maid of honor?"

I get up and walk to the couch, sitting down and hugging my friend. "I would love to be your maid of honor, and I'm so touched you asked me." I know Renee has two younger sisters and a bunch of girlfriends, so she has plenty of options.

"There isn't anyone else worthy of the job," she teases, hugging me back.

"No pressure or anything," I laugh, wondering how I'm going to manage to be maid of honor without bringing my husband, because the last thing any girl wants is a notorious criminal at her wedding. But I'll figure something out, because I don't want to let my best friend down.

It's Friday night, and I'm packing up my things when there's a knock on my office door. When I open it, I'm not altogether surprised to find Kaden standing there with a cocky grin on his face. I peek out into the corridor, checking it's empty before I usher him inside. It's been a long while since I officially tutored him, and he's no longer one of my students, so it might look suspicious that he's here.

"Kade." I eye him warily.

"Wow. What an enthusiastic greeting." He tilts his head to the side. "Tell me, do you greet all the men you love with such ambivalence?"

My lips twitch involuntarily in response to his cocky confidence. "I couldn't tell since you're the only one I've ever loved."

A flash of heat darkens his eyes. "And yet you refuse me." He rubs his jaw. "How long are we going to keep this charade up?"

"For as long as it takes it to sink in, Kade."

"That'd be never then," he quips.

"I'm trying to be strong here."

He steps forward, tipping my chin up. "I know that, honey, but that's my job. Let me worry about it for the both of us."

I reach up, removing his hand, and his gaze darts to my wrist. A muscle ticks in his jaw, and all trace of his good humor fades. "Is he doing this to you?" Gently, he takes my wrist, and the tender gesture is at complete odds with the thunderous look on his face.

"I thought we already discussed this," I say, slowly removing my arm.

"No, you avoided answering the question. But if you don't tell me right now, I'm going over to your house to ask that bastard for myself."

I gasp. "You wouldn't!"

"Try me." He folds his arms over his chest, drilling me with a determined look. He's just stubborn enough to do it too.

I sigh. "All right. Sit down." I shake my head as I walk to the couch. "Why do I always cave to your demands?"

"Because I'm too hard to resist."

His lips tip up into a smug grin as he plops down on the couch alongside me. Heat rolls off his body in waves, and I'm acutely aware of his potent, raw masculinity. I'm so attuned to his presence, and my hormones are throwing the mother of all parties. I bark out a bitter laugh, but I don't attempt to deny what's as obvious as the nose on my face. "Jeremy wants to start a family, and he's determined to knock me up as fast as he can," I blurt, because there's so way of sugarcoating the truth.

A muscle clenches in his jaw, and he digs his fingernails into his thigh. "You can't have a baby with him."

"I agree, and he doesn't know about the contraceptive implant I still have."

His shoulders loosen a little. "That doesn't explain the marks." His eyes lock on my bruised wrists.

"Doesn't it?" I whisper, not really wanting to articulate it.

Shock splays across his face. "He's physically forcing himself on you?"

I close my eyes, because I can't look at him and say this, but I don't want to leave him with a falsehood either. I don't want Kaden barging into my house and accusing Jeremy of rape, because that's a surefire way to ensure a bullet in his skull. "I don't fight him, Kade. I let him do what he wants because it's the easier option." My eyes blink open of their own accord. "But he has certain ... tastes."

All the color drains from his face. Twisting around, he cups my face tenderly. "I can't stand the thought of you being subjected to that." Rage returns the color to his skin. "You need to get away from him." He presses his forehead to mine. "Run away with me, Eva. Leave him, and we'll escape abroad." He eases back, peering into my eyes. "This isn't a flippant offer. I've thought of little else all week. You don't have to stay with him. I love you, and I want to protect you. All you have to say is yes, and I'll set everything in motion."

"Kade—"

He cuts me off with a passionate kiss, and I instantly melt into his arms, as if no time has passed between us. As if we were never apart. His kisses are a mix of fear and panic and unrestrained need, much like my own.

Remembering the door isn't locked, I reluctantly break the kiss, planting my hand on his chest to hold him at bay. "Someone could walk in."

He nods, reaching out and taking my hands in his warm ones. "It feels like I've waited forever to kiss you again."

I touch my tingling lips, bathing in the familiar sensations coursing through my body. "Me too."

He smiles before pressing a slow kiss to my forehead. He eases back, pinning me with a serious look. "I meant what I said, Eva, and I've given this a lot of thought. My life doesn't mean anything if I don't have you in it."

"You'd leave everything behind for me?" The incredulity is evident in my tone.

"Yes." Steely determination glints in his eyes. "I'd give everything up for you."

"I can't let you do that."

"You can't keep making decisions on my behalf!" he snaps, frustration getting the better of him. "I'm a grown man, Eva, fully capable of deciding these things for myself. The only thing you need to consider is whether you want that with me."

He makes it sound so simple when it's anything but. "You would be walking away without your degree. Leaving your whole family behind. Eventually those decisions would haunt you, and it'd destroy us."

He raises our conjoined hands to his lips. "No, my love. They wouldn't." He kisses the tips of my fingers. "I'm entering into this knowing full well what's at stake. I've already searched my soul, and I choose you. It will always be you."

Tears prick my eyes. No one has ever fought for me like this. No one's ever fought for me. Period.

"What if you fall out of love with me? And then you're stuck with me and we end up hating one another."

His answering smile is amused. "Damn, you're so fucking cute." Glancing quickly at the door, he drops a brief kiss on my lips. "I have loved you from the first minute I laid eyes on you. It hasn't faltered despite the time apart. If anything, it's grown, which is how I know I'll always love you, Eva. I'm secure in our love. That is the one thing I have no doubts over."

"Kade." This time I'm the one kissing him with reckless abandon, and he's the one easing back after a minute, chuckling. Then his expression turns grave. "All I ask is that you seriously consider it. I won't ever force you into doing anything against your will, but I need you to look deep into your heart and soul and ask yourself if what we have is worth taking this risk. I believe it is." Those penetrating blue eyes of his pin me in place. "Now it's up to you."

I'm still reeling from Kade's proposal five days later. Staring in the mirror, I wonder if the woman looking back at me has the balls to seize the kind of love she's always craved. It's right in front of me for the taking, but I'm still plagued with fears and worries. Years of suppressing those dreams can't be undone in a handful of days, regardless of how tempting it is to say yes. *How can I pull Kade away from his family? His future?* If I say yes, it'd be the most supremely selfish thing I've ever done. But he's asked me to stop making decisions on his behalf, and when I take my guilt and fear out of the equation, I'm left with little argument.

Checking my bedroom door is locked, I retrieve the burner cell Kade gave me the other night from under the hidden panel in my jewelry box. He's assured me it's untraceable, and I trust him. I switch it on and send him a text.

*Are you really sure about this?*

The reply is instantaneous. *One hundred percent.*

Butterflies flood my chest as I drop onto my bed, pulling my legs up to my chest. I want to say yes, but I'm still hesitant, still feeling selfish. But I've got to send something back, because he's waiting.

*Give me another few days to think about it.*

*Whatever you need, honey.*

I hug the cell to my chest, closing my eyes and allowing a tiny sliver of hope to slip through. The cell pings again.

*Are you okay?*

*I'm fine.*

*I love you.*

*I love you too.*

The word "yes" lies on the tip of my tongue. I'm so tempted to text it to him, but I owe him more than a knee-jerk reaction. I'll take another few days to consider all the repercussions before making a final decision.

But, as I return the cell to its hiding place, I can't contain the bubble of excitement filtering through my veins.

# *Chapter Fourteen*

## Past – Sophomore Year of College

### *Kaden*

Eva's completely professional, and it both impresses me and pisses me off. When I show up for my first study session after we fucked in the bathroom at the club, I expect we'll pick up right where we left off, but she has other ideas. She greets me coolly, wasting no time getting stuck into the lesson. Every time I open my mouth to ask her what the fuck she's playing at, she drills me with a look that shrivels the boner in my pants and has me cowering like a five-year-old being scolded. I'm having a hard time concentrating, so I'm plotting this big speech in my head. Once the lesson ends, I'm going all out. Convinced she's changed her mind, I have a list of arguments prepared to support why we should do this.

But I don't end up needing any.

The instant the hour is up, Eva races around her desk, bolting the office door and drawing the blinds.

My mouth is hanging open when she lunges at me, straddling me in the chair as she smashes her lips against mine.

Hells yeah. This is more like it.

I take her ardent kiss and multiply it, fisting my hand in her gorgeous hair and tugging her head back as my lips move from her mouth to her exposed neck. I plant lingering kisses up and down the column of her elegant neck, rubbing my nose against her flesh and inhaling her intoxicating scent.

"I'm not wearing panties," she moans as my tongue licks along her collarbone. My boner strains painfully in my pants when I slide one hand up under her skirt, discovering the truth for myself. I almost come on the spot when my fingers brush against her hot, wet folds.

"Jesus Christ. Are you trying to kill me?" I tug her head back, staring at her flushed face and dark eyes with a certain amount of pride. "You mean to tell me you sat across that desk lecturing me about the finer points of theoretical probability with a bare pussy?"

She bites down on her lip, nodding, and I move my hand around to her ass, firmly squeezing her cheeks.

"That's very naughty, Eva." I stand up, holding onto her effortlessly. Shoving the chair away with my foot, I brush papers and books off the desk with one clean sweep of my hand. She whimpers as I press her, face forward, over the edge of the desk. "And worthy of punishment."

"What are you going to do?" she asks in a husky voice that fucking slays me.

I unzip her skirt, tugging it down and kicking it away. She moves to slide her shoes off, but I stop her. "The heels stay on." This is like the embodiment of every fucking wet dream I've had for the last year. "And to answer your question, I'm going to slap your cunt with my cock. For starters."

My hand comes down firmly over her ass, and I spank her a few times. Wetness leaks out of her pussy, starting to drip down her legs, and I slide two fingers inside her as I pop the button on my jeans. "God, you're so wet."

"I've been thinking of this all week," she admits, turning her face to the side and looking back at me. "I haven't been able to think of anything else."

I drape my body over hers, capturing her lips in a searing hot kiss. "Believe me, I know."

"Well, hurry the fuck up then," she commands, and I snort.

I love her bossy attitude. "Are you always this impatient?" I ask, removing my cock and stroking myself. Beads of precum ooze out of the tip, proving I'm every bit as aroused as she is.

"Never. This is all you."

Well, hot damn. To hell with restraint.

"This is going to be hard and fast because I'm about two seconds away from shooting my load," I tell her as I suit up.

"Sounds perfect," she murmurs, and the glow on her face and the satisfied smile on her lips confirms it.

I slam into her without warning, and she shrieks. I'm betting, in the right circumstances, Eva's a real screamer.

"You need to stay quiet, honey."

She fists a hand in her mouth, nodding as I pick up my pace. Her walls tighten around me as I thrust in and out, and blissful tremors have me biting back my own moans. I pull her back a little, reaching around to rub her swollen clit, and she muffles her cries with her fisted hand. My balls tighten, and I know I won't last much longer.

"Fuck, Eva." I press my thumb onto her clit, exerting more pressure. "I can't hold off."

"Don't stop," she moans. "Almost there."

My balls pull up, tightening and constricting, and I pivot my hips, grinding into her as a flash of lightning bursts behind my eyes. I pinch her clit, and she bucks underneath me as my own release powers through me, intense and all-consuming, fiery tingles zipping up and down my spine.

Our joint ragged breathing is the only sound in the room for a couple of minutes. I pull out slowly, tossing the used condom in the trash, and help her into an upright position. Brushing strands of tangled hair back off her face, I check her face for any regrets. "Are you okay?"

Circling her arms around my neck, she smiles at me, a happy, sated smile that floods my insides with relief and pride. My cock twitches with fresh need. Leaning up, she kisses me. "You are so good at that." She nips at my lower lip, sucking it into her mouth, and my cock surges to full life, nudging against her stomach. She looks down, and an alluring smile pulls up the corners of her mouth. "And so incredibly sexy." Wrapping her hand around my cock, she strokes me slowly and sensually.

I thrust into her hand, needing more. Unbuttoning her blouse, I unclip her bra, freeing her massive breasts. Burying my head in them, I nuzzle her flesh, my tongue flicking out to taste her. "I can totally say the same about you." I suck her nipple into my mouth, and her hand tightens around my cock, moving faster. I lavish equal attention on her tits, while she works me expertly with skillful touches.

After a couple minutes, I take her hand and pull her over to the couch. Pulling my shirt up over my head, I toss it aside, along with her blouse and bra, until we're both buck naked. There is something so thrilling about being with her like this when some of her colleagues are still milling about the building. I don't know how the fuck I got so lucky, but I'm not going to question it or look a gift horse in the mouth. "Sit back and spread your legs wide," I demand, sinking to my knees on the floor.

She does as I ask without question, and I part her folds, licking up and down her slit as she writhes and moans on the couch. I dive in, and the sweet, salty taste of her is addictive. Replacing my tongue with two fingers, I pump in and out of her hard and fast while my mouth suctions over the sensitive bundle of nerves. She orgasms powerfully, her body jerking and arching as waves of pleasure roll over her.

I have a condom on in record time, and then I'm lying her down flat on the couch and pushing into her again. The look of ecstasy on her face blows me away, and while I'm trying to take my time, she's making it difficult. Her legs wrap around my waist, and she digs her hands into the cheeks of my ass, pulling me closer and grinding against me, meeting me thrust for thrust.

My lips capture hers in a drugging, deep kiss, and I'm like an animal as my mouth, my hands, and my cock devour her. Eva moves her hands up and down my spine, clasping my ass cheeks and tightening her thighs against me. Slapping sounds and quiet moans fill the air, and as she clamps her pussy around my cock, stars burst behind my eyes. I'm on the verge of heaven again, and I want to slow this down, but my body has other ideas.

"Kade," she whispers, and I open my eyes. "I want to see you when you come." She slides a hand between our bodies, rubbing herself, and that sends me over the edge. She joins me a few seconds later, and we climax together, our eyes locked on one another. It's the singular most intimate moment of my life and the moment that confirms the extent of my feelings for her.

This is more than lust or a teenage fantasy come true.

I'm in love with this woman.

And I don't care that society says it's wrong.

It can't be.

Not when it feels so unbelievably right.

Eva's paranoid about someone finding out, so she refuses to meet with me outside her office, and she also insists that I can't show up more than twice a week. Anything else would arouse too much suspicion.

But she underestimates the Kennedy determination, and when I show up at her office every night, she doesn't turn me away. I know it's risky, but this woman is my new drug. I *can't* stay away.

We're watching a movie on her laptop after a couple of rounds of energetic sex when I raise the subject. "I wish I could take you out. On a proper date."

She drags her attention away from the screen, quirking a brow. "You know we can't. It's too risky."

I scrub a hand over my jaw. "I've been thinking."

She twists around, slanting me with an amused smile. "Should I be worried?"

"Hardy har." I playfully elbow her in the ribs. "Do you think you could get away for a weekend? My parents have a property on Nantucket. It's very private and no one would find us there." I thread my fingers through hers, looking deep into her eyes. "I want to make love to you in a bed, go for long walks on the beach, to take a shower with you, to wake up beside you." All the normal stuff most couples do.

I've only just realized how difficult being with her in secret is, and I've been racking my brains trying to think of a way to be together without having to worry about prying eyes.

Her eyes glisten as she sits up, wrapping her arms around my waist and resting her cheek against my chest. "That sounds wonderful, but I don't know if I can get away."

My chest tightens, and I smother my sigh of exasperation. I knew what I was getting into when I signed up for this, and I don't want to start bitching and moaning now. That wouldn't be fair, and she'd most likely kick me to the curb.

I keep waiting for that to happen—for the moment she realizes I'm too young and not worth the trouble. I look down at her, running a hand through the thick strands of her hair as I press a kiss atop her head, praying she doesn't grow tired of my immature ass even though a part of me expects it.

Her eyes expand. "Hang on a sec." She tips her chin up, looking at me with excited eyes. "I'm scheduled to attend a conference in New York the weekend after next. It's already set up, but maybe I could fly to Nantucket from New York, and no one would be any the wiser. I can get the organizers to email me the slides and study the session notes in my own time."

Her obvious delight is infectious, and I grab her face, smashing my lips to hers. I continue kissing her with every overexcited emotion I'm feeling. "I'll borrow my dad's jet and wait for you on the runway in New York. I won't put your real name on the flight manifest."

"You can do that?" she interjects.

I tweak her nose. "Yep. Don't worry about a thing. I'll fix it so no one knows you are with me."

As I leave her office that night, instead of the usual gut-wrenching feeling, I'm virtually walking on clouds, busy making plans in my head.

Spending a full weekend with Eva is like a dream come true, and I don't plan on wasting a second of it.

# Chapter Fifteen

## Present Day

## Evelina

Jeremy knocks on my bedroom door as I'm applying the final touches to my makeup. "Evie? Our guests have just arrived at the gate. I would like to welcome them at the door."

"I'm ready," I say, opening my door and stepping out into the corridor. Jeremy looks handsome in his tailored black suit and crisp white button-down shirt, but the sight of him doesn't arouse even a minuscule amount of attraction.

It's like I'm immune to him.

Running his hands down over my body, he eyes me from head to toe. As usual, I want to curl up and cower away from his heated stare, but I plant a pleasant, albeit forced, smile on my face. "Elegant. I approve." He offers me his arm, and I loop mine through his, flicking a switch and putting my imaginary perfect hostess persona on.

One would swear Jeremy grew up as lord of the manor by the way he fixates on airs and graces. Any time we have guests over, dinner is always a very formal affair. Appearances mean everything to him, and he likes to showcase his wealth through grandiose gestures and extravagant displays of greed. In the same way, I must present the perfect image of the doting, well-maintained wife, and it's exhausting, but I've done what I've had to in order to survive this world.

Jeremy claps Daniel on the back proudly, ushering him into our home. I have a genuine smile for Cheryl as I greet her with a hug. I'm struck again by the similarities between us when she steps nervously inside our house, glancing around with an awestruck look on her face. I remember how overwhelming it all seemed to me at first.

Camille prepared a lavish spread before retiring for the night, so Jeremy hired waiting staff for the occasion. Which is completely ridiculous. I am well capable of serving a five-course meal to four dinner guests, but Jeremy wouldn't hear of it. It's the same any time we host dinner parties, which, thankfully, isn't too often. Like I said, it's all about appearances.

We chat casually over the dinner table, and once we have finished, Jeremy and Daniel disappear to the study to talk business while Cheryl and I take our wine out to the formal living room.

"You have a beautiful home," she supplies as we settle ourselves on the stiff couch.

"Thank you," I politely reply even though I don't agree. This place has always seemed more like a mausoleum to me. All we're missing is the entombed body of the first Mrs. Garcia to make it official.

"How are your studies coming along? And your part-time job?" I inquire.

She groans a little. "This final year is tough, but I'm enjoying it, and the job is fantastic. I'm learning so much."

"The year will be over before you know it. It seemed like my college experience was over in the blink of an eye."

"Daniel told me you graduated early, were top of your class, and are one of the youngest professors in Harvard history."

I arch a brow, surprised Daniel would know that. It's not like my husband brags about it or anything. At times, it almost seems like he's embarrassed by it.

"Yes, but I'm only actually an assistant professor right now. I'm really hoping for tenure in the next year."

"I bet you'll get it. You seem like a high achiever and the type Harvard would want to hold onto."

"Thank you, Cheryl. That's very nice of you to say."

We sip our wine, quietly looking out the window over the landscaped grounds, and the silence is companionable. She clears her throat, glancing briefly at the door. "Could I ask you something?"

I put my glass down on the coffee table, giving her my undivided attention, only slightly on edge over her impending question. "Of course."

"Do you know any of the Kennedy brothers? From Wellesley?"

Blood rushes to my ears, and I'm not sure what expression is on my face, but her expression turns to one of alarm, and she rushes to explain. "I grew up in Wellesley and, um, I knew the family quite well. I've heard several of the brothers attend Harvard, and I was just wondering if you knew them."

My panic reduces a couple of notches, but I'm still wired and careful about what I say. While none of the bodyguards are visible around the house, and they are all most likely out prowling the grounds, you can never be too sure. I compose myself and deliberately keep my voice calm and low. "Kaden Kennedy was one of my students at one time."

Her face brightens. "I know Kaden well."

That raises a whole bunch of new emotions to the surface, but I keep a neutral expression on my face. "You dated him?" I ask, guessing that's the reason for her exuberant reaction.

Her cheeks flush a little. "God, no! Kaden was like the big brother I never had. I had some issues in high school, and he was always there to defend me."

Relief washes over me like a tsunami, along with a surge of pride. "That sounds like Kaden. He's an intelligent, caring young man and very dedicated to his studies." I cringe at how formal I sound but needs must.

"It's been years since I saw him or Kev."

A despondent look crosses her face, and it's one I recognize. "So, you dated Keven Kennedy?" I guess again.

She nods. "He was my childhood sweetheart. I thought we'd be together forever."

"What happened?"

"My family moved." She's very tight-lipped, all of a sudden, and I'm sensing that's not the full story, but I'm not one to pry into things that are none of my business. However, it does give me an idea.

Cheryl is far too sweet to be dragged into this lifestyle, and I want to warn her. There was no one to warn me, not that it would've made much of a difference, because I didn't have a choice in who I married.

But she does, and if I can help her from making a mistake then it's worth speaking up.

"Come with me," I suggest, getting up and walking around the vast room to the windows at the side of the property. I stand in front of the glass, surreptitiously scanning the grounds for signs of any guards, and discreetly checking the room, but we're alone. Nonetheless, I'm not taking any chances. I lean in close to her, whispering in her ear. "Keven goes to Harvard too. You should look him up and ask him to tell you about Jeremy." I've never asked Kaden to tell me exactly what he knows about my husband and his dealings, but he has mentioned previously that his brother was the one to fill him in, so I'm sure Keven will be able to tell Cheryl everything she needs to know.

She gives me a funny look, and I don't blame her. I'm acting weird, but I have to be circumspect with my words in case she tells Daniel about this later.

"Why would you tell me that?" she asks, frowning.

I look over my shoulder again. "Because there are things you need to know," I whisper. "Things I can't tell you, but Keven can." I squeeze her hand. "Talk to him, and sooner rather than later."

The sounds of approaching footsteps alert us to the men's presence. When they step into the room, the look on Jeremy's face sends shivers up my spine. He looks like someone just spit in his coffee or took scissors to his favorite shirt.

"Time to go, Cheryl," Daniel confirms, shooting me a funny look as he walks to his fiancée, sliding his arm around her waist.

"Oh!" Cheryl sounds as surprised as I am. The night is still young, and I didn't think they'd be leaving so soon.

We wave them off at the door, and Jeremy is like a volcano ready to erupt at my side. The instant the door is shut, he slams me against it, putting his angry face in mine. Everything locks up inside me, and all I can think is he's somehow found out about Kaden. Which would be ironic because apart from the kissing last week, Kaden and I haven't touched in a long time.

"I want to know why you lied to me," Jeremy says through gritted teeth, and I swallow the lump of fear in my throat.

"What?" I hate how my voice trembles, but the look in his eyes is scaring me.

"How is it that Daniel knows my wife was attacked and I know fucking nothing about it!" he roars, slamming his fist into the wall by the door.

"I didn't want to worry you," I lie.

He snorts out a laugh, gripping my chin painfully. "No, you didn't want to lose your precious freedom," he snaps.

He starts pacing the corridor, and I spy Vincent approaching from the other side of the house. Jeremy's shouting must have brought him here. "It's okay, Vincent," Jeremy barks. "You can leave us."

Taking my elbow, Jeremy practically drags me upstairs, hauling me into his bedroom. It's been years since I've stepped foot in this room. He flings me onto the bed, towering over me with a vicious glint in his eye. "Tell me everything," he demands, taking off his belt and unzipping his pants. "Leave nothing out."

I have no choice but to give him an edited version of events. I tell him some random man passing by stepped in and saved me, because I'm too scared to leave that part out of the story, unsure exactly how much Daniel relayed.

"You have no idea how weak this makes me look!" he yells. "I should have retaliated immediately, and my inaction speaks volumes."

"I'm sorry," I whimper, flinching when he yanks me up and spins me around, tearing my dress apart with his hands rather than unzipping it. He throws the ripped shreds of my gown aside, and I can't stop shaking.

I've seen him mad before.

Watched him enact vengeance when his enemies dared to strike previously. That time ended up with over thirty bodies being dug out of a mass grave not too far from this house.

But he has never turned that rage on me, and I'm petrified.

"Strip," he demands, yanking at his own shirt. Buttons pop off, flying around the room.

"Please, Jeremy. I'm sorry. Don't do this."

"I've fucking run out of patience with you, Evelina. I forgave you for tossing your virginity away on that worthless little prick. I gave you your freedom to study and work. Hell, I've spent years fucking whores instead of my wife! But I'm done. From now on, I call the shots, and you will do what I tell you to do or suffer the consequences."

Impatient at my lack of undressing, he rips my bra and panties off in a fury.

I'm quaking all over, trying to cover myself with my arms when he kicks off his pants and strides naked to his walk-in closet. Briefly, I think about fleeing to my room and locking my door, but I know that wouldn't contain him. Not when he's in such a rage.

He returns holding a studded black leather paddle, and tears leak out of my eyes.

I zone out as he bends me over his knee, spanking me firmly time and time again, experiencing no pleasure, only pain.

When he thrusts inside me, he slams in and out, venting all his anger and rage. His hands close around my neck, squeezing and constricting, and I silently encourage him to do it—to put me out of my misery.

Three hours later, I limp back to my room, as naked as the day I was born, sore all over, and sobbing uncontrollably.

Jeremy saw the state I was in, but he didn't care, warning me not to embarrass him again before telling me to get out.

I slide under the covers of my bed, curling into a fetal position as I continue to sob. Years of trapped emotions run loose, and I know I'm close to my tipping point. He didn't even ask if I was okay, if my attackers hurt me. All he cared about was his reputation and the fact I'd made him look weak. Doling out his sick form of punishment only proves what I've felt all along—that I mean nothing to him. I'm a possession. A piece of arm candy. A baby-making machine. And nothing more.

But, more than that, his reaction tonight proves he's becoming unhinged.

And confirms to me that I'm not safe, even if I stay here.

# Chapter Sixteen

## Present Day

### Kaden

I'm chatting with Duke and a couple of other buddies outside the Littauer Building on Monday morning when I spot Eva making her way across the employee parking lot. My mood darkens as I watch her slow progress. Eva usually walks briskly and with purpose, but she's virtually dragging her body along the sidewalk this morning.

*She's hurt.*

It's the first thought that springs to mind, and I know my instincts are correct. Making excuses to the guys, I sprint in her direction, catching up to her just as she's about to enter the staff door at the rear of the building. "Professor Garcia!" I call out, and she stops walking, stiffening as she slowly turns around.

"Mr. Kennedy." She won't meet my eyes, pretending to fumble in her bag for something. "What can I do for you?"

"What's wrong?" I whisper, ignoring the urge to envelop her in my arms.

"Nothing," she mumbles, still refusing to look at me.

"Look at me, Eva." I glance around quickly, and no one is watching. Tipping her chin up, I'm shocked at her pale features and bloodshot, red-rimmed eyes. "What the fuck did he do to you?" I grind my teeth to my molars as red-hot anger sweeps through me.

"Not here, Kade. Please." Her lower lip wobbles, and tears prick her eyes.

I break apart inside.

Eva is usually so strong, and this vulnerable side isn't something I'm used to seeing.

I take out a book, pretending to show her something. "Tell them you're sick," I say in a low voice, discreetly sliding my keycard into her purse. "Then take a taxi to my place, and I'll meet you there."

"I can't," she says, but the words lack bite.

"Yes, you can." I drill her with a determined look. "You've never missed a single class. Go in and tell them you got sick on the drive here and you're returning home." She chews on the corner of her lip, and I know I have her. "I'm not taking no for an answer. Go do it now and I'll see you soon."

She nods, and more tears glisten in her eyes. I want to reach out and touch her, comfort her, so badly, but I can't. Not yet.

I watch until she's disappeared, and then I hightail it back to my Jeep. I stop at the store for supplies on the way, and then I park in the garage and wait for Eva to show up. The taxi appears ten minutes later, and I'm out of my Jeep and by her side in a jiffy. I stuff a fifty in the driver's hand, and then I open the back door, helping Eva out. I take her bag, keeping her close to my side as we walk through the garage and into the lobby of the building. I want to do more but I daren't risk it. The building has cameras all over the place, and I won't compromise her safety.

But the minute I close my penthouse door, I dump the bags on the floor and gingerly draw her into my arms. She bursts out crying, fisting her hands in my shirt as she sobs uncontrollably. My heart is breaking, and I'm terrified of what she'll tell me. Scared I won't be able to restrain myself from seeking out her husband and beating his ass, which wouldn't be smart, because I'm no use to Eva if I'm dead.

She clings to me, and I hold her close, running my hand up and down her hair, whispering assurances. When she stops crying, I scoop her into my arms and carry her to the couch. Placing a blanket over her shivering body, I brush hair back off her face, perching on the edge of the couch. "What happened, Eva?"

"I ... he ..." She breaks down again, and I hug her, fighting strong emotions. This helpless feeling is something I haven't felt in a long time.

"It's okay," I reassure her. "You can tell me when you're ready."

When she has composed herself again, I lean down, peering into her anguished eyes. "What can I do? Do you want something to eat? To drink? Or can I run you a bath? Put on a movie?"

She thinks about that for a minute. "A bath sounds good," she croaks, her voice hoarse from crying.

I nod, getting her a glass of water and a box of tissues before I head to the bathroom.

Mom gave me some aromatherapy oils when I pulled a muscle in my back, and I add those to the tub before leaving a few fluffy towels on top of the cabinet for Eva.

When I return to the living room, she has replaced the water with whiskey, and that does little to ease my concern. It's not even ten a.m., and if she's hitting the liquor I fear this is even worse than my worst suspicions.

"I needed something stronger," she says, noticing my reaction. "Hope you don't mind."

"Of course not. Whatever you need." I kneel down in front of her. "I already hate him, and I don't even know what he's done."

She smiles sadly. "I spent most of yesterday plotting ways to kill him."

"We should swap notes sometime. I have a lengthy list of possible ways to make him go away for good."

And that's no word of a lie. I've thought of it, but the difference is, I'd never follow through. Because Eva deserves a better man than that.

I stand up, extending my hand. "Come on. Your bath awaits."

After I've shown her where everything is, I step outside, closing the door and giving her privacy, even though every cell of my being begs to stay inside and take care of her. By the cumbersome way she's moving around, I know she's physically injured, and all the murderous thoughts I've been trying so hard to suppress flood my system, making my blood boil.

A loud rap on the front door startles me. I check the peephole and briefly consider not letting him in.

He thumps the door. "I know you're in there, Kade," Kev hollers. "Open the fucking door."

Sighing, I open the door, and my brother comes barreling into the hallway. "You're a fucking idiot!" he yells, pushing me.

I slam the door shut and then glare at my younger brother. "You picked the wrong day for this, Kev, so I suggest you leave before I do or say something I'll regret." I'm pumped full of unspent anger, and it won't take much to rile me up. Usually, I'm pretty level-headed, but thinking of all the things that asshole could've done to Eva has me twisted into knots.

Ignoring me, he storms into my living room and I follow him. "You've started up with her again, haven't you?" he asks, rounding on me.

"Like I told you in Ireland, it's none of your business."

Kev and I ended up trading blows in Ireland while on family vacation after he admitted to reading text messages between Eva and me. I hadn't even been seeing her at the time, but we'd bumped into each other shortly before I left for Ireland and had begun exchanging flirty texts. After we'd both cooled down, Kev took me aside and told me everything about her husband. I know he was only trying to protect me, but invading my privacy wasn't the way to go about it; however, it did upset and confuse me enough to put a halt to my texting with Eva at the time. Things haven't been the same between my brother and me since, although we have managed to hold civil conversations, but the closeness we shared is long gone. I miss that, I really do, but I'm sensing we're on a slippery slope again, that it's unlikely Kev and I will ever reclaim what we once had. And that's a damn shame, but, as I told Eva, if it comes down to my family or her, I'll choose her.

And I don't say that lightly, because family means *everything* to me.

But she means more.

It sticks in my gut, and I wish I didn't have to make a choice, but if it comes down to it, it will be Eva. There's no contest.

"The hell it isn't!" he shouts, scrunching handfuls of his hair.

"You need to calm the fuck down," I demand, anxiously looking over my shoulder. The last thing Eva needs is shouting and aggression. "Lower your voice, or I'll call security to escort you off the premises. I mean it. I'm already fucked up enough today, and I don't need this shit."

I watch Kev deliberately get a grip on himself. I say nothing else, waiting patiently while he gains control of his emotions. Kev doesn't lose his temper often, but when he does, it's like fireworks on the Fourth of July.

"I know she's here," he says after a bit, thankfully keeping his voice low.

I nod. "She is, but it's not what you're thinking." He broods for a bit, and I know that face. He's thinking about how to tell me something. "You came here for a reason, and if you won't leave, then just say it."

"Do you want to get yourself killed? Because if you continue this madness, that's what will happen."

"I don't need to hear this again, Kev. I haven't forgotten a word of what you said in Ireland."

He shakes his head. "Is that so? Well, I guess I can add stupid to the list of adjectives I use to describe you."

"You don't understand."

"No. You're right. I don't." He leans into my face. "I told you who her husband was and the things he's involved in. The circles he runs in. Putting a hit on you would be as easy as breathing for him. You don't mess with these guys, Kade. Not ever."

"Contrary to what you think of me, I have a plan. I'm not going to risk my life or hers."

He examines my face carefully. "What plan?"

"We're leaving the country." He doesn't need to know Eva has yet to agree to this plan, but that's neither here nor there. After this, I won't back down until she does agree.

Kev starts pacing the room. "You've fucking lost it, Kade. You're insane! You don't run from those guys. They always catch up to you. *Always*."

"I'm prepared to take that risk," I coolly reply. I'm not getting into the pros and cons with my brother. I've already run the analysis and made up my mind.

Kev stops and looks at me, really looks at me. "You love her that much? Enough to leave everything behind?"

I eyeball him as I reply. "Yes. I love her like I know I'll never love any other woman, and I can't stand by and watch her in pain anymore." His eyes pop wide. "She didn't sign up for any of this, Kev. She was forced into marrying him, and she's never loved him."

"Does she love you?"

Eva hasn't exactly said those three little words, but her recent admission is as good as. I'm opening my mouth to respond affirmatively when she does it for me.

"Yes." She pads to my side, curling her hand around mine. "I love your brother very much."

I lower my head as she raises her face to meet mine. Her skin is flushed from the bath, her hair swaddling her face, damp at the ends and brushing the edge of the tiny towel she's wearing. Her trusting eyes shine with love, rendering me speechless.

"Then you need to let him go," Kev quietly says, and I whip my head around, glowering at him.

"Get the fuck out, Kev. No one asked for your opinion."

Eva's tormented expression speaks volumes. "No," she whispers. "He's right. It's what I've tried to do, but I keep failing." Nervously, she tucks her hair behind her ears, away from her face, and I see the marks. Angry, thick red welts mar her slim neck, and bruising thumbprints are glaringly evident, confirming that bastard had his hands around her.

"Fuck." The thought is mine, but the word comes out of Kev's mouth.

She notices where our eyes are focused, and she hastily covers her neck with her hair again, her cheeks staining a dark red. "I'm, ah, just going to get dressed and then I'll leave."

Gently, I reach out, pulling her into my arms. "No, baby. You're not going anywhere. The only person leaving is my brother." I caution Keven with a grave look, and he nods. All the blood has leached from his face.

"Don't do this, Kade," she beseeches, trying to shuck out of my embrace, but I refuse to let her go. "I don't want you to fall out with your family."

"No, it's okay," Kev says, rubbing the back of his neck. "I'm intruding in something I shouldn't. I'll go. Let you two talk."

"Wait here." I eyeball her. "I'll be right back."

I walk Keven to the door, and both of us are silent, tension clogging the air. When he's out in the corridor, he turns around, gulping. "I'll call you later."

I nod, closing and locking the door, and return to Eva. She's sipping her whiskey, shaking and shivering on the edge of the couch. I grab my robe from the back of the bathroom door, silently handing it to her. She puts it on without protest. Then I pour myself a scotch too and sit down beside her.

"Jeremy found out I was attacked," she whispers. "And he was furious. Apparently, I made him look weak."

I stare at her with shock splayed across my face. "You didn't tell him?"

She shakes her head. "I was afraid he'd find out you saved me, and I don't want you on his radar, at all."

Her whole body is trembling, and I put my drink down, cradling her against my chest. "I love you for trying to protect me, but you've got to let me take care of *you* now."

"I'm scared, Kade. For the first time, I'm really, really scared. He was so cold toward me. Like it was my fault."

"How did you get those marks, Eva?"

She shakes her head, tears streaming down her face unbidden. "I can't tell you," she chokes out. "Please don't make me."

My imagination is going crazy, and the urge to commit murder is back, but Eva needs me to be in control, to comfort her, and my own feelings will have to go on the backburner. Now would be a great time to jump in and beg her to agree to leave, but she's too upset, and I don't want to push her when she's so fragile.

"I'm not going to let him hurt you again," I promise, holding onto her more tightly, and pressing a fierce kiss to her temple. I don't know how to ensure I can keep that promise, but I'm prepared to fucking die trying.

After I get some food into Eva, I tuck her up in my bed, urging her to sleep. I doubt she's done much of that lately, and it doesn't take long for her to nod off. Closing my eyes, I kiss the top of her head, inhaling her sweet scent and promising I'm going to keep her safe. Then I leave a note explaining I need to run a few errands and head out with a new sense of purpose.

I return a few hours later feeling like I've made progress. Eva is still sleeping, so I prepare a lasagna and put it into the oven, sitting down to go through my purchases.

"Hey," a sleepy voice says from behind me a short while later. "You're back." She yawns, dropping down on the couch alongside me. Her nose wrinkles. "Something smells yummy."

"It's lasagna. Hope you're hungry?"

"Starving," she admits, swinging her legs up onto the couch.

My eyes are like heat-seeking missiles zoning in on the expanse of smooth, bare tan skin. "Is that my shirt?" I ask, and she blushes.

"Yes. I was too hot to sleep in the robe." She moves to get up. "I can get changed."

I pull her down into my lap, placing my hands softly around the back of her waist. "I wasn't complaining. Far from it. You look sexy in my clothes." I nuzzle her shoulder, sighing contentedly when she relaxes against me.

Neither of us speaks for a while, but it's far from awkward.

"I like being here with you," she says softly. "I like it a lot."

"I like having you here." I gaze into her eyes, happy to see them looking clearer and less bloodshot. "I wish you never had to leave."

She cups my face. "Me too." Leaning in, she kisses first one cheek, and then the other. "I meant what I said earlier." Her eyes lock on mine. "I love you, Kaden. I think I fell in love with you the first day I met you, but it took me a long time to realize that, and then I kept that secret in my heart because I want to do the right thing by you, but it's so difficult when I want you so much." She repositions herself so she's straddling me. "I don't know what the right thing is anymore. All I know is how much I crave you. How happy you make me. How safe the world feels when I'm wrapped in your arms."

My cock is rock hard in my pants, and my eyes keep darting to her lips. Every cell in my body cries out for her, but I won't go there. She's injured and hurting, and I won't ever make demands on her. "I love you, Eva. So Goddamned much it hurts. I can't bear the thought of you being his, not when I know you belong with me."

"I've never been his, Kade. Never. My heart has only ever belonged to you." She eases back, slowly removing my shirt, until she's sitting on me completely naked.

Christ. I'm not sure my willpower extends this far, but I've got to at least exercise some restraint. "Eva," I groan. "I only have so much control around you, and you're hurt. I don't want to add to that."

She takes my hand, pulling it to her breast. "The only way you can hurt me is if you say no." Tears moisten her eyes, and she draws in a shaky breath. "He hurt me, and I want to erase the feel of his hands, his touch. I need you to demonstrate how much you love me. I need to feel you again, Kaden, because the only time I've ever felt cherished is when you're making love to me, and I need that so badly right now."

I kiss her tears away, and then I take her mouth, slowly and tenderly, pouring every emotion into the kiss. "Are you sure?" I peer deep into her eyes, watching as she nods her head vigorously.

Then I stand up, cradling her against my chest, and walk us to the bedroom.

# Chapter Seventeen

## Past

*Evelina*

"Oh my God, it's so beautiful here," I admit, already completely in love with the island. We are out on the patio area of his parents' vacation home, and the view is simply breathtaking. Leaning against the wooden railing, I look out over the stunning beach below. "I can only imagine how gorgeous it is in the summer."

Kade wraps his arms around me from behind, sheltering me from the blustery wind. It's freezing and definitely not the ideal time to visit Nantucket, but there's nowhere in the world I'd rather be right now. "Summer's definitely the best time to visit, but I like it off season. It's less hectic and less crowded, and I don't mind the cooler temps."

"I've never minded the cold either. There's something about a walk in brisk, fresh air that's always appealed to me. I like feeling that little sting against my cheeks."

He smiles. "Me too." Taking my hand, he raises it to his lips, planting a quick kiss against my knuckles. "Let's check on dinner and maybe we can take a walk on the beach after?"

"I'd love that." I circle my arms around his waist, falling into a slow step alongside him as we walk back to the house. I love that I can touch him at will, without fear, and I haven't stopped touching him since we arrived at the house. I can scarcely keep my hands off him.

"Your mom has great taste," I say, trailing my hand along the back of the comfy couch as I drink in all the homey little features. "It's not really what I was expecting." I've seen photos of the Kennedys' Wellesley house in one of those home and garden magazines, and it was all cool, clean lines and slick interiors. This house is the complete opposite, full of old-world furniture and cluttered with personal mementos and trinkets. Don't get me wrong, it's still very stylish and tasteful, but it feels more like a family home should. The Wellesley house looked like a show house, although it could've been presented that way on purpose. I don't know. I've never been there.

Nor am I likely to ever visit.

A pang of sorrow spears me straight through the chest at the thought.

If this was a normal situation, I think of how different things could be. Of how I could have a proper relationship with Kade. Obviously, the whole student-teacher issue would still be a concern, but that'd pale into the background compared to the other obstacles.

I sigh, and he notices. He's so observant like that. Even when I don't spot his eyes on me, which is rare because he's always focused on me, he seems to know what's going through my mind.

He hands me a glass of wine, brushing some stray strands of hair back off my face. "Stop thinking." He plants his hands on my shoulders. "We have this weekend, and God knows when we'll be able to sneak away again. Let's just enjoy our time together with no regrets and no doubts."

I put my wine down on the table, reaching up to cup his face. "How did you get so wise?"

He shrugs and smiles, but it's a little off. "I've had to grow up a lot these last couple of years."

"Are things still tense at home?"

Now it's his turn to sign. "Yeah, but I don't want to talk about it. I meant what I said. We leave all that shit at the door this weekend."

"Sounds good to me," I say, kicking off my shoes and sinking into the couch. Kade sits down beside me, handing me my wine again.

He toys with the ends of my hair as we chat about everything and anything, and I love how normal this is. "Are there any golf courses on the island?" I ask him as an idea comes to me.

His answering grin is amused. "Plenty. Why'd you ask?"

"I've always wanted to learn to play golf. Could we go for a game?"

His brows climb to his hairline. "Seriously? You want to play golf?"

I slap his arm. "Don't be so sexist."

He threads his hand into my hair, chuckling. "That's not it." He shakes his head, and the look of adoration on his face does strange flippy things to my stomach. "Just when I think you can't get any more perfect, you go and say something like that." He leans in, brushing his lips against my cheeks. "I would love to teach you how to play golf, but winds are high this weekend, and you're better off starting with some practice shots on the driving range. I can totally take you there, if you like."

I press a soft kiss to his lips. "I would *love* that." I put my wine glass down on the table.

His fingers tighten in my hair, and he wraps his other arm around my back. "Is it weird that the thought of *me* teaching *you* something really turns me on?"

I smile. "Not at all. I get a massive kick out of teaching, and the idea of you teaching me something *is* hot."

Kaden growls, and that's the only warning I get before his mouth collides with mine in a wild kiss. I don't need any encouragement, and soon we're ravishing one another, pawing at our clothes, desperate to get closer. We don't even last until dinner. Kade switches off the stove, lifting me effortlessly into his arms as he leads us upstairs. He plants soft kisses all over my cheeks and my neck as he walks us into his bedroom before tenderly placing me down on the bed.

Silently and slowly, we undress one another, our usual frenetic coupling traded for something more intimate, more sensual. We don't have to rush, and as Kade slowly makes love to me, over and over, all night long, I offer up a silent prayer that I somehow get to keep him, to keep this, to never have to relinquish the only thing that brings me any joy in this life.

We are both ravenous the next morning, and we make breakfast together, feeding one another across the long dining table that overlooks the outside pool and deck area. He joins me in the shower, fucking me quick and hard, making my legs tremble all over again. Dressing warmly, we head down to the beach, walking barefoot and hand in hand along the damp, golden sand. Wind whips my hair all over my face, and I'm quiet as I listen to Kade telling me stories of summers spent here, days full of bicycle rides and surfing and nights getting drunk at beach parties.

"It sounds magical," I admit wistfully.

"I have a lot of fond memories of this house," he supplies. "This place always felt more like home than our home."

"Why is that?" I inquire, straining to see him through the knotted strands of hair covering my face.

"Mom was a mom when she was here, and she always seemed more carefree. I guess that rubbed off on us, and I came to associate this house with fun."

"She must've had her hands full when you were all little. You're so close in age."

He shrugs, holding my hand more tightly. "She wasn't around much growing up. She traveled a lot for business, and Dad was the main parent." He makes a noise, and it sounds bitter. "And he isn't even my dad." Kade had previously explained the situation, and I know it's all still raw for him, especially now they've discovered Kyler also isn't James's son.

"He's your dad in all the ways that matter," I quietly supply, believing whole-heartedly that the blood flowing through your veins doesn't automatically qualify anyone for parenthood. How you interact with and care for your children is the only important thing. Letting them know they are loved, listening to them, helping them understand their fears and concerns, encouraging and fostering independence, and guiding them as they make their own way in this world. Or, at least, those are the things I believe are important. The things I was largely denied during my own youth.

Anyone can make a baby, but that doesn't mean they are a parent in the ways that count.

Look at my own mother.

His chest heaves, and my heart aches for him. "I know you're right, and I was just coming to terms with it when the latest bombshell was dropped, and now I'm fucking furious all over again." He shakes his head. "I'm so worried about Kyler and ..." He trails off, pulling me to a halt and enfolding me in his arms. "We're not going to do this. Not this weekend. This weekend is about you and me."

I rub my hands up and down his arms. "I don't mind. If you need to talk about it, then talk." He kisses the tip of my nose, and it's a sweet gesture. "I'm always here if you need to get stuff off your chest."

He kisses me softly, and I find myself falling deeper and deeper with every glide of his lips. When we stop kissing, I let my head rest naturally against his chest, while his arms hold me close. "I know that, and you're the only one I've spoken to about it, besides my brothers."

"You will deal with it, in your own time, and things will work themselves out." I try to reassure him. "I know I haven't met your family, but I can tell you're all close, and I know how much family means to you. It will right itself in time."

"I hope you're right, because things are pretty messed up with my family, and my parents are on the verge of divorce, and everyone is struggling to deal with this stuff." He presses a kiss to the top of my head. "I hate feeling like life is spiraling out of control, but that's what it feels like at the minute."

I squeeze him tighter, wishing I could remove his uncertainty and his pain. "At least you have your brothers, and they have you. Take comfort in that fact."

I had no one growing up, and, at times, I felt like the loneliest girl in the universe.

"I know, and we're lucky we have each other. I may want to throttle them on occasions, but I know they've always got my back, like they know I've always got theirs."

I leave him on the beach a couple of minutes later to head back to the house to grab a tie for my hair. The wind keeps tossing it all over my face, and it's driving me freaking insane, but I don't want to cut our walk short because I can't see over the hair hat I'm wearing.

When I return a couple of minutes later, I spot Kaden talking to two girls a bit farther along the beach. I hang back, not sure who they are or what he might have told them about why he's here. I sneak sly glances at them, hating how my chest flutters at the sight of the girls' obvious flirting. Not that I can blame them. Kaden is hot, and a great guy, and I'm guessing he's never short of offers. An ugly, twisty sensation floods my belly, accelerating as I watch the pretty blonde put her hand on Kaden's arm, moving in closer to him. He reacts immediately, removing her hand and taking a step back. Glancing over his shoulder, he spots me, and his body locks up.

I look away, tightness slicing across my chest as a sense of helplessness overtakes me. I don't know why I do it, because Kade hasn't done anything wrong, but I retrace my steps, making my way back to the house, running the last few yards when I hear the pounding of his feet chasing after me.

"Eva! Wait!" he calls as I dart into the house. A few sneaky tears are rolling down my face, and I swipe at them, angry and confused. Kade catches up to me, snagging me at the waist and lifting me up into his arms.

"Put me down, Kaden." I'm horrified when my voice shudders. It's like I've returned to my teenage self, and I don't understand the conflicting emotions running riot throughout me.

"Not until you listen to me. Nothing happened."

My arms go around his neck of their own accord. "I know it didn't. That's not why I'm upset."

He plonks down on the couch, keeping a firm hold of me so I can't escape. I wriggle in his lap, resting my head on his shoulder and sighing. "I'm being stupid. Ignore me."

He smooths a hand up and down my back. "Leann and I go way back," he starts explaining. "Her family owns the house three doors down, and we spent a lot of summers hanging out with them. She has four younger sisters, I had six younger brothers, so you can imagine how messy it got when we were teens. I fooled around with her a few times, but it was always casual, it meant nothing to either of us, and I haven't been with her in years. I told her I was here alone to study, and she took that up the wrong way."

He nudges my head up, studying my eyes. "When she hit on me, I told her straight up I had a girlfriend, and she backed off. It's not what it looked like, I swear." It's sweet that he looks worried, and I hate that I'm acting like a lovesick teenager.

"Did you sleep with her?" The words are out before I can stop them, and I want to punt kick myself in my lady parts. *What the hell has gotten into me?*

146

He tries to stifle his amused smile, but he fails. "You're adorable when you're jealous." I scowl at him, and he laughs. "And, no, I never had sex with Leann."

Relief floods me, and I'm back to questioning my sanity. "God, Kade. I'm so sorry. This is embarrassing, and you have every right to talk to whomever you want without me getting jealous."

"I like that you're jealous," he admits, rubbing his thumb against my bottom lip. "It shows you care."

"It shows how crazy and immature I am." I shake my head, and then his words properly sink in. "Do you doubt I care about you?"

He shrugs, trying to look unaffected when he speaks, but I see the truth and the vulnerability behind the words and his gaze. "Not really, but I'm wondering why and how long it'll take you to wise up and realize you don't need me in your life."

Part of me is fucking furious that he thinks that, but another, bigger part of me understands it. I cup his face. "Trust me, Kaden, when I say I need you, more than you could ever realize, and you have no idea how much happiness you bring into my life."

"You mean that?" he whispers, and, for the first time, his youth and his vulnerability shine through.

"Yes. I don't know what this is or where it's going, but right here, right now, you are the most important person in my life, and I care about you. Deeply." I suspect my feelings run way deeper, but I'm not prepared to admit that to myself, let alone him, but the incident on the beach has raised the ugly truth to the surface, and I'm not sure I can contain it any longer.

My presence in Kaden's life stops him from leading a normal existence.

Stops him from being with girls his own age, girls who are available and come without baggage, and, for the first time, what we're doing feels completely selfish and very wrong.

I try to shake those thoughts aside and enjoy the rest of the weekend, because I want this one weekend to feel carefree, to enjoy being with a wonderful guy who rocks my world, but that dose of reality has done a real number on me, and I don't know what to do with all these confusing emotions. Or, I do, but I'm not ready to accept it yet, so I try my best to push them aside and cherish the rest of my time with Kaden.

We head to his golf course Sunday morning, and, thankfully, the driving range is very quiet. I've never hit a golf ball before in my life, and I'm sure I'm about to embarrass myself. Kade is remarkably patient as he explains the basics of golf to me, praising my swing and calling me a natural despite how many times I actually fail to even connect the club with the ball. But he's a great teacher, and soon I'm even managing to hit a few shots.

We eat a delicious lunch in the clubhouse before heading back to the house to pack up our stuff. I shoot a lingering look at the gorgeous property as we pull away in the taxi, my heart heavy with the acknowledgment that I most likely won't ever be here again.

"Do you regret coming away with me?" he asks as we wait in the departures lounge a while later, waiting for our flight to be called.

Looking around quickly, I lace my hand in his and nuzzle his side. "Not at all. I had a great time."

He scrutinizes my face. "Don't lie to me, Eva." His Adam's apple jumps in his throat. "You haven't been yourself since I ran into Leann on the beach."

I guess I wasn't so successful at hiding the turmoil inside my head, and I figure I owe him some honesty. "You should be with someone like Leann, Kade. Someone who is free to love you the way you deserve to be loved."

A muscle spasms in his jaw. "I don't want to be with Leann. I don't fucking love her. I love you."

Shock splays across my face, and he misunderstands my reaction, pulling away from me and shoving his hands in his pockets. He leans his head against the high glass window, avoiding making eye contact with me.

"Kade." I cautiously approach him. "You can't love me," I whisper softly. "I'm not a free agent." I wish I was, and I wish I could tell him I love him too, because I'm fairly certain that's what I'm feeling.

"You can get a divorce," he murmurs, looking sheepishly at me.

This isn't the first time he's brought this up, and it pains me to see the subtle hope in his eyes. "I can't." I shake my head, and a blanket of sadness covers me.

"I see." He grits his teeth, his jaw clenching, and all hope dies in his eyes.

A flash of red in the corner of my eye briefly captures my attention, and I glance over Kade's shoulder. Everything turns to ice inside me as I instantly recognize the woman in the expensive red coat and the tall dark-haired man standing beside her.

"Oh my God," I rasp, quickly turning my back to them.

"What?" Kade is alerted to my panicked tone, placing his hand on my shoulder.

I fling his hand off. "Don't touch me!" I back away from him. "And you need to stay away from me," I whisper-add. "I've just spotted a colleague of my husband's and his wife."

Kade emits a string of colorful expletives. "Did they see you?"

"I don't think so ... I don't know."

"Okay. Stay calm," he whispers from a couple feet away. He's staring out the window, making it look like he's not talking to me. "I'll leave and wait by the plane. I'll have a member of staff call you when the pilot is ready for takeoff, and she'll escort you inside."

I subtly nod. "Thank you."

When Kaden leaves, I walk to the farthest side of the room, doing my best to make myself inconspicuous. When the commercial flight to Boston is called and the man and his wife leave, I release the breath I'd been holding, but the tight knots in my stomach and in my chest remain, and they are still there when we land in New York an hour later.

We were both quiet on the flight back, and I'm guessing Kade's rethinking everything the same way I am.

Setting out on Friday, I had high hopes for this weekend, but as I return to my house, to my marital bed, I force myself to face some hard facts.

Staring this affair with Kaden was selfish and dangerous. Kaden doesn't need to be saddled with someone like me, and the longer I prolong this affair, the more I risk ruining his life.

He deserves to find a good woman who is free to love him.

A woman who doesn't selfishly take what she wants, knowing it can lead to nowhere but trouble.

A woman who doesn't place the only man she's ever loved in harm's way.

As the saying goes, if you love someone, you should set them free.

And as I break Kaden's heart the following week, telling him we can't do this anymore, *lying* and saying the relationship has run its course, I hope I'm strong enough to do the right thing—to let him live his life without me holding him back.

# Chapter Eighteen

## Present Day

## *Kaden*

"Are you sure about this, Eva?" I ask her one final time, stretching above her on the bed and holding my naked body still.

"Yes." She maneuvers herself underneath me, reaching around and tracing a hand up and down my spine. Pleasurable shivers course through me. "Make love to me, Kade."

All my restraint is gone, and I, carefully, press my body to hers, planting my mouth against her tempting lips. I take my time, worshiping her mouth, before snaking a trail of kisses along her jaw, her neck, and down lower. I taste every inch of her silky, smooth skin, reveling in all the breathy little moans she emits as I flick my tongue against the hardened peaks of her nipples, gently sucking her ample breasts into my mouth. My body urges me to go faster, but I deliberately hold myself back. One, she's hurting, and I want to be as gentle with her as possible, and two, this is the first time in almost two years that I've had the woman I love underneath me, and I intend to savor every second of it.

I tease her supple flesh with my tongue and my hands as I move lower and lower. Nudging her legs apart at the thighs, I blow across her hot flesh, and she trembles. Slowly, I insert two fingers inside her, moving gently in and out.

"Faster, Kade," she murmurs, arching her back and writhing on the bed.

I pump my fingers faster, and my cock strains with unadulterated desire as my patience dies and pure need takes control. I suck on her clit, persistently lapping at that sensitive bundle of nerves while continuing to tease her pussy with my fingers. When she explodes on my face, she is screaming and crying out my name, and I can't wait a minute longer. I soak up every last cry, every whimper, and then I'm reaching for my nightstand, grabbing a condom and rolling it on.

Eva stares up at me, and I love that I've put that flushed, sated look on her face. "My God," she moans. "You are too damn good at that."

I send her an arrogant grin as I line my cock up to her entrance. "There is no such thing as too good when it comes to sex." I rub my hard cock up and down her slit, teasing both of us.

"Kade." Her voice contains a mix of pleading and warning.

I peer into her eyes, pinning her with a serious look. "Are you still okay with this?"

Her answer is a sharp slap to my butt. "If you back out now, I will scream from the top of my lungs in frustration."

Grinning, I push inside her, very slowly, inch by inch, and she gasps. "I won't ever leave you frustrated. That's just not my style." I lean down, capturing her mouth in a searing hot kiss. "I love you," I whisper, nuzzling the sensitive spot just under her ear. "I love you so much."

"Kade!" She groans as I start moving quicker, in and out, pistoning my hips and pushing all the way to the hilt. "I love you too."

And those are the last words spoken for a very long time.

"I'll have to leave soon," Eva says, drawing circles on my bare chest as she snuggles in closer to my side. "But I don't know how I can. I never want to leave this bed. Leave you."

"Then don't." The words fly out of my mouth, even if we both know the way it has to be.

She sits up, flattening her palms on my chest and staring at me for so long I wonder if she's in a bit of a daze. Biting her lip in that sexy way of hers, she leans in closer to me. "I want to say yes, Kade, and I'd give everything up to run away with you, but I can't be that selfish. Your brother is right. I can't take you away from your family and everything that's important to you here. I just can't do it."

I sit upright, pulling her into my lap and wrapping my arms around her waist. We're both still naked, and strategically aligned in the best way, but I force all greedy sexual thoughts aside and focus on the words coming out of my mouth. "We talked about this before. I'm not asking you to make decisions for me, just like I'm not asking to make the decision for you. I've already thought about this, Eva, and you mean more to me than anyone or anything in this world. I want to do this because I can't live my life without you in it, and that's our only choice right now. But I'm hoping it won't always be like that. That we'll have more options in the future."

"And what if we don't? Are you happy to never see your family again?"

Maybe I'm more of a glass-half-full kinda guy, but I don't see that happening. I'm confident I'll find a way to make this work, that this *will* only be temporary, but I don't want to articulate that, because the reality is I don't know how this is going to end. And I've already considered all scenarios. As fucking horrible as it is to think I may not ever see my family again, I'm prepared for that.

Eva means that much to me.

"I wouldn't be happy, no, but I'm prepared to accept that," I reply coolly. "If it means I get to have you, then it's a sacrifice I'm willing to make."

She looks torn. Tears pool in her eyes, but I can't tell if they're happy or sad ones. "I can't ask you to sacrifice everything for me."

I shake my head, touching her face. "You haven't asked me. I'm telling you that's what I'm prepared to do for you. You need to consider whether you're prepared to do that for me." I press a kiss to the back of her hand. "All you have to decide is whether you can leave everything behind and run away with me. If you are prepared to face the consequences of that decision for you *personally*. Feeling guilty about my decision has no bearing on yours, or it shouldn't, and vice versa."

"It's not that easy to separate them out, Kade."

"Sure it is." I cup her face. "You just accept my decision is already made and then think about your own situation. That's it."

She rests her head against my shoulder, and I cradle her to me, offering up prayers to every deity known to man. "I tried to escape once," she whispers, placing her hand on my chest. "I thought I was being careful with my plans, but I didn't really have a clue." She looks up at me. "When Jeremy found out, he beat me. Badly. It's the only time he has been purposely violent toward me. He told me point blank that if I tried anything like that again he would kill me." Her chest heaves. "If we decide to do this, and we don't pull it off, he will kill both of us, Kade."

"I'm well aware of the risks, which is why we will take our time planning every aspect down to the minutest detail."

"No plan is foolproof."

"No, but careful planning and determination will go a long way."

Her eyes penetrate mine, but she doesn't respond, laying her head back on my shoulder. We stay like that, both absorbed in thought.

After a few minutes, I, reluctantly, slide her off my lap, standing up and pulling a pair of sweats on, loving how her eyes greedily follow my every move. "Look, I'll go heat the lasagna up and give you some time to think about it. I don't want to pressure you, Eva, but the thought of sending you back to his house without some type of plan in place makes me nervous. So, take some time, grab another bath or a shower, and then let me know what you're thinking."

I'm remarkably calm as I fix dinner and set the table. Perhaps I'm delusional, but I have faith Eva will make the right call.

I've just plated up our food when I sense her presence. Looking up, I smile, watching her watching me.

"You're very domesticated," she says, sauntering toward me fully dressed. "It's a huge turn-on."

Holding out a chair for her, I laugh. "Wow. You're easily pleased."

She pecks my lips briefly before sitting down. "I am. The simple things mean the most to me." She reaches up, holding onto my waist. "You taking care of me today, in all the ways you have, means more to me than anything you could ever buy me."

I lean down, kissing her mouth upside down. "I want to look after you every day for the rest of our lives."

Tears spill out of her cheeks. "God, Kaden."

I crouch down in front of her. "What, my love."

She sniffles, and tears cascade down her cheeks. "You're too good to be true." She attempts to laugh, but it comes out as a half-laugh, half-cry.

"I just love you." I shrug before sitting down in the chair beside her. "And I'm far from perfect." She arches a brow, and I grin. "Underneath this exterior is a slob waiting to burst free," I joke, encouraging her to eat. "You haven't seen this apartment when I haven't cleaned it for weeks or when I'm too lazy to do laundry and I'm picking through the pile of dirty clothes on my bedroom floor for something to wear. I leave the toilet seat up all the time, I'm moodier than a girl with PMS a hell of a lot, I'm stubborn, I've had several instances of road rage, I get a bad dose of verbal diarrhea when I'm smashed, and—"

"Oh my God, enough!" She laughingly covers my mouth. "None of those things bother me. Like, at all. You could tell me you're a cross-dressing leather-pant-wearing alien in disguise, and I'd still love you. Still think you're perfect."

I lean in and kiss her. "Then it's official."

She frowns a little. "What is?"

"Either we're both rocking a one-way ticket to Insanityville or we're in love."

Her expression turns whimsical again. She puts her knife and fork down and takes my hands in hers. A host of different emotions flickers across her face. "We both know the only crazy we are is crazy in love."

I lift our conjoined hands, kissing the back of her hand.

She draws an exaggerated breath. "And I've thought about it. Your proposal. And my answer is ... yes."

I blink several times, staring at her in shock, wondering if my ears heard correctly. "Yes?"

"Yes," she says, more resolute this time. "Yes, I'll run away with you." Her eyes shine with potent emotion. "Yes to forever with you."

I'm out of my seat before I've even processed the movement, sweeping her up into my arms. I press a fierce kiss to her temple while hugging the shit out of her. "You won't regret this, and I'll do everything in my power to keep you safe." I feel like fist pumping the air. I can't believe she agreed. That we're doing this. That we'll finally be together.

She eases back a little. "I know you will. I trust you." She plants her hands on my chest, right over the spot where my heart is somersaulting in my chest. "I trust you completely."

I drag her back into her chair when her stomach emits a loud grumble of protest. "You need to eat," I command, "and then I'll run through what I have planned."

We're sitting on stools at the island unit in the kitchen going over everything I purchased today. Eva is staring at me like I hung the moon or something. "You should see the look on your face," I say, tweaking her nose.

"How did you do all this all ready?" Shock resonates in her tone.

"Well, I was pretty confident you were going to say yes," I lie. I hoped she'd say yes but I was skeptical. However, that didn't stop me from checking out a few things and starting to make plans. The rest of the stuff I purchased today.

I hand her the Prada bag with the wig and the new clothes I bought before sliding the set of keys to her. "So, it's agreed. You'll come here every day after work ends. I've parked your new car in the parking spot I purchased on campus. It's only a three-minute walk from the rear entrance of your building and once you're wearing the wig and dressed in different clothes, no one should notice it's you. And if your husband has someone checking, they'll still see your car parked out front and assume you're working late."

A nervous breath escapes her mouth. "How long do you think it'll take to set up everything else?"

I rub soothing circles on the back of her hand. "A few weeks, most likely. I don't want to rush and mess up. I've already connected with the guy who'll produce our fake IDs, and I'm in the process of setting up several offshore accounts in different names."

"It's like I've wandered onto the set of James Bond or Jason Bourne," she jokes, but it's not far off the mark. It's such a pity I can't confide in Kev, because he'd know some shortcuts, but he's the last person who'd help me with this.

"It won't always be like this." I try to reassure her, even if I'm not sure it's the full truth. We're going to have to move around a lot, and I'm guessing we'll always be watching our backs, which will take some adjustment.

"I don't care if it is." She squeezes my hand. "Once we're together, we can handle anything that comes our way."

# Chapter Nineteen

## Present Day

*Evelina*

Jeremy hasn't darkened my door since last weekend, and I couldn't be more grateful for small mercies. In fact, he hasn't been home much at all, and we've barely spoken in days. If he's assigned a bodyguard to watch over me, he's being extremely circumspect; still, I'm hugely self-conscious as I leave my office in disguise on Thursday night to travel the short distance to Kaden's place. Keeping my head down, I hurry to the secondhand Audi A1 hatchback Kaden bought me, quickly unlocking the car and getting in. I smile to myself as I think of all the covert ways he's trying to protect me. If I didn't know better, I'd almost say he's enjoying himself, but I know he's not. I know he'd much rather we didn't have to do this.

But the decision is made, and I'm not dwelling on it anymore.

It's like Kaden said—we've both independently made up our minds to do this, and there's no looking back. I've been surprised at how guilt-free and regret-free I've been this past week. It's like a considerable portion of stress evaporated when I made this decision.

Now I'm chomping at the bit to escape.

"Honey, I'm home," I joke as I enter Kade's apartment fifteen minutes later, yanking the short blonde wig off my head and tossing it on the table in the hall. Kade is on top of me in a flash, like every other day, and his obvious happiness in my presence never fails to delight me.

He reels me into his arms, capturing my mouth in an urgent kiss. "Missed you," he murmurs, nibbling at my lips. "Missed you so much."

My husband has never shown me such blatant affection, and I bask in Kaden's adoration, reveling in the glow of his love. The kiss quickly transforms, moving from urgent to frantic in a split second. My hands slide under his shirt, my greedy fingers trekking all over his delectable body. Kaden's time at the gym has sown benefits I'm more than happy to reap. A low groan rips from the back of his throat as he lifts me up, and my legs automatically go around his waist. Sweeping the contents of the table onto the floor in one expert brush of his hand, he plants my butt on the cold marble, sliding a hand up the inside of my thigh. I kick my shoes off, and they drop to the ground with a noisy clang.

My fingers fumble with the buttons on his shirt in my hurry to get the damn thing off him. Yanking his lips from mine, he effortlessly pulls it up over his head, flinging it aside. I suck one finger into my mouth, curling my tongue slowly up and down my flesh as I eyeball him with wicked intent. He curses, moving his hand to cup me down below, and I jerk on the table as liquid lust dances over my skin.

Still sucking my finger, I reach out with my other hand, popping the button on his jeans. Using my knees and feet, I shove the denim down his legs, desperate to get at him. His erection is poking out the front of his tight black boxer briefs, making my mouth water and my core ache painfully.

Cool air washes over my heated flesh as he pushes my dress up to my waist, tugging my nylons and panties down in one fluid move. I grab him to me, wrapping my legs around his body and pulling his lips to mine. My tongue explores his mouth, welcoming the fresh, minty taste and the expert way his tongue tangles with mine. Kaden kisses like a starving man, greedy and extreme, taking everything but savoring it wholly at the same time. My hands roam his body, slipping into the back of his boxers as I grab hold of his firm ass. He laughs and a growl gurgles from my throat. "I love your ass," I admit in a husky tone, licking a line up the side of his neck while squeezing his butt cheeks and closing my eyes in sheer bliss.

"I love your ass, too," he replies, thrusting two fingers inside me. "But I love your tits more, or maybe your pussy because it's always so fucking wet for me." I cry out at the welcome intrusion, riding his hand in unashamed abandon. "Hot damn. I've changed my mind. I love the way you react to my touch; I fucking love it." He holds the nape of my neck with his other hand, crashing his mouth down on mine. We're devouring one another, and his hand is doing wonderful things to my body, but it's not enough.

I yank his boxers down, and he chuckles against my mouth. "Impatient much, baby?"

"Shut up and fuck me," I rasp, taking hold of his hard, hot length and stroking it fast.

Kade lets loose a volley of expletives, dropping to his knees, grabbing his jeans, and pulling a condom out of his wallet.

The instant he thrusts inside me, my muscles equally tense and relax. I've never felt so comfortable with any man, and a deep sense of content-ment floods every cell, every nook and cranny of my body whenever I'm connected with Kaden like this. But my body demands more, tightening around his rock-hard length as he pushes in and out of me, twisting his hips in a way that ensures I feel every part of him as he worships me. I lock my legs more firmly around his waist, squeezing his butt cheeks and grinding my hips against his, increasing the friction and heightening all my senses. The table slams into the wall, and I briefly wonder if it might break, but all rational thought flees my mind as a series of heavenly tremors rip through my body, electrifying every part of me. He moves faster and faster, and momentum is building and building inside me until I shatter, explosively, powerfully, the orgasm whipping through me like lightning. I scream his name, over and over, holding him against me as his own release comes, his body shuddering and shaking as I press tiny kisses to his chest.

We stay locked in position, holding one another, while our heart rates return to normal and our breathing settles down.

"You sure know how to make a greeting memorable," I tease, sliding my hands up around his neck.

"We aim to please." He smirks, tenderly smoothing my dress back into place as he bends over to pick up my underwear.

"We?" I lift a brow, hopping off the table and leaning against the wall as I pull my panties and nylons back on.

"My cock and I," he smoothly replies, and I burst out laughing.

He moves in front of me, palming my face. "God, I love that sound. My new mission in life is to make you laugh like that each day."

My heart melts all over again. How can one man always know the right things to say? "My new mission is to make you happy each day."

Buttoning his jeans, he smiles at me. "Well, that's easy. All I need is to wake up with you by my side, and I'm the happiest man on the planet."

I stretch up and kiss him. "Have I told you how much I love you?"

His grin turns proud. "Maybe a time or two."

"Well, I haven't told you enough. I love you. I love you. I love you." I kiss him again. "I love you more than anything in this world."

"More than prawn chili masala?"

I pretend to consider it, laughing as he mock-scowls. "Definitely more than prawn masala."

"I take it back," I tell him an hour later, groaning as I rub my sore ribs. I'm lying flat on my back on the mats Kade laid out on the living room floor, silently kicking myself for my lack of finesse when it comes to self-defense. Kade's insistent that I continue my training, and I know it makes sense, but I suck badly at it. The problem is, I'm too distracted by all the sweaty, glistening male skin on display, and I react a split second too late. Every. Damn. Time.

"Take what back?" he asks, extending his hand to help me up.

"My professions of love," I say, teasingly. "You're a hard taskmaster."

"It's in your best interests, and I might not worry as much if I know you're able to defend yourself."

I want to argue that I'm not completely defenseless, but when you consider the people we're up against, it's a weak argument, so I just nod, picking myself back up and starting all over again.

"Make sure to get here as early as you can tomorrow," Kade says, as we stand just inside his door, attempting to pry ourselves from one another. "They said it'd take a few hours to get all the shots they need, and I'm still hoping we can squeeze in some alone time."

Kade has arranged for some people to come here tomorrow to take whatever photos are needed for our fake IDs.

"I'll be here. Don't worry." I squeeze him tight before reluctantly shucking out of his arms.

"And you have that untraceable cell I gave you?" he asks, as he does every night.

"Yes, babe. I have it hidden in my room, and I'll use it if I need to." I stretch up on my tiptoes and he meets me halfway, ravishing my mouth in a brutal kiss, one laced with passion and fear and a million other things we're both feeling.

He presses his forehead to mine. "Parting is such sweet sorrow," he murmurs in that deep, seductive voice of his.

"And ... he quotes Shakespeare." I press a hand over my chest. "Be still my beating heart." I caress his cheek. "And you say you're not perfect." I shake my head, smiling and touching his face again.

His lips curve up at one corner. "I'm not sure I said it quite like that, more like I'm not perfect *all the time.*"

I dart in and peck his lips one last time. "Good to see you still have a healthy ego."

He shrugs. "You call it ego. I call it confidence."

"Well," I say, glancing in the mirror and tucking a few wisps of stray dark hair under the blonde wig. "Whatever the label, it's good to hear. We're going to need to cling to that sentiment in the weeks and months ahead." I turn to face him, putting my hands on my hips and pouting. "How do I look?"

"Like a blonde bombshell." His eyes darken as he drinks me in. "And now I'm hard as a rock again." He sighs.

I run my hand up his arm. "It won't be like this for much longer."

He hugs me one final time. "I know, and it's the only thing that's keeping me sane."

I'm on edge the next morning when I find Jeremy waiting for me in the kitchen. I eye him warily as I fix my usual coffee, fruit, and a bagel. He doesn't speak, but I feel his eyes following me around the kitchen, making me incredibly uncomfortable. When I'm seated with my breakfast, he clears his throat, eventually saying what he waited to say. "We're going to the Carlisles' for dinner tonight. Be ready to leave by seven."

My heart sinks as I numbly nod.

"Wear the red dress—the short one—and put your hair up."

My heart plummets to my toes. Although the bruising has faded around my neck, marks are still clearly visible, and by the way he's currently staring at me, he knows it too. All the tiny hairs lift on the back of my neck, and I'm wondering what's going through Jeremy's mind these days. He's acting weird and it's in no way reassuring.

I wait until he's in the car to rush back to my bedroom, retrieving the hidden cell and stowing it in the inside pocket of my bag. Then I make my way to work.

Once inside my office, I power up my computer and call Kaden to explain.

"Can you get out this afternoon instead?" he asks, as I scan my email inbox. "I can call my contact and see if we can bring the session forward."

"I don't think so," I say, frowning as I open up a group email from the head of the department. "The big boss has called a staff meeting this afternoon. There's no way I can not show up." There isn't much they can do to me if I don't go, not now I'm leaving, but I'm reluctant to do anything out of the ordinary or anything to draw attention to myself, in case Jeremy does have people watching me, so I think it's best I attend. From the wording of the email, I can tell it's a serious issue.

"Okay." Kade's calm voice is unruffled. "I'll rearrange things. Don't worry about it."

"What do you think this is about?" Renee asks me later that day as we make our way through successive corridors en route to the conference room where the staff meeting is being held.

"No idea," I say, distracted a little with thoughts of the dinner tonight. And I say "dinner" in vague terms, because they are always just an excuse to drink to excess. Since Michael married Jenna ten months ago, she seems intent on turning their home into party central. I've lost count of the amount of invites we've received. I've managed to avoid attending a few of her events, but I know I won't be able to get out of this one tonight.

The Carlisles' parties are definitely an acquired taste, and it's bound to be a long night, because they've most likely invited a big crowd and the party will drag on into the small hours. But I'll grin and bear it, because I won't have to put up with this for much longer. Excitement bubbles in my veins, and I let it loose for a few seconds, but then I shut it down.

I won't allow myself to get excited or hopeful or to celebrate prematurely.

Not until we're on board a plane headed far away from the United States.

Then, and only then, will I allow myself to believe in it, to taste freedom, to finally breath.

"Hey, are you okay?" Renee asks, her brow furrowing as her gaze slips to my neck.

Self-conscious, I pull my scarf up higher, shooting her a reassuring smile. "Never better." I loop my arm through hers, deploying a tried and tested diversion tactic. "How are the wedding plans coming along?"

We chatter about wedding stuff as we make our way into the room, muting when we notice all the solemn faces and the apprehensive atmosphere in the room. Renee and I trade puzzled expressions. Most of our colleagues are already seated, and there are only a few vacant chairs left around the table, so we're forced to sit across from one another. Unfortunately, that means I'm seated alongside Jesse, and I wonder if it's the universe's way of punishing me. I can feel his eyes boring a hole in the side of my head, but I ignore him, opening up my pad and jotting down a few notes.

The big boss man arrives a couple of minutes later, and a deathly hush settles over the room. He wastes no time getting down to the bones of the matter. Standing at the top of the table, he doesn't sit down, slowly perusing the men and women in front of him. "Harvard's excellent reputation and stellar results have been built on the foundation of structure, discipline, and always striving to be the best. We are a pillar within our community and an example to all those who wish to follow in our footsteps."

He slams his palms down on the table, and my heart jumps behind my ribcage. Thunderclouds roll over his face as he stares each of us down.

"The rules by which we govern are there for an important reason. To protect the sanctity of the brand and our reputation and to safeguard our staff and our students." He rakes his gaze around the table again, and I'm growing uncomfortable in my own skin. "The no fraternization policy is in effect because it is absolutely abhorrent to use your position in this university for personal sexual gratification."

All the blood drains from my face as I realize where this is going.

"To take advantage of any student, irrespective of the circumstances, is an abuse of power and one which is not tolerated by this faculty." He straightens up and his gaze lands on my side of the table. Bile swims up my throat, and I worry I'm about to hurl up the contents of my stomach.

"Unfortunately, such a scenario has been brought to my attention recently. Upon investigation, it appears there is merit in the allegations that have been made. One of your colleagues, an assistant professor, has been engaged in intimate sexual activity with a student." His voice booms around the room, but I barely hear it over the blood thrumming in my ears.

Wiping my sweaty palms down the front of my skirt, I'm struggling to contain the violent shaking that has overtaken my body. If this comes out now, it will ruin everything Kaden and I are hoping to do. While he isn't my student any longer, and technically the policy doesn't apply to our current situation, that won't matter if it comes out that we started our affair when we *were* student and teacher. And the fact I'm married, and to *whom* I'm married, would cause a big enough scandal to bring plenty of heat on the department.

No, if this comes out now, it would not be good.

That nauseating feeling intensifies, and I clamp my lips shut, cautioning myself to calm down.

"You may feel this should be dealt with privately with the individual concerned," the department head continues, "and the human resources department may very well agree with you, but this is *my* department, and I will handle things the way I want to. I'm doing this today, in front of all staff members, because I want this to be a warning. To all of you." Those steely eyes roam the room again, and I have to force myself to keep my chin up and my eyes fixed straight ahead. "I will not tolerate noncompliance with any of our policies, especially this one. To take advantage of a student under your charge is most heinous and has the potential to significantly damage Harvard's reputation and the reputation of my department."

He swings his gaze back around, leveling a ferocious look in my direction. "That is why I am calling the culprit out in public." His eyes narrow, and I shift uncomfortably in my chair. Sweat coasts down my spine, and little beads of moisture dab at my brow. "What do you have to say for yourself?"

# *Chapter Twenty*
## Present Day

*Kaden*

I check my cell for the umpteenth time, frowning at the lack of new texts. I haven't heard from Eva since yesterday afternoon, and I'm growing increasingly worried. I know she said she had an important staff meeting to attend and then she was going out with that thug she's married to, but surely she could've found some opportunity to message me back?

I crick my neck from side to side, trying to loosen my stiff shoulder muscles, but nothing's working.

"No cell phones on the golf course," my dad, James, says, sending me a dark look. He's a complete stickler for the rules when it comes to golf. Pity he didn't share that same sense of obligation when it came to his marriage. Then he may never have gotten involved with that witch Courtney, and my parents might still be together.

I slip it into the back pocket of my golf pants. "Sorry."

"What's so important you have to check it every five seconds?" my brother Kyler asks, squinting as he watches Dad's ball rise high into the sky. We're at the fifteenth hole, preparing to tee off, and this is turning into the longest game of golf ever. Between Kyler continuously ending up in the bunker and the length of time it takes Kev to line up and take each shot, it's dragging out unnecessarily, only adding to my nerves. The eighteenth hole can't come quick enough.

"Nothing," I murmur, pulling a driver out of my golf bag.

Kev sends me a knowing look, and I hold his stare, daring him to let the cat out of the bag, but he holds his tongue, knowing full and well what shitstorm he'd unleash if he went there.

An hour later, we're finally finished. Dropping our bags off at our cars, we walk into the clubhouse together. Dad wanders off, chatting to a couple of his golf buddies while Kev, Kyler, and I walk to the dining room, securing a table for lunch.

"So, who's the girl?" Kyler asks once we're seated with drinks, idly reading the menu.

"There is no girl." I keep my eyes on the menu, so I don't have to lie to his face.

"Please tell me you're not back with Tiffani," he groans.

"Tiff and I are permanently finished. I told you that." I lift my chin and meet his gaze head-on.

"I've heard that a few times," he retorts, leaning back in his chair with a smirk on his face.

"He means it this time," Kev interjects, taking a sip of his beer. Our eyes lock briefly.

Kyler's eyes narrow as he assesses us. "What don't I know?"

"Nothing. How's Faye?" It's a deliberate attempt to steer the conversation to safer topics.

He squints at me, knowing exactly what I've done, but he can't help talking about his girlfriend. He's completely infatuated with her.

A goofy smile slips over his mouth. "She's good." Sitting up, he leans his elbows on the table. "Did you hear I'm permanently living with her now?" I arch a brow, and he continues explaining. "Shit kinda came to a head with Brad, so I moved in with Faye, and Rachel moved in with him."

"Do Mom and Dad know that?"

He snorts. "Don't know, and don't care. We're both twenty next year, and there isn't anything they can do about it. Besides, they know how we feel about one another."

"And everyone knows they're screwing each other's brains out any chance they get," Kev adds, earning a slap to the back of the head from Ky.

"Shut it, ass face. That's my future wife you're talking about."

"When're you planning on using that ring you bought?" I ask, and shock splays across Kev's face.

"What?" Kev splutters, leveling an incredulous look at Kyler. "You have a ring? Since when?"

Ky shrugs, but he can't keep the grin off his face. "I went shopping with Kal last summer and ended up walking away with an engagement ring for Faye. It was a spur of the moment thing, but I'm not sorry I bought it."

"Wow." Kev is virtually speechless for once. I never thought our younger brothers would be the first to get engaged, but Kal's loved Lana virtually his whole life, and Kyler fell head over heels for Faye the minute she showed up on our doorstep.

"When you find the one, you just know," Kyler confidently says, and I'm so proud of my brother. He's come a long way in the last two years.

"I'm happy for you, Ky. For both of you. She's a gorgeous girl, and you two belong together. I hope everything works out."

Kev's sharp gaze flashes to mine, and I know how that came out.

Like a goodbye.

"Thanks, man." Kyler flushes with pride. "Even if all the shit with Brad doesn't go away, I've decided I'm going to propose at Christmas. I'm done waiting. I want my ring on her finger so every asshole who wants in her pants knows she's mine."

Kev barks out a laugh. "Spoken like a true possessive douche. I'm not sure Faye would be too pleased to hear your motives."

"Don't be a jerk." Ky discreetly flips him the bird. "You know I'm asking her because I fucking love that girl to death, and I want to make sure I get to spend every minute of the rest of my life with her, but there are other obvious advantages too."

"I'm only messing around," Kev says in a somber tone. "We all see how you feel about her. How you feel about one another."

A pang of sorrow hits me in the chest. My family is never going to see how that exists between me and Eva too, and I hate that. Hate that they might never get to meet her, to get a chance to know her.

Dad appears then, putting an end to that particular conversation. I spend the rest of lunch locked in my troubled mind, sneaking glances at my cell every chance I get, growing more and more alarmed at the silence glaring back at me.

Kev hovers around my Jeep as we say goodbye to Dad and Kyler. "Make sure to call your mother," Dad cautions me, giving me a quick hug. "She wants to confirm numbers for Christmas, so you need to let her know if you're bringing a plus one or not."

My chest tightens again. I'm hoping we'll be out of the country for Christmas, because the longer we leave it, the more likely Jeremy Garcia is to find out about our affair and our plans. Forcing a fake smile on my face, I hug Dad again, slapping him on the back. "I'll call her. Stop fretting." Dad gets in his car, and Ky and I knuckle touch before he slides behind the wheel of his SUV.

They haven't even started their engines, when Kev rounds on me. "We need to talk."

I open my Jeep door. "Get in."

Gripping the steering wheel tight, I'm psyching myself up for lecture number three hundred and sixty-three.

"Are you really doing this?" Kev asks quietly, eyeballing me.

"Doing what?"

"Running away with her."

I nod, and air expels from his mouth in a noisy outburst. He stares out the side passenger window, and you could cut the tension with a knife.

Slowly, he turns to face me. "I didn't understand before, but I think I do now." My brows lift. "You love her, and she loves you. Like Faye and Ky. Like Kal and Lana."

I drag my hand through my hair, slowly nodding. "Yeah. It's like that."

"Then I'm happy for you, man."

My jaw hangs open, and my eyes blink wide as I stare at the stranger sitting in the car beside me. "Come again?"

He smiles. "You can't help who you fall for, and I had her figured out all wrong."

"I tried to stay away from her, Kev. I tried real hard, but it's always been Eva for me. I didn't care that she was my professor or that she's married. We just have this connection. It's been there from the moment I met her, and the more I get to know her, the harder I fall. There won't ever be anyone else for me. I need to keep her safe, and I can't do that here."

A dark look crosses his eyes. "Does he do that to her a lot?"

I know what he's referencing. "She says it's only a recent thing, but I'm not sure it's the truth."

"I want to help."

For the second time in minutes, my mouth sags to the floor. "What?"

"I'll help. You'll need to be really clever to disappear without a trace."

My heart swells in my chest, and my voice is a little choked when I speak. "You've no idea how much it means to hear you say that, but no." I shake my head. "I don't want you involved. I don't want any of my family involved. I want nothing that could lead from me to you. Not just because that prick might trace us if he finds a connection to you, but more so that he doesn't go after any of my family for colluding in our escape. You can't get anywhere near this, Kev."

"I don't have to be personally involved. I can hook you up with—"

"No," I cut across him, vehemently shaking my head. "Any of your contacts could lead back to you, and I can't have that on my conscience too. I'll have enough to worry about without worrying about you or any of my family. Promise me, Kev. Promise me you'll stay out of this."

"But—"

"No." I interject again. "I have this in hand, and I'm not completely clueless. I'm working with some good people who know what they're doing, and I've hired people who will keep us safe."

Reluctantly, he nods. Then he leans his head back against the headrest, exhaling noisily. "I can't believe you're leaving. That I might not see you again." He twists his head around to look at me, and I'm startled by the display of naked emotion on his face. "This is going to kill Mom and Dad. You do realize that?"

I rub an aching spot between my brows, sighing. "I know, but I don't have a choice. And I'm hoping it won't be forever. The guy who's helping me get out of the country has put me in touch with an organization overseas run by a guy who is ex-CIA. He has a bunch of really experienced guys working for him, most ex-CIA, FBI, and Homeland, and they run security missions all over the world. I'm going to speak to him about getting a crew on Garcia and his operation. All I need is some concrete piece of evidence against him, and we can use that to take him down. If he goes away, the threat goes away, and we can come back home."

"There's a lot of ifs in that scenario."

"I know, but I'm not going to give up, and everyone makes mistakes sometime. I'm going to ensure one of my guys is there to capture the moment Garcia fucks up, and then I'll take great pleasure in helping the authorities take him down." I clamp a hand on his shoulder. "We *will* see each other again. I firmly believe that."

"I'm sorry," he abruptly says, surprising me for the third time today. "For all that shit in Ireland and for not making more of an effort to patch things up between us. I'm not going to apologize for spying on you, because I did what I had to do to protect my brother, but I'm sorry things have been shitty between us. I never wanted that, and I don't want you to leave with any bad blood between us."

"Ah, shit, man. You're going to make me cry."

He laughs, punching me in the shoulder, and it fucking hurts. Kev has one mean left hook. Not that I'm telling him that—the competitive Kennedy gene is still alive and kicking.

"Are we good?" he asks, sobering up.

I grip his shoulder. "We're good, Kev, and our separation was as much my fault. I've regretted so much of what was said."

"Me too, but I'll always have your back, Kade. Always. Because that's what brothers do."

I'm pacing the length of my living room floor later that night, ready to throw caution to the wind and storm over to the Garcia house when my cell finally pings with a text from Eva. It's ridiculous how fast I'm on it.

*"I'm sorry for not replying sooner. Been out of the house since last night. I'm okay. I'll talk to you Monday."*

*"Can you talk now?"* I text back, needing to hear her voice. To know for sure everything is okay.

*"No. He's here."*

*"I'm worried about you."*

*"Don't. Just rearrange the meeting for next week, the earlier the better."*

*"Consider it done."*

*"I've got to go. I'll see you Monday."*

*"Don't forget how much I love you."*

*"I know, and I love you too."*

But as I lie in bed that night, tossing and turning, helpless and frustrated on my own, I can't help feeling like something bad is waiting right around the corner. Something that will change everything. And those worrisome thoughts keep me awake most of the night.

# Chapter Twenty-One
## Present Day

*Evelina*

I'm still rattled as I make my way into the building Monday morning. The stress of that meeting on Friday stayed with me all weekend, compounded by Jeremy's probing questions in the car on our way out that night and that screwed-up gathering at the Carlisles'. It's not like Jeremy to pry into my working life, so his loaded questions about what detains me so late at the office these days has me petrified. Does he know something or he's suspicious?

Renee is waiting outside my office with two coffee cups in hand. "Hey, girlfriend," she says, kissing me on the cheek. "I come bearing gifts."

I unlock my door and let her inside. "Thanks." I take a cup from her. "I so need this. I barely slept a wink last night." The stress of everything that happened on Friday kept me awake most of the weekend. An intense shudder whittles down my spine as I recall my horrific weekend. I was right about one thing—Jeremy is definitely becoming unhinged. Either that or the pressure of running his criminal organization is finally starting to get to him.

Renee kicks the door closed with her foot, walking to my couch and dropping down into it. "Can I ask you something?"

"Sure." I sit down beside her.

"At that meeting on Friday, you thought it was you, didn't you? You thought the boss man was looking at you, not Jesse."

I can't lie to my best friend anymore. Not when our time together is coming to an end. I pin her with a serious look. "Was it that obvious?"

She shakes her head. "Not at all. I only noticed because I was focused on you, and I know you. Know your little mannerisms and tells." She timidly sips her coffee. "How long did you have an affair with Kaden Kennedy for?"

My eyes almost bug out of my head. "What? You knew? You know?"

"I had a strong suspicion. I worked late a couple of Friday nights, and I knew he was still in your office with you. I never heard or saw anything, but I wondered. A couple of times, I interrupted a few of your study sessions, and I could tell the guy was smitten with you."

I can only look at her in shock. "Well, damn. I guess we aren't as careful as we need to be."

Her brow puckers a little. "Back up there a sec." Realization creeps over her face. "Are you telling me it's still going on?"

I slowly nod.

She curses. "Tell me everything."

"Are you sure you want to know? Guilt by association and all that."

She puts her coffee down, taking my hands in hers. "I know a lot more than you realize." I eyeball her sharply. "I know who your husband is, Eva. It's no big secret to anyone. And I also know you're miserable and unhappy in that marriage, and, if I had to hazard a guess, I'd say you didn't marry him by choice."

I gawk at my friend, amazed at how astute and observant she is despite how hard I've tried to mask the truth from her. "I didn't," I finally admit. "And you're right, about all of it."

"Tell me." She glances at the clock on the wall. "Neither of us has class for two hours, so tell me. Tell me everything."

And I do. Unburdening it all. How I ended up married to that monster and what he tried to make me do on the weekend. Her eyes pop wide, and she stares at me in blatant shock. "He did what?"

I gulp over the stream of nausea building at the back of my throat. "The Carlisles like to party excessively. The other times I've been to their place it was dinner and drinks and a few lewd remarks, but this weekend was some kind of planned orgy, except Jeremy neglected to mention that in advance." I shudder at the memories.

"And he made you watch when you wouldn't participate?" She looks like she's going to be sick.

I nod. "Yeah. He was furious that I wouldn't agree to any of it. I thought he was going to make me, but he didn't want to look like a total prick in front of his colleagues, so, instead, he made me stay in the room while they all fucked one another."

"That is seriously sick shit."

I shrug. "It was consensual, and they all seemed to enjoy it."

"That's not what I meant. Your husband forcing you to watch him fuck other women, when he knew you weren't into it, is horrific."

I lean forward, propping my elbows on my knees. "To be honest, Renee, I was just glad it wasn't me. I can't bear his hands on me. My skin literally crawls anytime he touches me." A forceful shudder travels up my spine. "Those other women, wives of his colleagues and his employees, had no such qualms. They've always hated me anyway, and I didn't miss the smug looks sent my way as they let my husband do all manner of kinky shit to them." I crank out a hoarse laugh. "They didn't realize I really couldn't care less. The only part of it that truly scares me is how much Jeremy seems to be losing control. For years, he's sheltered me from all this stuff, but he seems hellbent on bringing me further into his world, and I'm petrified of that. Of what it means going forward."

"What are you going to do? And how does Kaden fit into everything?"

I pick up my story, telling her how I fell for Kaden and how I tried to do the right thing by ending things and pushing him away. I even tell her how we've reconnected and what we're planning to do. Her reply knows the socks off me.

"Do it!" She grips my hands tighter. "Run away with him! By God, if that man loved me, I would've never been able to refuse him." Tears glisten in her eyes. "This is what you've always wanted, Eva. The type of love that only comes around once in a lifetime. He's willing to give it all up for you." She swoons. "It's so romantic."

"It's also hugely dangerous," I add, lest she's forgotten that part of the sordid tale I've just spun.

"He's got the money and contacts to keep you safe." She slants me a wicked grin. "Not to mention his brute strength. Don't think I didn't notice how ripped he is now. I almost jumped him myself that day he showed up here. If anyone can protect you, he can."

"Wow. You really think it's a good idea?"

"Yes." Tears well in her eyes. "I will miss the hell out of you, and I wish you could be at my wedding, but I want you to be happy and safe, and that's more important."

"Kade says he's going to do everything in his power to fix it so we can return."

"Well, then, I'll hold fast to that and believe that this won't be goodbye."

A noise from out in the corridor causes my heart rate to rocket to unhealthy levels. I stare, wide-eyed, at Renee, and she shoots me a puzzled look. Apprehensive, I get up, heart racing when I spot the tiny open crack in the door. "Shit!" I spin around, pinning panic-stricken eyes on Renee. "The door wasn't properly closed! Do you think someone heard us?"

She gets up, walking briskly out into the corridor and quickly checking the adjacent doors. "No one else is here. You know most of them show up later on a Monday or they are already at class."

"But I heard a noise."

"It might've just been the door easing open, because I'm pretty sure I closed it properly." She squeezes my shoulders. "I know you're on edge, and I understand why, but calm down. No one heard anything, and I'm not going to breathe a word to another living soul."

"Okay, you're right." I shift my neck from side to side, attempting to release some stress. "I feel like I'm constantly watching over my shoulder."

"At least you don't have that douche canoe Jesse to worry about anymore." She saunters back over to the couch. "I know he's a slimy, sleazy, sexist pig, but even I didn't think he'd go there."

"I'm hardly in any position to throw stones." I perch on the edge of the couch. "But it was a big shock. I swear when the boss man said his name and not mine I almost wept with relief. I thought he'd been eyeballing me the entire time, but it was Jesse."

"I'll bet. Kristin says he was sleeping with at least three or four of his students, and they suspect he's been pulling that shit for years, so there's no fear he'll be back here any time."

"Is it hypocritical of me to say the asshat had it coming?"

"Nope. Your situation is completely different. You fell in love with one of your students and you tried to do the right thing. Even when you were lusting after him, you still didn't renege on your professional responsibility to Kaden and you never let your feelings influence how you treated him as a student. Jesse was sleeping with students in exchange for good grades, and his fuck buddies were as interchangeable as the weather."

"I'm not sure the administration would see it like that. Especially the boss man."

"Probably not, but they're never going to find out, and if they do, you'll be long gone."

Tears sting the back of my eyes as I turn and face my friend. "I'm really going to miss you, Renee. So, so much."

She jumps up, hugging me. "Me too, but let's make a promise that it's not going to be forever."

And we make that promise, even though I've no way of knowing whether I can keep it or not.

# *Chapter Twenty-Two*
## Present Day

*Kaden*

A few weeks pass, and the closer we get to D-day, the more excited and nervous I feel. Eva is, understandably, walking on eggshells at home, and I'm pushing my contacts to get the last few pieces in place so we can make our move. At least we get to spend a few hours every week-night together, even if we've had to cut her visits short. For a while, Eva was really scared her husband was on to us, but his probing questions died off, and she says he hasn't been around much, which pleases me. However, she's still highly strung, and we need to put our plan in motion before stress tips her over the edge. Most nights, I'm able to help her unwind and leave some of her stress at the door.

Saying goodbye to her is torture every night, and I can't wait for the day when we don't have to separate. While she's better equipped to defend herself, and she says Jeremy hasn't come near her in weeks, I still worry.

Which is why I find myself at the gun range again tonight. Kev first suggested it a couple of weeks back, and it was a smart idea. My fists and upper body strength will only get me so far with the kind of gangsters Garcia employs, so I'm learning to shoot. I tried to persuade Eva to come along, but she drew the line at a gun. Not that I can blame her. She's explained a few scary incidents that have happened over the years, and I know, in her mind, she'll always associate guns with her husband and the murdering criminals he hangs around with.

"Your aim is getting better," Kev says, surveying the target sheet in front of me with expert eyes.

"I'd like to think so. I've been coming here every evening for two weeks straight."

He looks over his shoulder, lowering his voice. "How much longer?"

"I should have everything in place by the end of the week," I whisper. "I'm hoping to leave Sunday."

He looks off into space, and awkward silence fills the gap between us.

"I knew this was coming, but, damn, that's not easy to hear," he murmurs after a bit.

"I know. How do you think I feel?"

I accept what I need to do, and I have zero regrets or doubts, but it's still hard preparing to walk away from everything and everyone I know. I've been writing letters for each member of my family, and that has proven tremendously difficult. This is going to come as a massive shock to all of them. Excepting Kev, no one even knows about Eva.

This will crush Mom. And thoughts of missing out on Kyler and Faye's engagement, Kal and Lana's wedding, and not being around to see my cute nephew, Hewson, grow up, is killing me. Guilt is starting to eat away at me, but I have my own life to lead, and I need to do what feels right for me and my future. Plus, I refuse to believe this is goodbye forever. I have plenty of cash, and I've been working on setting up my online golf business—something which I can do anonymously from behind a computer in any part of the world—so I'm confident I'll have the resources to enable us to return home at some point.

Perhaps I'm kidding myself, but I need to cling to that hope or I might falter. Eva is relying on me, and I need to be strong for her. I won't let her down.

"I'm scared for you, brother," Kev admits in a rare burst of vulnerability. "If anything happens to you ..."

"It won't. I've taken months to plan this methodically, leaving nothing to chance."

"How do you know the prick isn't on to you?"

"I wouldn't be standing here if he knew about me or our plans."

"Maybe you should've put someone on him."

"I tried, but my guy wouldn't assign any of his operatives to watch either Eva or Garcia. He said it was too risky. He's too well-guarded and if any of Garcia's men made his guys, it would be a virtual bloodbath. When he explained it like that, as much as I hated it, I realized Eva is safer without a bodyguard shadowing her."

Kev rubs a hand behind his neck. "Lack of protection makes me nervous. I could always contact Dad's guy?"

I shake my head. "No, Kev. No ties to the family. I made that very clear weeks ago. And I'm not unprotected. I have guys watching my place 'round the clock, and they haven't noticed anything untoward. I'm sure Garcia doesn't know. Besides, he's been away a lot. Eva says he's very preoccupied lately and very stressed. She senses something big is going down."

Kev nods his head. "Yeah, I've heard some rumors."

My jaw tautens. "What kind of rumors and why am I only hearing about this now?"

"Don't take that fucking tone with me, Kade." Kev glares at me. "If it was something you needed to know, I would've told you. I've been keeping an eye on the situation, and if it impacted you, Eva, or your plans, I would've informed you straightaway."

I curse under my breath. "What the hell, Kev? I told you not to do anything! What part of that didn't you understand?!"

"Cool your fucking jets, Kade," Kev says, looking anxiously around, but the only other two guys in the place aren't paying us one bit of attention. "You know I was mixed up in some dodgy stuff a couple of years back, and while I extricated myself from that mess, I still keep tabs on all parties in case anything goes down that could trace back to me. I've been scanning some of the covert boards, and there's a turf war brewing between Garcia and his main rival. Apparently, Garcia took out his second in command a couple weeks ago, and they're preparing to retaliate."

"Fuck!" I put my gun away in its case and take off my safety glasses. Kev does the same, and we are both quiet as we make our way outside. "You won't know this, but Garcia's rivals attacked Eva a few weeks ago. I happened across them and stopped it before they could seriously hurt her. She kept it quiet from Garcia because she didn't want to implicate me, but he went crazy when he found out."

"That's what those bruises were about?"

My brother has always been sharp. "Yeah. And he's been acting weird since then, Eva says. It's obviously all tied up with that."

"Word on the street is it's an all-out war. A few of Garcia's trucks ran into difficulty crossing the border, and then they were ambushed. He lost millions, and he's preparing to bring out the big guns in response. It's good you're getting Eva out of this before it becomes World War fucking Three, because shit is about to hit the fan, big time."

Kev's intelligence does zilch to ease the tight knot in my chest. But I say nothing to Eva later that night, not wanting to worry her any more than she already is. We'll be out of the country before she can get caught in the crossfire.

It's Saturday night, and I'm getting ready for my date with Eva when the buzzer pings. Duke makes a goofy face into the small video screen, and I roll my eyes, chuckling as I press the button and let him up.

"Yo, man." He raises his fist for a knuckle touch. "Where da fuck you going dressed like that?" He gestures at my custom black suit, his brows nudging up.

"Dinner with the fam," I lie. "What's up? I'm under pressure for time." I pull up the collar of my shirt, slinging the tie around my neck.

"I know when I'm not wanted," he jokes, smirking. "I was actually just passing and spotted something weird, so I pulled over and parked."

My fingers stall on my tie. Now I'm intrigued. "Okay. You have my attention."

"I noticed Tiffani pacing the sidewalk outside. She kept looking up here and then knotting her hands in her hair, walking up and down like a bone fide stalker. Seriously that chick needs psychiatric evaluation."

I frown. I haven't heard a thing from Tiffani in weeks, and the couple of times I've bumped into her on campus, she's purposely gone the opposite way. I thought all that was behind me, and I really don't have time to deal with her shit today. Not when Eva's most likely already on her way. "Damn it. I'd better go face her."

"No need, man. She's gone. She flipped her shit when she saw me and took off running before I even opened my mouth. Total nut job."

I frown again. "That's … weird."

He lounges against the wall. "Or maybe not. She was at the bar last weekend, smashed and falling all over the place. A couple of the guys overheard her talking to some of the girls, and she was crying over how much she loves you, telling them she was going to win you back. I'm guessing she's getting ready to make her play."

I shrug, opening the door, and Duke steps out into the corridor. "I hate to shove you out the door, but I'm really running late. If Tiff has something to say to me, she'll be back."

"No doubt." He props against the doorframe. "Anyway, I just wanted to warn you she was hanging about."

"Thanks, man. I appreciate it." I slap him on the back, somehow managing to speak over the sudden lump wedged in my throat. This is most likely the last time I'll speak to Duke. I left a letter for him too, but he'll be so pissed I bailed without a word. There is a lot I'd like to say to him in person, but I can't risk it. Instead I throw out a casual statement. "Catch you later, dude."

All concerns about Tiffani, and nostalgic thoughts about Duke, evaporate once I'm in the chauffeur-driven car with Eva a half hour later. The privacy screen is up, and we spend most of the journey draped around one another, making out like we're teenagers. I'm tempted to pull her into my lap for a quick fuck before we get to the restaurant, but I manage to restrain myself. We never get to do this, and tonight is important.

It's the start of the rest of our lives, and I want it to mean something. I don't want to reduce it to hot sex in the back of a hired car, when tonight symbolizes all the other ways in which our relationship is important. Eva deserves to be treated like a goddess, and that's what I'm going to do tonight.

"Are you sure this is a good idea?" she asks as we make our way inside the exclusive members-only restaurant. I understand her concern, and it took a colossal amount of skill to coax her into agreeing to this tonight.

But, between the tinted windows of the Merc, the shielded underground entrance to La Grotte Secrete, and this establishment's notoriety for protecting the privacy of their patrons, I'm confident we won't be recognized.

I lift her hand to my lips, kissing her delicate skin. I've always been fascinated with Eva's hands, and now I know how exquisite they feel exploring my body I'm an addict for life. "I wouldn't bring you here if I thought it placed you in any kind of risk. Your husband is out of state, his bodyguards think you're with Renee, and this restaurant doesn't approve membership for known criminals, so no one will see us. But, to be on the safe side, I had my guy hack into their system and vet the bookings list to ensure there was no one here tonight with any connection to your husband or any of his rivals. He confirmed we're safe. You can relax, baby." I kiss her cheek as the waitresses guides us to our table.

I hold out Eva's chair and then sit down across from her, taking a moment to appreciate how fucking amazing she looks tonight. She's wearing a sophisticated, strapless black dress that could be considered plain on anyone else. But, on Eva, it glides over her stunning curves like a glove, accentuating her beautiful body to perfection. With her hair down, and minimal makeup, she's naturally stunning, carrying herself with a quiet confidence I find very attractive. God, she's incredibly gorgeous, and I can't believe she's going to be mine.

"I would just prefer to celebrate after we're out of the country," she whispers, anxiously knotting her hands in her lap and glancing warily around the room.

Fuck, maybe I made a mistake doing this tonight, but we could both use the distraction, and I thought going out for dinner, in a safe, private, environment, would help put us at ease. If I sit at home, I'll just be thinking of my family and how horrified they're going to be in a couple of days when they receive my letters and realize I've left the country with no intention of coming back anytime soon. And, despite the calm façade I'm presenting to Eva, I *am* worried about the plans for tomorrow and constantly praying nothing goes wrong.

"We can leave right now, honey, if you're not comfortable. I wanted to do something special because I never get to spoil you, but you only have to say the word and we can go."

"No, it's okay." She sends me a tentative smile. "I trust you, and it's better than sitting in an empty house fretting over everything."

I order a bottle of the most expensive champagne, and we chat quietly over our drinks, holding hands the entire time. "I can't believe this time tomorrow we'll be far, far away," she whispers, after the waitress has cleared away our entrees. "I'm so excited and completely on edge too."

I rub soothing circles across the back of her hand. "I'm feeling all that too, but it's going to be fine. The guys have done this countless times. They're pros at this stuff, and we're in safe hands. I won't let anything happen to you."

Her eyes glisten as she leans across the table toward me. "When I was a little girl, *this* was the type of love I dreamed about—finding a man who consumed my world, who I lived and breathed for. Someone who loved me back with the same intensity. Someone I visualized myself growing old with. A man who would do anything for me, be anything for me, as I would do for him." A little tear sneaks out of the corner of one eye. "I gave up believing in that dream a long time ago, but here you are. Here we are. And I find myself believing again."

She reaches across the table, kissing me passionately. "I thank whoever brought you into my life, Kaden Kennedy. Someone up there was looking out for me." She caresses my cheek affectionately, and the adoring look in her eyes almost undoes me. "Thank you for loving me enough to risk everything for me. And, for as long as I live, I will do everything in my power to make sure you know your sacrifice wasn't in vain. I will love you so completely, as long as there is breath in my lungs and blood flowing through my veins. You never have to doubt that."

"Eva." My voice is gruff, and I wish I could take her into my arms right now. "You complete me, in every way, and I love you more than I ever thought it was possible to love another person. Never doubt that you have my full heart and you have it for life."

Eva is laughing freely by the time dessert arrives, buoyed up by a couple of glasses of champagne, and a fabulous meal. I'd like to think my charming company was a factor too, but that could be my healthy ego speaking.

I'm glad we did this tonight.

That I'll be sending her home for the last time tonight more relaxed than when she left.

"I don't think I can stomach another bite," she moans as I raise my spoon to her mouth.

"You have to try this. It's to die for. Best chocolate mousse I've ever tasted." I feed it to her, and the little sounds she makes has me instantly hard. Reaching across the table, I capture her lips in a demanding kiss, swirling my tongue around her mouth, tasting the creamy, rich chocolatey flavors still lingering in her mouth.

"Wow!" Her face is flushed as she looks at me. "Your kisses are to die for. I've never enjoyed kissing anyone as much as I love kissing you."

"I should hope so," I tease as prickles of apprehension crest over me. I discreetly check out my surroundings, catching the eye of someone familiar. Twisting my head, I lock eyes with Brad McConaughey. Brad is my brother Kyler's best friend and someone who practically grew up in our house. He's virtually gained adopted Kennedy brother status by this stage. His hand rests on the back of his date, a girl I also know. Rachel is Faye's best friend from Ireland and now Brad's girlfriend and roommate.

Brad glances briefly at Eva and then back at me. I know he knows who she is and that he's wondering what the hell is going on. I send him a pleading look, and he nods, letting me know he'll keep my secret safe.

"Who is that?" Eva whispers, her voice trembling as panic takes hold.

I send Brad one final nod, before focusing on the love of my life. "No one you need to worry about." I cup her face, rubbing her cheek tenderly. "He's one of my brother's best friends, but he won't say anything. I promise. He's a good guy, and he won't get involved."

Eva is still worried when the car drops me back at my place. I wanted to drop her home first, but she won't hear of it. It's too risky with the guards on the gate. So, the driver will drop her home last. I took the precaution of booking a new car company this time, and I made the reservation in a fake name, so if anyone questions Eva or the driver, nothing will lead back to me.

I kiss her for way too long in the car, but I hate having to part. I wish our date was ending with her spending the night with me, so I could take my time worshiping her body, making love to her all night long. But we can't risk it. If one of the guards reported her absence to her husband, he might return home and ruin all our plans.

"I love you," I say, leaning into the car as I attempt to drag myself away. I kiss her one last time. "I'll see you at the rendezvous point in the morning. If anything happens, or anything changes, call or text me. And you have the emergency number I gave you?"

She nods. "It's on my cell, but I also memorized it, just in case."

"Good, that's good, baby." I kiss her again. "God, I hate saying goodbye."

"This is the last goodbye, and that's something to celebrate." She offers me a genuine smile, and I get a grip of myself.

"It definitely is. See you tomorrow, honey. Sleep well."

I close her door and watch until the Merc is out of sight.

An ominous sense of dread skates over my skin as I step into the hallway of my apartment. The light automatically switches on when my foot hits the floor, but the illumination does little to assuage my sudden fear. All the fine hairs on my arms lift. My body is on heightened alert as I cautiously make my way to the living room, cursing the fact my gun is in my bedroom and so far out of reach.

Bile swims up my throat as I step into my living space and freeze on the spot. My mouth is frozen in horror as I stare at the three bloody bodies mounted in a sloppy heap on the hardwood floor. Instinct kicks in, and I turn around, racing for the door, but I'm a fraction too late. Someone slams into me from behind, and I crash face-first into the door. The butt of a weapon is pressed against the back of my head. "Going somewhere, asshole?" a gravelly voice says as my hands are jerked behind my back and roughly tied. I attempt to shove the jerk off, but the clicking sound of his gun stalls my movement. "Try it, jerk face. I'd love an excuse to put a hole through that pretty-boy skull of yours."

"Fuck you."

He viciously slams my head against the door and I see stars. Then I'm yanked back, and the gun pokes firmly into my back as a black cloth cover is placed over my head.

Pain explodes in my skull as I'm hit full force from behind, and that's the last thing I remember before I black out.

# Chapter Twenty-Three

## Present Day

*Evelina*

I've had a horrible sense of foreboding from the minute I left Kaden last night, and it hasn't gone away. Especially since I'm at the agreed meeting place, and Kade is nowhere to be found. As I watch the minutes tick by on my watch, I grow more and more distressed.

Something has happened.

I feel it in my bones.

Kade told me to give it ten minutes and if he hadn't shown to call the emergency number and someone would come get me. It's been twenty minutes and he's still a no show. My hands are trembling as I stab the numbers on the phone. I won't leave without him, but, for now, I'll follow the agreed plan and call for backup. Without warning, someone makes a grab for me from behind. I react instinctively, dropping down and shoving my elbow back into my assailant's thigh while stomping on his foot. A string of colorful expletives filters through the air, and his hold on me relaxes. I wriggle out of his grip, but I lose my footing on the gravel underneath, wobbling precariously as I attempt to run way. The cell flies out of my hand, skittering across the road, and I'm powerless to stop myself from falling. I throw my palms out in front of me at the last second, holding myself up, mere inches from the stony ground.

A hand fists in my jacket before I can get away, and I'm yanked painfully to my feet.

"That wasn't very nice, Mrs. Garcia." His menacing tone sends chills down my spine, and my stomach lurches to my toes. Intense fear whittles through me. Holding me against him, with my back flush to his chest, he grasps my chin firmly, pinching my skin. "If you're looking for your boy toy, I'm afraid he's otherwise indisposed." My breath shuttles out in panicked spurts, but I say nothing, knowing better than to antagonize hired guns. I don't recognize the voice, but that doesn't mean he isn't one of Jeremy's guys. Or it could be the same crew who tried to take me previously. I'm not sure whether it matters much—the end outcome is most likely the same.

When he hauls me back through the gate of the abandoned warehouse, I'm almost choked as he keeps a meaty arm wrapped around my neck. Terrifying thoughts are bouncing through my brain, and I'm so scared for Kade. I know he's strong and skillful with his hands, but none of that means shit if they crept up on him the same way they crept up on me. Because I didn't hear a thing until they were on top of me.

My legs are kicking up dirt and dust as I'm dragged across the empty wasteland, and a strangled, gurgling sound slips from my throat. The sliding of a door pricks my ears, and I catch a glimpse of the gruesome scene before something dark is placed over my head. I'm thrust into the back of the van, stumbling in panic as I almost fall over the two dead bodies on the floor. I'm guessing they are part of the team Kaden hired to help us escape, and my anxiety reaches new heights. *What if Kaden is already dead?* I'll never forgive myself if he's lost his life because of me.

Someone shoves me onto a hard seat or bench, and my hands and feet are tied tightly. A fretful, fluttery feeling presses down on my chest, constricting the flow of oxygen to my lungs. A body drops into place alongside me, a heavy thigh resting against mine, making no effort to put any distance between us. Disgust and dread crawl over me, and I'm working hard to keep my shaking to a minimum. I've been around these sick bastards long enough to know they get off on obvious displays of fear. Hands brush against my breasts, and my breath falters in my chest, as all manner of hideous scenarios flit through my mind.

"Don't touch her," a different male voice says. "You know what we were told."

"Be patient," another male says. "And your reward will come."

A few guffaws ring out, and my heart starts pounding against my ribcage as sheer terror consumes me.

I'm jostled from side to side as the van moves over uneven terrain. Apart from a few low whispers, conversation is almost nonexistent, and the silence seems even louder against the screaming in my head. Although I knew there was always a risk we'd be discovered, Kaden had been so careful, considering all the angles and hiring guys who supposedly knew what they were doing.

But none of that matters now, because someone has gotten to us.

And my money is on my husband.

The van screeches to a halt a while later, and I'm dragged outside. One of the men keeps a firm hold of my arm as I'm steered forward. The dark covering is still over my head, and I trip several times, unable to see where I'm walking. A blast of cold air swirls around me as we descend steps, going lower and lower. I stumble several times, falling into the man in front of me, while the one behind me curses, roughly yanking me back.

We're back on flat ground, and I'm being propelled forward. The air is even colder at this level and a shiver skips down my spine. I focus on making my limbs move, forcing one foot in front of the other and it feels a lot like walking to the gallows.

A piercing scream filters through the cold, dank air, and everything freezes inside me. That was a female scream, and it was full of unrestrained anguish. My stomach lurches queasily, but I draw deep breaths while counting to ten in my head, doing everything I can think of to keep my composure and my wits about me.

Something cold and hard juts into my lower back, and I'm prodded forward with more urgency. My heart is jackhammering against my ribcage, and every nerve ending on my body is primed and on high alert. My ears are pricked and paying attention, hearing the muted whimpering sounds coming from somewhere close by and the scuttling of rats racing across the floor.

A door creaks open, and I'm shoved forward. Losing my balance, I take a tumble, but someone snatches me up, at the last second, digging fingernails into my arms. Biting back a cry, I grit my teeth and mentally plead with my body to stop shaking. At this point, I can't tell if I'm trembling from fear or the cold or a mixture of the two. My jacket is stripped off me, and then I'm manhandled into a seat. My wrists and ankles are tied to the chair, and then the cover is lifted from my head.

I blink my eyes open, shaking my head from side to side, trying to see through the messy strands of hair shielding my face. Cold, calloused fingers sweep the hair out of my eyes. I look up, wincing as the glare from the overhead light startles me. I take a quick look around, making out a few things through my blurred vision. We're in some kind of empty cellar or basement. The exposed walls are crumbling, the brickwork cracked in several places. As my eyes slowly adjust, all the blood drains from my face.

It's as I suspected.

"Hello, darling," Jeremy hisses. "Surprised to see me?"

"Not really." I pin the full extent of my hatred on him. "Disappointment is more the emotion I'm feeling right now."

My head jerks back with the force of his slap, and my cheek stings.

"Don't fucking ... touch her," a choked voice says in between exaggerated breaths. I whip my head around, in the direction of his voice, crying out as I spot Kaden restrained in the corner of the room. All I can think is, thank God, he's still alive.

*For now*, that nasty little devil on my shoulder taunts, but I ignore the evil voice.

Kaden is tied to a chair at the wrists, ankles, and across his upper torso. His chin is resting on his chest, his head bowed. His upper body is bare, but his lower body is still encased in the black pants and dress shoes he was wearing last night. Cuts and bruises cover every inch of naked flesh, and bile floods my mouth. Tears well automatically in my eyes.

Jeremy's eyes narrow scornfully. Turning around, he stalks toward Kaden, slamming his fist into his stomach. "I think that's my line, asshole." He grabs Kaden by the hair, yanking his head back, and I gasp at the sight of his beaten and bruised face. One eye is completely closed, swollen and painted in different shades of black and blue. A deep gash in his cheek oozes blood, and his lips are dried and cut in several places. A large, round purplish bruise is mushrooming on his other cheek. It's obvious they've had him for hours, and God only knows what they've been doing to him.

My entire body quakes in fear. For him. For me.

"You should've kept your filthy hands to yourself," Jeremy snaps, punching Kaden in the stomach again.

"Stop! Don't hurt him. This isn't his fault." I'm frantically clasping at straws, struggling to concoct some version of the truth that will seem plausible while making it look like this wasn't really Kade's idea.

Jeremy strides across the room, crouching over me and putting his face in mine. Although every instinct roars at me to pull back, I don't move an inch, not even when the putrid warmth of his nasty breath oozes over my face. "Lying at this point is completely futile, *my love.*" He snarls the words, hissing in my face, and I've never seen so much rage, so much hatred, on anyone's face before.

The stark reality of what we're facing hits me like a wet fish in the face.

We're not getting out of here.

Not alive.

Everything I'd hoped to protect Kaden from is coming true. He's going to lose his life because of my selfishness. So, I do the only thing I can, even if a big part of me knows it's not going to make any difference.

"He means nothing to me," I tell Jeremy, eyeballing him. "He was a means to an end. A way to get out of the country. Nothing more." I snort. "He's only a fucking kid, for God's sake."

Jeremy pinches my chin forcefully. "Don't fuck me around, Evie."

"I'm not. I failed the last time I tried to escape because I didn't know what I was doing. Kaden had the right contacts, so I used him. I was planning on ditching him the minute I was overseas."

I know Kaden is smart enough to play along, but he doesn't. "Eva ... don't."

I glance at him, keeping my expression neutral even though it kills me not to react to the sight of the man I love tied up and beaten, looking defeated. "No offense, Kaden, but you're way too young and immature for me. You fell for my bullshit so easily." I send him a look that is part smug, and part faux-apologetic.

An amused chuckle wafts across the room, and my eyes follow the sound. Vincent is lurking in the shadows like the creeper he is. Three other armed men line the walls alongside him, their dark gazes fixed on me in a way that stalls the blood flowing in my veins. Jeremy darts forward, ramming his fist into Kaden's face, and I scream. Kade's head lolls back and then jerks forward as he loses consciousness.

Another snide chuckle bounces off the wall. Glancing sideways, I notice Michael Carlisle for the first time, flanked by two men on his left and two more on his right. All are heavily armed. All look scary as fuck, and they have this dangerous, bloodthirsty-slash-lustful glint in their eyes. He shares a look with Jeremy before prowling to my side. "You acted all high and mighty at our house, refusing to fuck anyone, but I knew it was an act." Michael sneers. "That you were a dirty slut all along."

He leans down, grabbing my crotch, and a new layer of terror takes hold of me. "I'm going to enjoy fucking you in front of your lover, and I'm going to make you bleed until you're begging me to stop." He presses his disgusting mouth to my ear, while his hand rubs back and forth along my crotch. My leggings are too thin of a barrier, and I thrash about in the chair, trying to shake his hand off, to no avail. "You will wish for death when I'm done with you," he whispers in my ear.

Another strong tremor rockets through me, and I'm visibly shaking, but I keep my nerves at bay as I speak. "Nothing you can say or do will defeat me." I eyeball him. "You think I haven't learned how to lock myself in my mind when my husband was fucking me? I'm a pro at blocking it out. Do your worst. It won't affect me." I shoot my eyes to Jeremy, who has returned to my side. "I've had years to practice the technique."

Jeremy backhands me again, but I barely feel the sting this time. My insides are starting to numb from the shock. "You disappoint me so much, Evie." His lips twist into a sneer as he shakes his head. "You've disappointed me from the very first minute I met you. Your slut of a mother coaxed me into sticking with the deal, promising you'd come around, but she underestimated your stubbornness. And your stupidity," he tags on the end.

"You should know better than to believe anything that comes out of her mouth," I retort. Jeremy is well aware there's no love lost between Mom and me.

"I happen to be very fond of your mother's mouth." He smirks. "She knows how to deep throat like a pro."

"What?!" A new layer of horror engulfs me.

He laughs, and it's a condescending sound. "I've been fucking your mother, right under *your* nose, and your father's, for years." He presses his face into mine, and his sour breath turns my stomach. "The broad may be getting on in years, but she knows how to please a man. She lets me fuck her wherever, whenever, and however I like. She exists to please me. What a shame she didn't instill that lesson in you." He pinches my nipples through my sweater and flimsy cotton bra, and my eyes water.

Kaden comes to, growling at Jeremy. The legs of his chair screech as he thrashes about. "Leave her alone! It's me you want to punish," he yells, his tone growing more agitated.

Jeremy ignores Kaden, keeping his focus locked on me. "All you had to do was spread your legs, look the other way with my business interests, and pop out a few brats. Do you know how many women would kill to be in your shoes?" He tweaks my nipple, hard, and tears leak out of my eyes. But I don't cry out. I won't give him the satisfaction.

"I would happily have traded places with any of them. I never wanted to marry you. I don't even like you, let alone love you."

A muscle pulses in his jaw, and I let him have it. Nothing I say now will change the plans for Kaden and me. If I'm going to die like this, I, at least, want him to know how I really feel. "Every time you touched me, I wanted to vomit. Your touch makes my skin crawl like a thousand fire ants invading my body. There is nothing even slightly attractive about you. You're a spiteful old bastard who'll get his comeuppance one of these days."

He kicks my chair over in a rage, and I fall backwards, my head slamming into the wooden slats as the chair crashes to the concrete floor. Kade is going crazy, screaming and roaring, until he's silenced, and the sound of fists pummeling flesh sobers me up.

"Get her up," Jeremy barks at someone, and my chair is lifted off the ground. He glowers at me. "I gave you fucking everything, and this is how you repay me?"

I soften my expression and my tone, deciding to try a different tack. "What did you expect, Jeremy? I was promised to you when I was *fourteen*.

I was only a kid then and barely an adult when I married you. You knew I didn't want this, but you chose to ignore that. It might've been different if we'd met under other circumstances."

"Save it, Evie." His fists clench at his sides. "It's too late." He looks over at Vincent. "Bring in the girl."

My gaze flicks to Kaden's again, and our eyes meet. So much passes between us in that one fleeting look, and I can tell how helpless he feels. How much he believes this is his fault for not protecting me better, but he's wrong. If I die here today, I'll die knowing what it feels like to be loved and cherished, knowing my man did everything in his power to save me.

Kaden hasn't failed me.

He's the only man who hasn't ever let me down.

Jeremy is on top of him before I've even blinked, landing blows on his face and his chest, as he releases the full extent of his rage. "You don't get to look at *my wife* like that!" he roars, continuing to pummel Kaden with his fists, and I'm terrified he's going to kill him with his bare hands.

"No!" A high-pitched wail fills the air, and I look around in time to see Kaden's ex-girlfriend thrown to her knees on the ground in front of him. "Don't hurt him!" She looks up at Jeremy as she struggles to stand—no easy feat with her hands tied behind her back. Her thin white tank is streaked with dark stains, and her nipples are poking out through the fabric, taut in the frigid air. The knees of her skinny jeans are torn, the denim similarly stained with the same dark, oily substance. Her hair is greasy, her normal vibrant curls hanging in frizzy clumps around her face. Her skin is blotchy, and her eyes are bloodshot from crying. "You promised you'd leave him alone!"

"Shut up, you stupid bitch!" Jeremy barks, grabbing her by the arm. She screams, and he backhands her. Vomit travels up my throat.

"What did you do, Tiff?" Kaden coughs out, his voice hoarse and cracked, spitting blood all over himself and the floor. Blood is pumping out of his split nose and leaking from open cuts in his mouth.

Jeremy slams Tiffani into another chair on the other side of the room, and one of his goons restrains her. "Tell him, *Tiff*. Tell him how you're the reason he's here today."

# *Chapter Twenty-Four*

## Present Day

### *Kaden*

"I'm really sorry, Kade," Tiffani cries, tears pumping out of her eyes. "I just wanted you back. Jesse said Mr. Garcia would deal with his wife, and I knew once she was out of the way, you'd come back to me." Her sniffles turn into full-blown sobs. "He said he wouldn't hurt you, and I believed him."

My head is pounding, and black spots dance in front of my eyes. Every part of my body aches like a bitch, and blood pools in my mouth. But that pales into insignificance compared to the chills tiptoeing up my spine.

I've no idea how long I've been here or how they got Eva, but I'm praying that Jonas—the guy who heads up the company I hired—has figured something is up by now and is trying to work out where we are.

"Jesse?" I croak, lifting my head to look at Tiff. Currently, I'm seeing four carbon copies of her head. She looks rough, and now I know who was doing all that screaming. I shiver at the thought of what they've been doing to her. "You mean Professor Sleazebag?"

Eva jolts in her chair, twisting her head so she's facing Tiffani. "Professor Roberts was involved in this?" She looks up at her husband, her brow creased in confusion.

Tiff sniffs, refusing to look at Eva as she answers. Her tear-stained panic-filled eyes lock on mine as she explains in a trembling voice. "He's been sleeping with Madison for months. After he got fired, he came to our apartment and told me he'd overheard Professor Garcia telling someone she was sleeping with you and you were planning to run away together. He knew I was really upset over our breakup, and he suggested this plan."

I'm not surprised Tiff's roommate, Madison, got mixed up with that douchebag. She has the shittiest taste in men and zero self-worth.

Eva looks completely shell-shocked, and her eyes widen as she stares at her husband. "You know that asshole?"

"Not personally," the dickhead supplies. "He went to college with Daniel, and Daniel set up a meeting with the girl." He walks to Tiffani's side, wrenching her head back, and her sobs grow louder and more hysterical. I want to warn her, to tell her to tone it down, but I can't see shit out of one eye, and my vision is completely unfocused out of the other. I can't send her any warning looks or hand gestures. "I already suspected you were up to something," the asshole continues, tugging sharply on Tiffani's hair while he eyeballs Eva. "I had Vincent watching you, and I was pretty sure you were trying to escape again, but it wasn't until the little slut came forward that everything slotted into place."

"You promised you wouldn't hurt Kaden, and I helped you! Why are you doing this to me?!" Tiffani blurts, her voice scraped raw.

"You should've known better than to get mixed up in things that are above your pay grade, little girl," he taunts, running his fingers lazily across her throat.

"Leave her the fuck alone!" I shout. "She was naïve, but she doesn't deserve to be punished for that." I can't believe Tiffani was so stupid. For a smart girl, she sure makes some piss-poor decisions.

I brace myself for the gut punch, so I'm not expecting the hit to come from behind. A fist slams into my temple, and I fall sideways, the chair dipping toward the ground as I start to lose consciousness again. Eva is screaming, and Tiffani is crying, but the sounds are muted. Fighting the invisible arms beckoning me to darkness, I force my eyes open, trying to see over the stars coating my retinas and the stabbing pain ripping through my skull. My chair is pulled upright before it hits the ground.

"I'm so sorry, Kade," Tiffani whimpers. "I didn't realize who he was when I came to talk to him. When Madison found out what I'd done, she freaked. She knew exactly who he was from stuff Jesse had told her and from campus gossip. I was so scared, and I didn't know what to do! I came to your place last night, and I swear I was going to tell you, but then Duke showed up, and I ran off, and they grabbed me and ..." She breaks down completely, sobbing and shaking, and I wish I could do something to help her, but I'm struggling to keep my eyes open, and I only have energy to focus on Eva.

"Let the girl go, Jeremy," Eva says, in a remarkably calm voice. "I'd ask you to let Kaden go too, but I know you won't agree to that."

Jeremy lets go of Tiffani and crouches down in front of Eva. "I'm glad you know something about me."

Tiffani is ugly crying now, flailing about and struggling against her restraints.

"We could've been happy, you know," Jeremy says, caressing Eva's cheek, and I want to charge over there and rip his filthy hands off her, but my body won't or can't cooperate, and I'm forced to watch helplessly from the sidelines. "If you had just tried."

"You can't force love, Jeremy. That's not how it works." Eva's voice is quiet but confident.

"And you think you love *him*?" He snorts, gesturing toward me.

"I do love him, and I'll do anything, *anything* to save him." She glances over at me, and I try to keep my chin up, to open my eyes and plead with her to not do this. No amount of begging is going to work, and she knows it too. But she's still going to do this, and I can't be mad at her, not when she's fighting to save me.

She eyeballs her husband. "I mean it. If you let him go, I'll whatever you want. I'll have your babies, give up my career, and you can keep me imprisoned in the house. I'll participate in the parties and the orgies, and I won't complain. I swear. I give you my word. Just let him live." She stretches forward in her chair, as far as the restraints permit. "Please, Jeremy. Please. I'm begging you. Please let Kaden go."

Tiffani screams obscenities at Eva in between bouts of tears, calling her every name under the sun. I'm guessing she's figuring things out, realizing Eva is the cause of my distraction and lack of commitment over the course of our relationship. And that fact is not sitting well with Tiff, but this isn't the time to go nuclear. Damn it. She needs to shut up and put up. Yelling insults at Eva and crying hysterically isn't doing her any favors.

I'm probably concussed, so I'm not sure if what happens next is in slow-mo, as it appears to be, or if it's quick. Jeremy stands up, a muscle ticking in his jaw. Reaching behind him, he pulls a gun out from the waistband of his pants and aims it in Tiffani's direction. A loud pop goes off in the room, and her head whips back. The crying and shouting stops instantly. Her arms go limp at her sides, and a line of blood drips down her face from the hole in the center of her forehead. I'm too out of it to properly comprehend the fact Tiffani is dead.

"Oh my God!" Eva's voice is rattled now. "I can't believe you did that! She was only a harmless, young girl!"

"She was an interfering bitch who didn't care what happened to you," Jeremy snaps. He hovers over Eva, scrubbing a hand over his jaw. "As for your proposal, my answer is no. I don't want a cheating whore for a wife. I should've realized sooner that the apple doesn't fall far from the tree—like mother, like daughter."

He runs a hand over his hair, casually smoothing it back into place. Walking to the side of the room, he retrieves his jacket, putting it on. He nods at someone over my head. A door opens and closes, and then a man squats down at my side, opening a box and placing items on the floor.

Eva gasps. "No! Jeremy! Please, no!"

Jeremy stalks toward her, removing a knife that is strapped to his ankle and leaning into her face.

Panic jumps up and bites me. "Get the fuck away from her!" I roar. Or at least I think I do, but who knows what garbled sounds are coming out of my mouth. I try to move in my chair, but my leg only shudders for a second before turning limp. My head throbs with the effort involved in holding it upright.

"You, of all people, know there are consequences, Evie. This is the price you will pay." In one quick motion, he rips her sweater in half, flinging the ruined pieces to the floor. Eva shivers in her thin bra and leggings. As out of it as I am, bile swims up my throat while alarm bells blare in my ears. He nicks her bra, cutting the strap in the middle, and the material drops away, exposing her to the room full of male vultures.

A primitive roar emits from my throat, and adrenaline courses through my veins. Jeremy laughs, and I want to flay the skin from his bones, slowly and painfully, one layer at a time.

He cups one of Eva's naked breasts, squeezing her flesh tight. "You have a gorgeous body, Evie, and I see how my men watch you. I could've taken you here, forced your lover to watch, but I won't lower myself. I won't touch you now you're contaminated with another man's seed. Instead, my men will take their pleasure, however they see fit, and Kennedy will watch it all. When they're through, they'll inject him with a lethal dose of heroin, but death would be too easy for you." He grabs her chin, forcing her face to his. "Once Michael is done with you, you'll be sold into slavery. No one will find you where you're going, and you'll wish you were dead every single day of the rest of your miserable existence."

Bending down, he kisses her. She tries to pull her face away, but he has her cheeks in a vise grip as he devours her mouth. I'm yelling, and rage is a red bull charging my insides with a much-needed injection of adrenaline.

He pulls back abruptly, and Eva spits in his face. Fisting his hand in her hair, he tugs her head back, holding the knife against her throat, and my heart stutters in my chest. I start thrashing about in the chair. "Tempting, but I'm getting a good price for you." He moves the knife to her left cheek, and she sucks in an audible gasp. "I could cut you, slice little lines out of your skin, and I'd enjoy hearing you scream," he taunts, "but the clients like their whores unblemished." He lets go of her and walks away. "She's all yours, boys. Have at her."

A man moves out from behind me, stalking toward her. I can't see his expression, but I see the naked terror on Eva's face as he approaches, unbuckling his belt as he walks.

Then several things happen all at once.

I rear up, the chair still strapped to my body, swinging left and then right, knocking the men that rush me to the ground in an unexpected move. The door to the room bursts open, and a line of armed men wearing government-issue vests floods the room. Gunfire breaks out, but all I see is Eva. I charge toward her as the guy in front of her swings around, drawing his weapon. I headbutt him, shoving him sideways, out of the way, and then I throw myself on top of Eva. Her chair falls back, and she winces, bracing herself for impact. I'm pressing awkwardly on top of her, and I know it's uncomfortable, but all I can think is to shield her with my body. Shots whizz over our heads, and it'll be a miracle if we get out of here alive.

"Stay down, baby," I croak. "Stay under me. It'll all be over soon."

Then a burst of red-hot pain enters my upper body, and the world turns dark.

# *Chapter Twenty-Five*
## Present Day

*Evelina*

"Kade! Kaden!" Hysteria underscores my words as Kaden slumps on top of me, his eyes fluttering shut as breath leaves his body in a rush. "Kaden! Baby, please talk to me. Say something!" I can hardly see over the tears flooding my eyes. I gasp as the pressure of Kaden's weight on top of me almost becomes too much. His body mass compresses my chest, restricting my air supply. In the room, shouts and traded gunfire continue to ricochet around me, but it's as if we're in our own little bubble, removed from the warzone around us.

Warm liquid drips down the side of my body. Twisting my head at an odd angle, I ignore the sharp twinge of pain as my eyes pop wide in horror. Blood is oozing from somewhere in Kaden's back, confirming my worst fears.

He's been shot.

And I don't even know if he's still alive because my stupid hands are still tied to the damn chair and I can't reach for him. Can't feel if his skin has turned cold with death or if a pulse still throbs in his neck.

"Help!" I scream. "Help him, someone, please!" Over and over, I shout the same words while a mantra is on repeat in my mind. *Please, God, don't let him die. Kaden can't die.*

"Miss, it's okay, Miss." A concerned voice stalls my avid screaming and I blink through my tears, staring into the kindly face of the man standing over me. "You're safe now. I'm Agent Wentward, and we're going to get you out of here shortly."

"Help him, please," I say, my throat scratched raw from screaming. "He's been shot, and I don't even know if ..." I trail off, unable to say it, and tears flow freely again.

Agent Wentward places his fingers on Kaden's neck before glancing over his shoulder. I follow his movement, noticing the swarm of men and women in SWAT and FBI vests milling around the room. An older man at the top of the room is barking out instructions, and a few others are on walkie-talkies and cells. "I need EMS in here now!" Agent Wentward hollers before turning back around to me. "He's alive, Miss, and we'll get him the help he needs. Are you hurt?"

"I ... I don't know. I don't think so." I'm sure my back is a smorgasbord of colorful bruises, but I can't tell if anything is broken, if I've sustained any serious injuries.

Two men and a woman enter the room, wearing beige shirts and brown pants, carrying a stretcher with them. Agent Wentward raises his hand, and they make a beeline for us. The agent steps back, but he doesn't leave, staying close by as the medics do their thing. The men attend to Kaden, while the woman checks my vitals, asking a few questions that I try my best to answer. I don't remove my eyes from Kaden, watching as one of the men gingerly inspects his back.

Then he's lifted off me and placed on the stretcher. I try to sit up, forgetting I'm still strapped into the chair. The woman cuts my restraints and helps me up, wrapping a blanket around my bare chest and another one over my shoulders. My gaze darts around the room, but the two men are gone with Kaden, and a new layer of panic sets in. "I want to go with him! I need to make sure he's okay."

The woman—I think she said her name was Sue or Suze or something like that—pats my arm. "Calm down, Eva. You will get to see Kaden soon. I promise you my colleagues will take very good care of him." Agent Wentward steers a wheelchair over, helping Sue get me into it. I want to protest, to demand they take me to Kaden, but the aftermath of the mad adrenaline rush has drained me, leaving me completely exhausted. I slump in the chair, barely noticing the row of dead bodies on the ground.

"Stop." I reach out, placing my hand on the Agent's arm to stall him. Leaning over the chair, I stare at the lifeless body of my husband, lying prone on the stone floor. His leg is twisted at an awkward angle, and one arm is slumped across his stomach. A large bloodstain extends across the front of his white button-down shirt confirming cause of death. His eyes are wide and vacant, staring up at the ceiling.

A massive sense of relief engulfs me, and I break down, my tears releasing years of caged stress and unhappiness. Anyone looking at me might believe I'm grieving my husband. But the few who know me, really know me, are the only ones who would understand the massive weight that has just been lifted from me.

I pass out in the ambulance on the way to the hospital, and when I come to, I'm in a private room, dressed in a standard-issue hospital gown, strapped to an IV and a bleeping machine. Movement out of the corner of my eye snags my attention, and I turn my head to the side. My parents are seated by my bed, looking pale and ashen.

Or, at least, my father is.

Mom looks annoyed, like being here is a major inconvenience.

"Dad," I croak, refusing to look at the woman who gave birth to me. "Where's Kaden? Is he okay?"

Dad gets up, holding a cup of water with a straw out to me. "Take a sip, sweetheart."

The water is cold and refreshing sliding down my dry throat. I look up at my father with pleading eyes. "Please, Dad." I lift my arm, weakly holding onto his. "I need to know Kaden's all right. Is he alive?"

Mom scoffs, and my eyes flit momentarily to her face.

"He's alive, sweetheart," Dad replies, and I sink into the bed in grateful relief. "A bullet went through his shoulder, but he had surgery and they removed it. He's in recovery, and you should be able to see him soon."

I cry. Can't help it. Dad slides his arm around me in an uneasy hug. "You love this man?"

I sniffle. "I do."

He nods. "I spoke to his parents outside. They seem like good people. It appears they didn't know anything about your relationship either."

"We couldn't tell anyone, for obvious reasons."

Mom makes a disapproving sound at the back of her throat, and I swing fierce eyes on her. "Do you have something to say, Mother?"

"Your husband is dead and the first words out of your mouth are concerns for your lover?" She glares at me. "You should be ashamed of yourself."

I try to sit up, wincing as my achy back protests the movement. "Help me up," I ask Dad, and he helps situate me so I'm sitting more upright in the bed.

I take another sip of water before turning my attention to my mother. "He told me, you know. Right before he stripped me and offered me to his men, Jeremy told me how you and he had been fucking for years right under our noses."

Dad doesn't even flinch, and there's no hint of surprise on his face. I eyeball him. "You knew."

Mom yelps as Dad nods. "I suspected as much," he says, looking only at me, "but I said nothing because I figured that took some of the heat off you."

In a funny way, Dad is probably right. Still, I'm sure my mother didn't start screwing my husband to make my life easier.

Mom huffs but we both ignore her. "I'm sorry, sweetheart." Dad tenderly touches my cheek. "I should've run away with you when you were a kid, when all this happened and I realized what I'd gotten myself into. Instead, I allowed your mother to manipulate me into staying, and I will regret that for as long as I live." His loving eyes stab mine. "I have failed you as a father, and I am truly sorry for not being the man you needed me to be. Watching you suffer all these years has been slowly destroying me. I wanted to find some way of freeing you, but he had so much stuff on me. I was in too deep." He presses a kiss to the top of my head. "I've had preliminary talks with the FBI agent in charge of the case. They might be able to do a deal. Limited jail time in exchange for my testimony. While most of the key players were taken out today, the business is up for grabs, and they'll all start turning on one another. I want to help the authorities bring as many of them down as they can, and I'll accept whatever punishment they deem appropriate. It'll be worth it. To know you are safe. Finally, free of that man."

I wet my dry lips. "I don't want you to go to jail, Dad, but I'm proud you're doing the right thing."

"Oh, puh-lease," Mom interjects sourly. "Don't pull that moralistic bullshit now. You both may have complained, but you were happy to take the perks."

I shake my head, flabbergasted at how deliberately ignorant and obstinate she is. "Most everything I have was paid for with my own hard-earned money. I never wanted anything from that man, and the authorities can take the glamorous gowns and jewels he bought me. I want none of it and no reminder of the man you forced me to marry."

She stands, planting her hands on her hips and sneering at me. "That act might fool others, but it doesn't fool me. I know who Kaden is. Who his family is. Why else would you bed a younger man, one of your former students, if it wasn't for his money?" Her face contorts into an ugly grimace. "You can look down your nose at me, but you're no better."

Nudging Dad, I ease myself out of the bed, gripping the headrest to help support my weak limbs. I want to be standing up, facing my mother head-on, when I say this. "I am worth a million of you, Mother. Because I love Kaden for who he is, not what he can give me. And I would never sell my daughter to a monster; I don't care how high the stakes seemed. When I have children, I will make them a priority. I will love them and care for them and keep them safe and protected. I will make them feel cherished in all the ways I should have been made to feel. But you can walk away, knowing you didn't undermine me. You didn't rob me of my self-worth, and your cold treatment made me a stronger person. So, I guess I do have something to thank you for after all."

She wants to hit me.

I see it in her eyes and the way her hand twitches at her side, but she won't dare it this time. "Now get out, and never come back. I never want to see you again."

Grabbing her bag and her coat from the back of the chair, she levels one final hateful look my way. "I never wanted children, and you've just reinforced all the reasons why. You won't see me again, either of you, and I won't shed a single tear."

"Leave, Isabel," Dad hisses, "or I'll find one of those FBI agents to forcibly remove you. You've said your piece; now go."

Dad and I spend another half hour talking through stuff that needs to be said, and when he leaves, I feel lighter than I have in years. I don't know how long it will take for us to have a normal father-daughter relationship, or if we'll ever get to that place, but at least we are both in the space where we want to try.

A nurse arrives a short while later to wheel me to Kaden's room. While I'm dying to see him, to see for myself that he's okay, I'm all kinds of nervous too. I'm expecting his family to be there, and this wasn't quite how I wanted to meet them. I can only imagine how angry they must be at me. I'm the one who dragged him into this, after all. If it wasn't for me, Kaden wouldn't have gotten shot.

We round the corner and turn left into a private suite of sorts. A bunch of people are sitting on couches in the plush waiting area, and all heads swivel in my direction. I will my heart to calm down as a woman I recognize—purely from photos—approaches me. The nurse stops, and I look up at Kaden's beautiful mom. She runs a hand nervously through her short blonde hair, and I decide to take the bull by the horns. I extend my hand. "Mrs. Kennedy. It's great to finally meet you, although I wish it were under different circumstances."

She clasps my hand in a firm handshake. "I agree, and you've got to excuse us if we're a little shell-shocked, Evelina. This has all come as a massive shock."

"Is Kaden okay?" I gulp anxiously. "I mean, he'll make a full recovery? That's what the nurses have told me."

She nods her head, and air streams out of my mouth in a rush of relief.

"He'll be fine. The bullet hit his shoulder, missing anything vital, and his other injuries will heal in time."

"He saved me," I tell her. "He threw himself on top of me once the gunfire broke out. I don't know how he did it. How he made it across the room when he was in so much pain." My eyes well up. "I'm so sorry. I never wanted any of this for him. I tried to push him away, more than once, but—"

She bends down so we're at eye level, cutting across me. "But my son's stubborn. Especially when it comes to something he wants." She takes my hands, smiling softly at me. "And from what Keven's told us, my son is very much in love with you."

I look sideways, and my eyes scan over the rest of the Kennedys. It's not difficult to identify Kaden's brothers because they all look so alike, and, holy hell, there is so much hotness in this room, I'm almost blinded. I don't know which brother is which, apart from Keven, as he's the only one I've met before. All of them share worried expressions, but only one is sending daggers at me. A brooding boy, leaning against the wall in the corner, wearing a moody scowl. He looks younger, and I'm guessing he's one of the triplets.

I focus on Kaden's mother again. "I love him very much, and this is the last thing I wanted for him. I never meant for him to get hurt."

"We understand that," a tall good-looking man says, holding out his hand to me. "I'm James. I'm Kaden's father."

"It's an honor to meet you, sir." I shake his hand.

"Please, call me James, and I think it's best we let you through to our boy before he tries to get out of that bed and injures himself further. He hasn't stopped asking for you since he woke up."

The biggest smile spreads over my face. "I'm glad to hear it. I've been asking for him too."

Two gorgeous girls send sympathetic looks my way as James wheels me past them, en route to Kaden's room. I'm guessing one of them is Faye, but I'm not sure which one or who the other girl is. One of the other brother's girlfriends, I suppose.

Kade's eyes land on mine the instant James pushes me into the room, and I burst out crying. God, all I'm doing lately is making a complete spectacle of myself, but my emotions are stretched thin over the events of the last twenty-four hours and the tense build-up over the last couple of months.

Kaden looks terrible, all bloodied and bruised, and half his upper body is tightly bandaged with his shoulder in a sling. But he's still the most beautiful man in the world to me.

"Shh, honey," he murmurs, opening his good arm for me. "Don't cry. It's okay. It's going to be okay."

James helps me up onto the bed. Kaden's uninjured arm wraps around me, and I gently hold him while my legs dangle off the side of the bed. "I'll leave you two to talk in private," his dad says. "Press the bell if you need anything, Kaden."

"I'm good, Dad," Kade says, pressing a kiss to the top of my head. "I have everything I need right here."

James smiles at his son. "I can see that." Then he quietly exits the room.

Kaden tips my head up, and our eyes meet. "How do you feel? Are you badly hurt?"

"Stop stealing my lines, and, no, I'm not badly hurt. My back is bruised, I pretty much ache all over, and I'm weak, but it's nothing a bit of rest won't cure." I cup his face, my expression faltering as I trace gentle fingertips over his bruised, cut-up face. His busted eye looks so sore. "God, Kaden. I'm so sorry for all this. What you must have gone through ..."

"I'm fine, Eva." He kisses the tips of my fingers. "I'm not going to lie, I hurt literally everywhere. I've a few broken ribs, and I'll have to wear this sling for a few weeks, but I'm alive, and so are you, and that is the only thing we should focus on now."

"I thought we were going to die," I tell him, running my fingers through his hair. "I really did."

"I know, honey. I was praying my guy would come through, but in the end, it was my brother who saved us."

I arch a brow. "What? Who? How?"

He smiles, and it's unbelievable how much that brightens up my world. I never thought I'd get to see that smile again. Get to snuggle with him like this. Have a future to look forward to.

"It's just as well Kev is as stubborn as me." He chuckles. "I told him not to get involved but he ignored me. Kev has monitored all our cells for years," he starts explaining and my eyes pop wide. "He has no qualms about boundaries and privacy, but his heart is in the right place, and he has saved our butts more times than I can count." He kisses my forehead, and I melt. "Anyway, Garcia's bastards smashed my cell and left it on the side of the road, so I knew there was no way my brother was riding to the rescue this time, but I underestimated him. Again."

He brushes my hair back, planting a soft kiss on my neck. "Don't ever tell him I said that though. His ego is worse than mine."

"Doubtful," I tease, kissing the underside of his jaw. "But that's a conversation for another day. What did Keven do?"

"I found him snooping in my bedroom a few weeks ago. Turns out he put trackers in the soles of all my shoes. Kev knew we were leaving, and he was up all night monitoring shit online. He had also discovered Jonas's identity and he was tapping his phones, so he heard how some of his guys were MIA, and he knew something had gone wrong. He tracked me to the warehouse and sent an anonymous tip to the FBI with our location."

"Wow. We owe him our lives."

"We do, and I don't think he'll ever let me forget it."

"Nor should he."

"He hacked into the FBI's communication channel and heard everything as it went down. I'm glad he was smart enough not to attempt to come after us himself because if anything had happened to him ..." He doesn't need to complete that sentence.

And that brings other memories to the surface. "Poor Tiffani."

He nods, and his Adam's apple bobs in his throat. "I can't believe she's dead. She didn't deserve that, even if she did throw you to the wolves."

"She didn't understand what she was doing."

"He was so cold when he took her out. Like she was an annoying insect under the bottom of his shoe." He shivers. "I'm so grateful you're free of him, and I wish you'd never had to endure the things you have."

"He's dead, and he can't hurt either of us again."

"I know. Kev updated me. He said there's an internal battle going on for control of his business, and he doubts anyone will be concerned with us, but I think we still need to take precautions. I hope you don't mind, but I've hired my dad's guys to watch over us."

While I hate the thought of more men with guns hiding in the shadows, I know it makes sense to take precautions until we know we're in the clear. "You won't hear any complaints from me."

He holds me tighter to his side, and I wish I could kiss him, but his mouth is all torn and bleeding, and I don't want to hurt him. Instead, I press a kiss to the sliver of exposed skin at his collarbone. "I love you, Kaden, and I'm so happy you're okay."

"I love you too, honey." He presses a soft kiss to my cheek. "And now we get to start living our lives the way we've always wanted." He peers into my eyes, and I fall in love with him all over again. "It's over, Eva. From now on, there is nothing standing in our way."

# *Epilogue*
## Present – Christmas

### Kaden

"Oh my God," Eva exclaims, beaming at me, "it's as noisy as a toddler's playground in here."

She's not wrong. Christmas dinner chez Kennedy is becoming quite the boisterous affair. Our family is growing, and the get-togethers are getting bigger. Faye's father is here along with her three half-siblings, as well as Brad's mother and two sisters, and Rachel and her dad. Although my nephew Hewson is the only actual toddler in the place, the way Kal and Keaton are shrieking and hollering as they chase him around the room makes it seem like we've a roomful of sugar-crazed, over-excited kiddies.

"I love it," Eva adds, looping her arm through mine and grinning. I lean down and kiss her on the lips, uncaring that my family surrounds us. I spent far too long hiding my love for her, and I won't shy away from PDAs or from telling her how much I love her. "This is what family is all about."

The last month has been blissful and strenuous in equal measures. We both had to give numerous statements to the FBI around the events in the warehouse, and Eva has had a lot of legal stuff to complete to officially sever all connection to Jeremy Garcia. Dan Evans, our family attorney, put a rush on things, and when the paperwork came through, we snuck off to the courthouse and got married.

It was, hands down, the best day of my life.

Eva looked so beautiful in her simple off-white knee-length gown. With minimal makeup and her gorgeous hair pinned up in an elegant bun, she was the most radiant bride. As long as I live, I will never forget the blissful, adoring look in her eyes as we made our vows. The moment the officiate said I could "kiss my bride" is forever imprinted on my heart. Kissing my wife for the first time was indescribable. It feels like everything we've endured over the last few years has been building to his point, and everything has come full circle, like it was supposed to.

Asking my wife to remove her new engagement and wedding rings today was difficult, but I know Kyler is making a big announcement after dinner, and I won't steal my brother's thunder.

The only two people who know we are married are Renee and Keven. Both stood with us, as maid of honor and best man, respectively. And both have been sworn to secrecy until we've publicly announced it. I don't like asking Eva to keep it quiet, but, frankly, I like having this time to ourselves. As soon as Mom finds out, she's going to demand a big, glitzy wedding, and she'll suck Eva into wedding planning before she knows it.

"I'm happy you're comfortable here." I wrap my arms around her as Mom smiles in our direction. "And I knew my family would love you." I was worried about her mental state today because her dad has just started his two-year stint behind bars, and I know she's going to miss him. Despite their history, he has really stepped up these last few weeks and come through for Eva. His testimony will put a lot of men away for a long time, and he's single-handedly removed any final threats to our freedom. No one in those circles cares about Eva anymore, and that's the way I like it.

She squeezes me tight. "You have a wonderful family, Kaden, and they couldn't have been more welcoming. I wasn't expecting them to be as open and forgiving."

If she realized half of the stuff my family has been through, she'd understand how our situation is almost the norm. At one time, it looked like Kyler was in love with his half-sister, and let's not forget the courtroom shit Kal's fiancée Lana put him through, so Eva's murdering ex-husband and her position as professor wasn't any more scandalous. "It takes a lot to shock my family," I admit, kissing her temple. Oriental scents of apricot, plum, and coconut swirl around me, and I inhale the hypnotic fragrance of her perfume.

It's new, like a lot of other things.

Eva insisted on turning her back completely on her old life, leaving most of her clothes and personal possessions behind. I offered to take her shopping, to buy her whatever she needs, but she wouldn't hear of it, and I didn't protest. I understand how important independence is to her after almost a decade spent living in a cage. So, as much as I want to shower her with gifts, and spend every spare second with her, I have taken a step back and given her the space she needs. I'm happy for Eva to set the pace, as long as I'm there for the ride.

Hewson darts past us like a whirlwind, his daddy and uncle chasing after him with glee. Hewson wraps his little arms around Eva's bare leg, looking up at her. The cutest little smile spreads across his face and his arms go out. "Up!" he demands. "Me want up!" Without hesitation, Eva scoops the little angel into her arms, tweaking his noise and making him laugh.

"You have that look on your face," my brother Kalvin says, smirking at me.

I play along. "What look, asshat?"

"The look of lurvveee."

I shrug. "I'm in love. I'm not hiding that."

Kal raises a brow, and Keaton makes his escape, any mention of love making him run for the hills, even if he is devoted to his long-time sweetheart Melissa. The triplets turned eighteen last month, and they're technically adults, but to me they're still my kid brothers.

"I think I might have to kidnap this little guy," Eva tells Kal, tickling a chuckling Hewson. He now has his arms latched around her neck, and the sight stirs something powerful inside me.

"You'll have to get in line," Kal replies. "And I think Faye would come to blows with you over it."

"Fact," I agree. "She's besotted with him. Both her and Kyler are."

"I know you're only home for Christmas break, but if you and Lana need any more babysitters, we'd be happy to help," Eva says, cooing at Hewson.

"It's like a feast or famine," Kal quips. "We only have a few friends we trust to babysit back in Florida, so we don't get out much. Then we come here and everyone's trying to push us out the door!"

"Take advantage of it," I say, plucking the little guy out of Eva's arms and putting him up on my shoulders.

"Kade." Eva's tone holds considerable caution.

Ignoring the sharp tug on my still-healing shoulder, I reach up and hold Hewson's little hands. "Relax, honey. I'm fine."

Leaving Eva chatting with Kal, I race around the room with Hewson still on my shoulders, delighting in every little chuckle and squeal coming out of his mouth.

"Should you be doing that?" Mom asks, stepping in front of me.

"I'm fine, Mom. I barely feel a twinge, and I'm fed up of taking it easy."

Hewson wriggles on my shoulders, and I carefully let him down. He takes off running straightaway, making a beeline for his momma. Lana lifts him up, pressing a loving kiss to his forehead.

"I have a feeling you might be the one to give me my next grandchild," Mom says with a twinkle in her eye.

I stumble back a little. "Steady on there, Mom. I know how you get, and don't go putting ideas in Eva's head yet. I only just got her to myself, and I want to enjoy this time together before we start a family."

"But you are planning that with her?"

I'm tempted to tell her about the wedding, but I spot Kyler out of the corner of my eye, holding Faye close, his eyes radiant with the news they're bursting to tell everyone, and I won't take this from him. "Absolutely." I circle my arm around Mom's shoulder. "Eva's the one, and I look forward to starting a family with her, just not yet."

Although, practicing is lots of fun, but I keep that thought to myself.

I haven't been of much use to her in that regard until recently. The first couple of weeks after I was shot, my injuries made it too difficult to do much, but I've been making up for lost time this past week.

"And you're happy, Kade?" Her eyes probe mine.

"Extremely." I kiss my mother on the cheek. "I didn't think I'd be here for Christmas. I thought Eva and I would be alone somewhere on the other side of the world, and while that would've been special in its own way, I would've missed everyone like crazy." I look over at my wife, laughing and joking with Kal, Lana, Keven, and Keanu, and my heart swells with love.

"I'm thrilled for you, Kaden." Mom palms my face. "And she's perfect for you."

"You don't care that she's older?"

"Pft." Mom waves her hands in the air. "Age is only a number when it comes to love. You're both adults and it doesn't matter if there's five months or five years between you. Besides, you're following in family tradition so I'm hardly going to complain." She winks, nudging my hip as she goes off to round everyone up for dinner.

I always forget that Mom is older than Dad, and I hadn't thought of it like that.

Keaton rubs his belly, groaning. "I don't think I can eat another thing," he tells the table. "I'm fit to burst."

"Well, you better make some room." I mess his hair up. "Eva spent ages making those cheesecakes, and it'd be rude to refuse to taste it."

"I'm stuffed," Kal admits, "but I'll always make room for cheesecake."

"You are like a bottomless pit," Lana proclaims, smiling as she shakes her head. "I don't know where you put it."

"I know," Faye pipes up, envy obvious in her tone. "I only have to look at cheesecake and it goes straight to my hips."

"You're gorgeous, babe, and you know it. Knock yourself out with the cheesecake," Kyler tells her, earning a chorus of groans from the guys around the table. The girls all predictably swoon.

"Jesus Christ," Kent moans. "If I—"

We all round on him, telling him to zip it, that we've heard it a million times. Whitney, Faye's half-sister, drapes her arm around Kent's shoulder, whispering something in his ear, much to the chagrin of her dad Adam. I don't know what it is with those two, but they've been carrying on for years, whenever they see one another. Kent is far from ideal boyfriend material, and I don't need to be a mind reader to know Adam isn't one bit happy about their relationship, even if it appears pretty casual.

"Hey, man," I say, nudging Keven's shoulder. He's seated on my left, while Eva has been sitting on my right. I clear my throat. "I have something I want to say." In all honesty, this should've been said weeks ago but I was drugged up and not thinking clearly in the hospital, and the last few weeks have been hectic, so this is the first opportunity I've had to properly thank Keven. I could've pulled him aside at the courthouse, but I didn't want to spoil our wedding by referencing anything about that awful day.

He arches a brow.

"I haven't properly thanked you for what you did for me and Eva. Neither of us would be here today if it wasn't for your super-stalking skills and your quick thinking." A messy ball of emotion clogs the back of my throat. "I owe you my life, brother." I lower my voice. "My wife owes you her life." I clamp a hand on his shoulder. "And I will never, ever forget what you did for us." I squeeze his shoulder. "I love you, bruh."

Kev surprises me, tugging me into a hug. "I love you too, man. And seeing how happy you both are is all the thanks I need."

Our uncharacteristic mushy moment is broken up when Mom and Eva return to the dining room with dessert. They are both laughing, and the sight almost brings tears to my eyes. Once everyone has their cake, Eva sits back down, grinning up at me. "Happy, honey?" I ask, kissing the tip of her nose.

"Deliriously," she confirms, leaning in to kiss me. "I love your family, and I love this day, and I can't remember ever feeling this happy. You have given me so much, Kaden." She flings her arms around me, and I love that she has no qualms about doing so in front of my family. Everyone is chatting, and eating their dessert, but I'm guessing all eyes are on us too. "I love you," she whispers in my ear. "And I'm going to show you just how much when we get home."

Home.

I never thought I'd love that word as much as I've come to. I gave Eva free rein to redecorate my penthouse however she liked, and she went to town on it, filling it with all the homey little fixtures and fittings it was missing, all the things that now give it that warm, welcoming vibe when you step foot in the door. I think she was glad to have something to do now that she's no longer working.

The day after the showdown at the warehouse, Eva resigned her position at Harvard. She felt like she had no choice once the news channels started reporting events, splashing both our faces over TV screens. At least this way, Eva's reputation is still intact. If she had stayed, an investigation would most likely have been launched into our relationship, and she probably would've been fired in a cloud of disgrace. As it is, the rumor mill is in overdrive on campus, but I refuse to confirm or deny anything. They can form their own opinions, and I don't care.

I hate that she's lost the career she loved so much, but she has come to terms with it a lot quicker than I thought she would. Now, she's getting heavily involved in my business idea, and she's going to conduct market research and put some of the structures in place while I finish out my degree and graduate. Then we're going to run my online golf business together, and Eva has a few ideas of her own that she'll most likely pursue down the line.

Everything has slotted perfectly into place, and life is good.

"Hey," she says, staring quizzically at me. "Where'd you go?"

I take her hand and press a kiss to her palm. "I was just thinking about how perfect my life is now you're officially in it."

"If you don't stop staying stuff like that I might just have to drag you to the bathroom before we leave," she whispers in my ear.

"And you think I'd have any issue with that?" I quirk a brow in amusement. "You can have your wicked way with me any time, any place, anywhere."

She bursts out laughing and the sound is like music to my ears. Grinning at her, I plant another quick kiss on her lips. Man, I can't stop touching this woman. I just love her so much.

Kyler clears his throat loudly, and we both sober up. Eva is aware of what's about to go down, although I made her promise not to say a word. I'm the only one Kyler told the news to, and I'm honored he trusted me enough to share it. He stands up, holding his hand over Faye's. They lock eyes, and a moment passes between them. A moment none of us misses. Mom is on the verge of tears, and I think she's just figured it out.

Kyler lifts his head, his gaze roaming around the table. "Faye and I have some news. We're getting married!"

The room erupts in a chorus of shouting, clapping, and cheering. Kyler pulls Faye to her feet, enveloping her in his arms, looking like he never wants to let go. Eva and I share a look, understanding the emotions my brother and his new fiancée are feeling. We move toward one another at the same time, our lips meeting in the middle, our hands finding one another.

"Oh my God," Whitney shrieks, "that ring is obscene."

Eva and I part, standing up as one and moving around the table. Whitney's jaw is someplace on the ground as she holds Faye's hand, staring enviously at the massive engagement ring on her finger.

"Overcompensating, bruh?" I joke, grabbing Kyler into a hug.

"Very fucking funny."

"I'm really happy for you guys," I say, grabbing Faye into my embrace as Eva moves to hug Ky.

"Have you set a date or anything?" Eva asks.

"Not yet," Faye says, slinging her arm around my brother's waist and grinning up at him. "But we don't want to wait, so we'll probably get married sometime during summer break."

Wow. Mom is going to sprout wings and fly when she realizes she has two weddings to plan next year.

"You should have a double wedding with Lana and Kal," Keaton suggests, tugging Faye away from Ky and wrapping her in a massive hug. "That would be fun."

"No fucking way," Ky says. "Faye isn't sharing her day with anyone else, and I'm sure Kal feels the same way."

"I hear ya, bro," Kalvin says, edging his way into the conversation. "And we're not planning on getting hitched for another couple of years yet. Between our little bundle of fun, college, and Lana's writing career, we have our hands full. We'll do it when we have time to plan it properly."

"I'm so excited for you," Lana squeals, taking her turn hugging Faye. "Now we're going to be legit sisters-in-law."

"I hadn't thought of that," Faye admits, "but that'll be so cool. And I'll have official auntie dibs on Hewson."

The doorbell rings as Rachel and Brad step up to offer their congratulations. Mom and Dad exchange nervous looks across the table, and I know what that means. We have a history of family celebrations being interrupted with shitty news.

Case in point.

Keanu returns from the front door with a horrified expression on his face. Officer Hanks steps into the dining room flanked by a man and a woman dressed in suits and serious expressions.

"What's going on?" Dad asks, stepping forward and addressing our local police officer. Unfortunately, thanks to Kent's shenanigan's and other family history, Officer Hanks is well-acquainted with our family. "What was so important you had to interrupt us on Christmas Day? Do I need to call my attorney?"

"That would be a good idea, sir," the woman says in a serious tone.

"These folks are from the FBI," Officer Hanks explains. "And they're here on official business."

The male FBI agent is eyeballing Keven like he's his next meal, and I'm terrified of where this is going. "We are here for Keven Kennedy. Come with us quietly, son, and we'll make this painless for your family."

Mom gasps, clamping a hand over her mouth, while Dad is already on his cell, calling Dan Evans, no doubt. Dad must have that man on a massive retainer, and we keep him plenty busy.

Keven leans in and kisses Faye on the cheek before slapping Kyler on the shoulder. "Congrats, guys, and I'm sorry to put a dampener on your news." Ky locks Kev in a fierce hug, whispering something in his ear. Then Mom comes out of her daze, rushing Keven, sobbing and hugging him while Kev ushers reassurances. "They just want to talk to me about a few things, Mom. It's not that serious," he lies.

"Is that really necessary," I hear Officer Hanks ask, and I swing my head around, watching the male FBI agent opening a set of handcuffs. "The young man is coming voluntarily with you."

Ignoring Officer Hanks, the FBI agent rounds the table, stopping in front of Keven. Mom is clinging to his side, tears glistening in her eyes. The agent shows his badge, reads Kev his rights, and then handcuffs him.

"Don't say a word until Dan gets there," I tell Kev even though he doesn't need to hear it. Kev knows more about his rights than any of us do. He's done some crazy shit in the past, and he's always feared this day would come, so I know he's prepared and he won't do anything to incriminate himself further.

I hold Eva against me while my brother is led away, rubbing my hands up and down her back, soothing her.

## Keven

Agent Dickhead shoves my head in the back of his SUV, strapping me in while the female agent, who has yet to introduce herself, gets in the other side to keep an eye on me. Jerkoff slides behind the wheel, starting the engine. I stare out the window, at familiar landscape, as the miles eat away.

I've always known this day would come. Despite how careful I've been, some things refuse to stay buried. I knew the risk I was taking the day I sent the anonymous tip to the FBI about Kade and Eva's location. There wasn't time to put the proper precautions in place, and I knew it wouldn't take too long before they discovered where the tip came from. I knew it would lead to further investigation, but, if I had my time over again, I'd still do the same.

My brother and his wife would have died that day if I hadn't intervened.

And if I end up going to jail, I won't have any regrets.

My brother is alive, and that's all that counts.

The silence in the SUV is deafening, but I sure as fuck won't be the first to break it.

We pull up at the back entrance of what I know is the local FBI field office. I cooperate as I'm removed from the car and led into the building.

They deposit me in a small room, cuffing my hands to the table and leaving me alone. Some time passes, and then the same two agents return with an older gentleman with thick dark hair. He removes the handcuffs from my wrists before dropping into a chair across from me, while the other two stand over in the corner like dutiful lackeys. "Good evening, Mr. Kennedy. I'm Supervisory Special Agent Andrew Clement, and I'd like to have an off-the-record chat with you before your attorney arrives." Slamming a heavy manila folder down on the table, he eyeballs me with a penetrating stare. "We've had our eye on you for some time, Keven." He raps his fingers off the table while I stare neutrally ahead. "You've been a very naughty boy." He flips open the file, skimming through documents. "Illegal online gambling. Identify theft and larceny. Illegal wire-tapping. Not to mention some of the undesirables you've been connected to in the past. The list goes on."

He has no idea.

Propping his elbows on the desk, he stabs me with sharp hazel eyes. "There is no denying how incredibly skilled you are with a computer, or your obvious intelligence, so I have a proposition for you."

I arch a brow, as the woman pulls a white screen down from the ceiling.

"Our analysis shows you have tried to mend your ways, and your most recent illegal activities have all centered on protecting family and friends. We know you sent us the anonymous tip which led us to the warehouse that day, and we're grateful." He pauses momentarily. "However, your actions are enough to put you away for quite some time unless you agree to come and work for us," Agent Clement says.

*Okay, what?*

I eyeball the guy like he's crazy. "Work for you?" I splutter. "Doing what?"

"We could use a good technical analyst like you on a special high-priority undercover case."

"And what? If I do this, you'll rip up those charges?"

Extracting a document from the file, he slides it across the table to me. "That's a contract of employment which also confirms that if you come to work with us we will drop all pending charges against you and shred your file, subject to certain provisions, of course."

"What if I don't want to come and work for you?"

"Then you'll be prosecuted to the full extent of the law."

I say nothing for a few minutes. "I need some time to think about it."

The man smiles, as if I've just told a joke. "This is a one-time offer, and you'll need to make your mind up now." He clicks his fingers, and the male lackey switches off the light as the screen powers up. "Perhaps this might help persuade you," Agent Clement says.

Photos of various well-known criminals appear on the screen, and he starts explaining. "Following the recent death of Jeremy Garcia, a drugs war has erupted on our streets, as various interested parties battle to take over what was his." More images fill the screen. "But that's not even the real problem. Most of the main players have their hands in several cookie jars. Narcotics is only one aspect of their business." The images on the screen shift, showing several large trucks, open at the rear, with young girls spilling out of the vehicles, crying, and in various stages of undress. "Sex trafficking is another lucrative source of income, and something that's been on our radar for quite some time, but we're struggling to find evidence to pin these guys down."

The images return to some of Massachusetts's most notorious gangsters. "The turmoil in the aftermath of Garcia's demise grants us an opportunity to infiltrate these organizations and start to build solid evidence against those responsible. With your background, and your skills, you could be a valuable asset to our team."

The screen changes again, and my eyes zone in on the pretty blonde outside the photography studio. My chest tightens as I examine the shot in more detail. She's looking up at a guy I don't recognize, and they're smiling at one another. "Who's that?" I ask, gnawing on the inside of my mouth.

"Daniel Stanten. A relative newcomer on the scene. He was being groomed by Garcia and word on the street is he's the one to watch."

"Who's the girl," I ask, although I already know her name.

"Cheryl Keeland. His fiancée."

"I'll do it," I blurt. "I'll come and work for you." Light floods the room, and Agent Clement stares at me in surprise. I reach across the table for the contract. "Where do I sign?"

He removes a pen from his inside jacket pocket and hands it to me. I don't even bother reading it. Dan Evans will string me up for this, but screw that shit.

I've spent years trying to get all thoughts and memories of Cheryl Keeland out of my head, to no avail. Torn through girls like they were a two-for-one special, but nothing or no one can erase the only girl who has ever owned my heart.

Cheryl was the love of my life growing up, and I never envisioned a future where she wasn't in it.

Until I fucked up.

And I lost her.

And I haven't been at peace within myself since.

I don't believe in kismet or karma or whatever the fuck you call it.

But right now, it feels like fate is sending me one-big-ass message.

And I'm not going to fuck up again.

Cheryl may be engaged to that guy, but she hasn't married him yet, so there's still time to warn her.

Time to tell her what I should have told her senior year.

Time to win back the heart of the only girl who has ever mattered.

Skipping to the back page of the contract, I scribble my signature in the field provided, sliding the document across the slick surface to a shocked-looking Agent Clement.

Grinning, I lean across the table. "When do I start?"

The Kennedy Boys series continues in *Forgiving Keven*, coming soon.

Visit this link to receive a free bonus chapter from *Seducing Kaden*:
https://claims.instafreebie.com/free/984R7D0U

# About The Author

*USA Today* bestselling author **Siobhan Davis** writes emotionally intense young adult and new adult fiction with swoon-worthy romance, complex characters, and tons of unexpected plot twists and turns that will have you flipping the pages beyond bedtime! She is the author of the international bestselling *True Calling*, *Saven*, and *Kennedy Boys* series.

Siobhan's family will tell you she's a little bit obsessive when it comes to reading and writing, and they aren't wrong. She can rarely be found without her trusty Kindle, a paperback book, or her laptop somewhere close at hand.

Prior to becoming a full-time writer, Siobhan forged a successful corporate career in human resource management.

She resides in the Garden County of Ireland with her husband and two sons.

You can connect with Siobhan in the following ways:

Author Website: www.siobhandavis.com
Author Blog: My YA NA Book Obsession
Facebook: AuthorSiobhanDavis
Twitter: @siobhandavis
Google+: SiobhanDavisAuthor
Email: siobhan@siobhandavis.com

# *Books by Siobhan Davis*

## TRUE CALLING SERIES
Young Adult Science Fiction/Dystopian Romance

*True Calling*
*Lovestruck*
*Beyond Reach*
*Light of a Thousand Stars*
*Destiny Rising*
*Short Story Collection*
*True Calling Series Collection*

## SAVEN SERIES
Young Adult Science Fiction/Paranormal Romance

*Saven Deception*
*The Logan Collection*
*Saven Disclosure*
*Saven Denial*
*Saven Defiance*
*The Heir and the Human*
*Saven Deliverance*
*Saven: The Complete Series*

## KENNEDY BOYS SERIES
Upper Young Adult/New Adult Contemporary Romance

*Finding Kyler*
*Losing Kyler*
*Keeping Kyler*

*The Irish Getaway*
*Loving Kalvin*
*Saving Brad*
*Seducing Kaden*
*Forgiving Keven^*
*Adoring Keaton^*
*Releasing Keanu^*
*Reforming Kent^*

## STANDALONES
New Adult Contemporary Romance

*Inseparable*
*Incognito*
*When Forever Changes\**

Reverse Harem Contemporary Romance

*Surviving Amber Springs\**

## ALINTHIA SERIES
Upper YA/NA Paranormal Romance/Reverse Harem

*The Lost Savior*
*The Secret Heir*
*The Warrior Princess*
*The Chosen One^*

\* Coming 2018
^ Release date to be confirmed.

Visit www.siobhandavis.com for all future release dates. Release dates are subject to change based on reader demand and the author's schedule. Subscribing to the author's newsletter or following her on Facebook is the best way to stay updated with planned new releases..

Made in the USA
Middletown, DE
22 November 2019